HOLIDAY IN BATH

Laura Matthews

WARNER BOOKS

A Warner Communications Company

*For Denise Marcil,
with thanks.*

WARNER BOOKS EDITION

Copyright © 1981 by Elizabeth Rotter
All rights reserved.

Cover art by Walter Popp

Warner Books, Inc.
666 Fifth Avenue
New York, N.Y. 10103

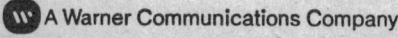 A Warner Communications Company

Printed in the United States of America

First Printing: March, 1981

Reissued: November, 1989

10 9 8 7 6 5 4 3 2

chapter one

"Now, Mama, we have been over all this before!" the young lady declared passionately. "You assure me that neither of you nor Papa would dream of forcing me into a disagreeable marriage, and yet every other word from either of you is Cranford's name. I *know* he is handsome, and that his papa's lands run with Papa's, and that he is intelligent and stable and all the rest of it. He is also insufferably dull! And old," she added as a scourging afterthought.

"Old!" Mrs. Storwood's countenance registered dismay. "Trelenny, he cannot be above eight and twenty! Why, of course he isn't, as you were born when he was ten and Lady Chessels and I..."

Trelenny cast her blue eyes heavenward. "Yes, Mama, you and his mother dreamed of the day we would wed. But those were daydreams, don't you see? The days when parents arranged matches for their children are dead! I am sure if he has said it once, Papa has said a hundred times that the young must depend on the older, wiser counsel of their relations, and I would not contradict him for the world But I haven't even *met* any other eligible young men! And I am only eighteen. Can't you see what would happen to me? I'd be stuck here all my life just like you." Guiltily she dropped to her knees beside her mother's chair. "You know I don't mean that quite as I said it, Mama. I know you and Papa have been happy, even with his illness. But . . . but you had a chance to live in London when you were young. You went to balls and plays and parties. And the friends you made! Would you not feel completely cut off from the world if you did not still correspond with Mrs. Waplington and Lady Sandburn? I haven't even any friends to write to, and God knows what I would tell them if I did. There cannot be many young ladies of my age who would be interested in my visits to the tenants or my rides about the mountains!"

Mrs. Storwood tucked back a straggling wisp of her daughter's blonde hair. "You write to Clare."

Although a great many retorts sprang to Trelenny's lips, she said only, "She and Lord Hinton live quite as retired as we do."

"Yes, but still she is your friend and no doubt you await her letters as eagerly as any I might receive."

Trelenny rose and paced agitatedly about the room. "I keep expecting her to tell me how she *feels* about things . . . but she never does. Do you think he mistreats her?"

Such a suggestion obviously had never crossed her mother's mind, and she stared blankly at her daughter for a moment. "Do not say such a thing even in jest, Trelenny! Lord Hinton is an admirable man and devoted to Clare. Whatever put such an idea in your mind? Did you not see how tenderly he treated her at their wedding?"

"At their wedding, yes," Trelenny said scornfully. "But you cannot have failed to notice that we have not seen them since, Mama. He carried her off to the wilds of Scotland immediately—not even to his seat! And they might as well have disappeared from the face of the earth after that. They've been married well over a year and he has never brought her to Ashwicke Park. Except for her letters, she might be dead for all anyone knows!"

"Don't be absurd!" Mrs. Storwood said sharply. "Her brother has visited her."

"Oh, Cranford. It's a wonder he could take his nose out of a book long enough to journey there, I concede. And what did he tell us of her on his return? Just exactly what anyone tells you when he has visited someone—they look well, seem happy, are busy, etc., etc. Why doesn't she come here to visit?" Trelenny came close to her mother and dropped her voice to a conspiratorial whisper "I'll tell you what *I* think. *I* think he is keeping her prisoner"

"Where do you get this fantastic imagination of yours?" Mrs. Storwood asked despairingly as she twisted her shapely hands in her lap. "It is not from your father, and it is certainly not from me. I have never heard anything more absurd in my life, Trelenny. Must you make a mystery of every common occurrence? She has had a child, for heaven's sake! You don't go jaunting about the countryside when you are carrying a child, and you don't order round your carriage the moment you are delivered of it!"

"Little Catherine must be six months old by now," Trelenny said stubbornly. "Lots of people travel with children."

"And more don't," her mother retorted. "Have you been reading some lurid novel about an imprisoned wife?"

"Now, Mama, I have to have something entertaining to read. It is just that book Mrs. Waplington sent you and you set aside. Surely there can be no harm in it when your dear friend sent it. You know, the one by Lady Caroline Lamb."

"Glenarvon? It is not meant for a child of your years, my dear. Surely you can find something more uplifting than that to read." Mrs. Storwood habitually used persuasion rather than firm injunction with her daughter, for nothing so surely set up that young lady's back as being told what to do, especially when there was the hint that it was her youth and unworldliness which prompted the instruction.

"Would you have me read the literature that Cranford brings?" Trelenny asked sweetly. "Perhaps you would like me to read aloud to you. Let me see. There is a very large tome on antiquities and another on the Romans. But no, you would probably prefer his own translation of Antoninus. That is the very thing . . . if you have some desire to nap! Imagine his thinking that I would be interested in such stuff. Well, he cannot possibly believe I am, for I have told him any number of times that I cannot read more than two pages without yawning."

Trelenny stood with hands on hips in a most unladylike posture, which her mother had frequently deplored. Of course, Mrs. Storwood could understand and share her daughter's vexation with a suitor who, himself fascinated by archeological exploration, seemed to think that others shared his enthusiasm. It was all very well for him to discuss tumuli and whatever with Mr. Storwood, but to enlarge on the subject of Roman cremation at the dinner table was going a bit far! There had been a time when the Honorable Cranford Ashwicke had not been such a pedagogue, when he was the despair of his mother and a drain on his father's purse. But after Lady Chessels' death he had settled down quite nicely—too nicely, Mrs. Storwood feared, to appeal to her effervescent daughter.

Perhaps it was the wildness surrounding her in the Westmorland countryside which inspired Trelenny to her hoydenish behavior. More likely it was the lack of polite society, with its polishing influence, which had such an effect. No amount of strictures and examples seemed to make the least impression on the girl. Like a pot on the boil, there was no restraining her spirits. It was a wonder, really, that Cranford would even consider her as a bride!

Not that Trelenny was not an attractive girl, in her way. The impish blue eyes were set in a face which had not entirely lost its girlish roundness, though her figure had now developed from its former chubbiness into a rather alluring fullness. And there was no hiding it in today's gowns, Mrs. Storwood thought uneasily. Not that there was anyone to see her emerging butterfly, more was the pity. It was really the greatest shame that Mr. Storwood's weak heart prevented them from taking the girl to London to enjoy a season and meet some people of her own age. Just to acquaint her with the world of fashion, Mrs. Storwood rationalized, as she could see the advantages of Trelenny's marrying Cranford every bit as well as her husband. And the freckles which sprinkled across her cheeks and nose would surely subside without the constant exposure to the sharp winds of the country. If not, they could be bathed with milk, which Trelenny would doubtless allow when she realized the great importance of being in fashion. The braided blonde hair, too, would be so lovely trained into one of those styles one saw in *Le Beau Monde*, rather than pinned tightly to her head to prevent its escaping when she dashed madly about the lanes on that frisky mare.

Mrs. Storwood sighed. "Yes, my love, it is vexing of Cranford to expect you to read such dry stuff, and I am sure he does not think to praise you for the effort you make to accommodate him. Yesterday I was astonished to find you poring over one of those old volumes of his for an hour or more."

A mischievous light danced in her daughter's eyes. "Oh, I found the most fascinating thing, Mama, and I intend to impress him with my endeavors when he calls this afternoon to take me riding."

"Do you, dear?" Mrs. Storwood asked uncertainly. "I'm sure that's very thoughtful of you."

"Yes, I think so," her daughter proclaimed righteously. "I shall change now, if you will excuse me."

And high time it was to show Cranford the futility of both his efforts to instruct and to woo her, Trelenny thought rebelliously as she allowed her maid to assist her into the most capacious of her riding habits, one of royal blue velvet with lace peeking out at her throat and her wrists. Imagine being married to such a stick! Not that she thought him the least enamored of her. There was something so mechanical, and so unloverlike about his courting that of itself it would have put her off, let alone his antiquarian leanings. He bore not the least resemblance to any lover *she* had ever read of, and having no personal experience, she could only rely on such novels as she came by, sent by her mother's considerate friends. The closest circulating library must be some eighty miles away, and she had only been to York twice in her life!

No, Cranford was only pursuing her out of the determined wishes of both their families, and he was doing a very poor job of it. It was time he learned a lesson, and she was just the one to give it. Aware that her mother and father would be shocked by her plans, she had bribed a stable lad to saddle her mare and take it to the copse by the stream, a spot which was not visible from the house. Still, a quaver of doubt assailed her when she surveyed Stalwart patiently standing under a tree, his reins loosely held by the boy.

"Is it . . . difficult to ride astride?" she asked breathlessly.

"Oh, no, ma'am," he assured her. "Easier than the sidesaddle, I should think. *You'll* be having no trouble. Just use your knees to grip and you'll be safe as houses."

"Very well, then. Hand me up, please."

For years she had watched men mount their horses, and it had seemed a very simple matter. And probably it was for them, unhampered by wide skirts as she was. The heel of her boot caught in the hem of the skirt as she attempted to swing her leg over the saddle, and she found herself ingloriously slung across like a pannier. Disgusted, she allowed herself to slip down to the ground once more. "You go back to the stables, Tommy, and tell Mr. Ashwicke to meet me here when he comes."

When the lad disappeared from view, she led Stalwart to a rock, raised her skirts immodestly, and gained a seat on the now restless mare. As commodious as the skirts were, there was no way in which she could settle them that they did not come above her short boots. She tugged and rearranged, an embarrassed flush staining her cheeks. Well, there was no help for it, and she certainly did not care what Cranford thought of her. So what if he caught a glimpse of her leg? It would probably be a unique sight for the stodgy old fellow. She was *not* going to abandon her plan.

Unaccustomed to sitting facing forward on a horse, she felt slightly unbalanced, though rather heady with her escapade. When Stalwart moved forward at her summons she found that her knees automatically gripped to give her a firm seat. How pleasant not to have one's back twisted about, she thought euphorically as she urged the mare to a gallop. Yes, decidedly it was a great deal more comfortable than riding the sidesaddle. She put Stalwart to a fence.

Now Trelenny knew exactly how to position herself for a jump in her customary fashion of riding, but she suddenly felt unsure as the horse tensed to leap forward. For one panic-stricken moment she did not think she would keep her seat, and then they were back on the ground and racing across the field. Amazing, she thought, that one should actually have so much more control riding this way, and inexplicably she grew very angry. Why had no one told her? What stupidity was it that kept women with their backs twisted, clinging to the tiny horn and knee rest? In mountainous country such as she lived in, the sidesaddle proved a precarious seat. Fuming with indignation, she headed the mare back to the copse.

Cranford watched her preoccupied approach with astonishment. Trust the little hoyden to do something outrageous! He had known, the moment they told him to meet her by the copse, that she was up to something. Whether it would be a race on donkeys or a raft built for the stream, he had not decided, but he had certainly not expected this. And her leg was showing above her boot, for God's sake! He dismounted and walked to meet her, grabbing Stalwart's bridle firmly. "Get down."

"I won't! And let go of my horse," she commanded fiercely.

"I do not ride with ladies seated astride."

"Then you need not ride with me, but if you don't release Stalwart I shall . . ." Menacingly, she waved her whip at him.

With one adept movement he reached out, clasped the whip, and twisted it from her grip. "Get down, Trelenny."

"Why should I?"

"For one thing, you are exposing an indecent amount of leg to the view of anyone who cares to look."

"Which I am sure you don't, and there is no one else abroad, so it cannot make the least difference."

"And I tell you it does, ma'am. You have had your little scene, so let's be done with it. Do I have to tell you again to get down or must I remove you forcibly?"

Trelenny glared at him but made an attempt to do as he ordered. Unfortunately, her boot heel once again betrayed her and became entangled in her skirt. While one leg hung down toward the ground her skirt remained high above with the other.

Drawing a sharp breath of exasperation, Cranford took hold of her waist and swung her off the horse as though she weighed no more than a saddle, allowing her feet to remain in the air until she had kicked her heel loose of the skirt. Then he desposited her unceremoniously on the ground. "Now, Trelenny, would you like to explain why you felt it necessary to put on such a display?"

"I don't owe you any explanation, though I assure you I had sufficient reason. And it is all your own fault!"

"I would be charmed to hear how that might be so," he replied with exaggerated gallantry.

"You wouldn't be charmed by anything but a dead Roman soldier in his crumbling gruesome coffin," she snapped as she grasped Stalwart's reins and began to walk towards the stables.

Unperturbed, he followed suit, not deigning to honor her castigation with a reply. After a while of stomping along, she glanced at him furtively. "I read something from one of the books you left me."

"I'm surprised to hear it."

"Well, I wouldn't have, but I heard Mama coming, and I didn't want her to know that I was reading *Glenarvon*, so I hid it under one of your wretched essays and just happened to see something of interest. Not interest, precisely, but something unusual. Ladies didn't use to ride sidesaddle, you know.

I learned that they used to ride astride just as men do. Fancy! And I thought I would show you how diligent a student I am by adopting the ways of your musty old Romans, or Greeks, or Egyptians, or whatever."

"You thought no such thing, my girl. Your only wish was to annoy me."

Trelenny turned her head aside and made a face. "Well, then, I succeeded."

"Admirably."

"I think it is wicked to make women ride sidesaddle when it is ever so much more comfortable riding astride. You know what these mountains are, Cranford. One has so much more control facing forward that it would be a great deal safer to ride about that way. I could have a skirt made full enough that it would come down to my boots. Or two skirts together, one for each leg so that they wouldn't ride up at all Yes, that would be even better. There could be no impropriety in that." She glanced at him earnestly.

"It won't do, Trelenny. You must realize your mother would never allow it."

His voice was slightly more sympathetic than it had been until this point, and she asked with some interest, "Would you approve?"

"No. I realize the sidesaddle gives a precarious seat over our dangerous, narrow roads, but ladies with breeding do not ride astride."

"The ancient ladies did."

"We pride ourselves on being a more cultivated society, Trelenny."

He sounded so inordinately stuffy that she was once again roused to anger. "Well, I think that your old Romans were not only uncultivated but stupid, bumbling paperskulls."

"But then, you haven't bothered to read anything about them," he said placidly.

"I have. I once read a guidebook on the various English counties. And there were enumerated all the antiquities in each one of them. And do you know how they often knew the Romans had been there?"

"Yes."

Ignoring him, she continued. "I shall tell you. They found coins. All kinds of coins, all over the place. From lots of different periods. Now, I am eighteen years old, Cranford, and I have never so much as lost a tuppence! There, you see?

What a bunch of dunderheads to be losing their money everywhere they went."

She glanced at him triumphantly, and he gave a roar of laughter and rumpled her hair. "Trelenny, you really are a goosecap. Imagine your using such powerful logic. Unanswerable, I promise you. I shall henceforth regard the Romans with a certain caution to my enthusiasm. How could it be otherwise after this major flaw in them has been pointed out to me?" His eyes danced with amusement.

"Now you're laughing at me. I see nothing funny in it. A careless group of people at the very least, and who knows what at worst?" Her very eyebrows quivered with her fervor.

"I could tell you, if you were interested," he teased.

"I'm not, thank you just the same." She turned her back on him and delivered Stalwart into her groom's hands. "I suppose you will wish to come in and take tea with Mama."

"She will expect me to do so, of course, but if it will inconvenience you . . ."

"Not in the least," she replied haughtily as she led the way toward the house.

"And, Trelenny, you should not be reading *Glenvaron*. You are far too young for such stuff, if there is any age for it, which I doubt."

"Little you know," she murmured; and, when he had been treated to her indifference over the tea table, she settled herself in the wing chair in her bedroom and finished the scandalous book. Not that she understood a great deal of its scandal because she had little knowledge of the people ridiculed and she had no intention of asking her mother for Mrs. Waplington's letter to decode the work.

The book was old hat to London society by now, having been out for some months, and Mrs. Waplington had debated the wisdom of sending it to her old friend; but the desire to exhibit her intimate knowledge of the participants had won over her better judgment. And though Trelenny believed that her mother had set aside the book as unworthy of her attention, in actual fact Mrs. Storwood had read every line with a horrified interest which would have astonished her daughter. After all, Mrs. Storwood had reasoned, she was not impressionable as her child was and she, too, knew Lady Holland and Lady Melbourne, if she had no acquaintance with the younger members of the cast. Sometimes it seemed to her, from the snippets of gossip her friends sent, that the *haut ton* had run mad and that she was better off in the country. At other times she ached with regret at her daughter's exclusion from the brilliantly lit ballrooms, the chatter-filled saloons, and the elegant playhouses. How well she remembered the days when Mr. Storwood was courting her against the backdrop of London's gaiety...

chapter two

"Wetherby, have we one of my sister's sidesaddles about still?" Cranford asked as he dismounted at the Ashwicke Park stables.

The groom rubbed a hand thoughtfully over his chin and cocked his head. "Mayt be, sir, and then mayt not. Want I should have a look-see?"

"If you would. I'll be back a little later. Is my father at home?"

"Yes, sir. Leastways, he's not rid out."

With a nod, Cranford consigned his horse to the groom and trod purposefully toward the house. There was no use allowing the viscount to believe that his son's suit with Miss Storwood was prospering, since it most emphatically was not. Although Cranford had not yet discussed the matter of marriage with the young lady herself, they were both well aware of his intentions. How could she not be, when he had approached Mr. Storwood for permission to court his daughter? Cranford was also aware that both Trelenny's parents were in favor of the match. Only the daughter was not! But it went against the grain to offer for her when she was so patently indisposed to his suit, and he refused to speak of it with her when she gave him not the least encouragement. The silly child had every intention of refusing him, he could feel it in his bones, and he had no desire to hear her say so, the ungrateful imp.

The warm September sunlight barely penetrated Lord Chessels' study, for he kept the draperies drawn while he worked there. There was no similarity between father and son. Lord Chessels was of only medium height and his son towered over him, while the harshly drawn features of the older man had found a kinder expression in the aristocratic nose, high cheekbones, and firm jaw of the younger. No lines of irritability scored Cranford's forehead, and his eyes although almost black, held none of the fierceness of his father's. Cranford, as always, wore an impassive countenance in his father's presence. Lord Chessels lifted preoccupied eyes from the accounts he was studying. "It's you. Have you been to Sutton Hall?"

"Yes, sir."

"And the matter is settled at last, I hope." Lord Chessels' questioning brow rose with a hint of impatience.

"No, far from it." It took an effort for Cranford to subdue the resentment which rose in him at his father's condescending attitude, and he walked to the far end of the room, where he idly twirled the enormous globe. "I have not yet asked her because she does not welcome my suit."

"Nonsense. How can you know unless you put the matter to her?" his father asked with undisguised annoyance.

Cranford clamped his teeth together and did not reply for a long moment. In his youth he would have spoken his mind with little regard for the respect due his father; he was more cautious now. His body still tensed with resentment as it always had, but he was more the master of his emotions now. "You have seen very little of Trelenny, of course, Father. She's as transparent as a pane of glass, and she finds me a very dull fellow."

The cold light in his father's eyes spoke volumes. "You are boring her with your antiquities. Ladies aren't interested in Roman ruins and Latin verses, Cranford. I would have thought *you* would know that . . . but perhaps you've forgotten." Lord Chessels drummed his fingers against the desk top. "Her parents are in favor of the match. She will do what they wish."

"I think not. They won't force her, and God knows I don't want an unwilling bride. They have some influence, of course, but she's a willful girl. Perhaps in time she will accustom herself to the idea, though I admit I am not particularly hopeful on that score."

"Ha! You would be delighted if she refused you," the older man growled. "I can't see what you have against the girl. Takes after her mother a good deal in looks, with that blonde hair and those blue eyes. And you can see in Maria Storwood that there is no fading over twenty years' time. Still a beautiful woman, with a fair understanding and considerable natural grace. What is there to balk at in that?"

"I take not the least exception to Mrs. Storwood, who is a lady of refinement and good breeding. Her daughter is a hoyden."

"She'll settle down when she produces an heir for you. They always do," Lord Chessels replied smugly.

Again Cranford's body stiffened and a muscle in his jaw twitched. "Do they, sir?"

The viscount raised his eyes sharply at the note of sarcasm in his son's voice. "Just see that you win the girl, Cranford. Remember, it was your mother's fondest wish."

The young man's eyes dropped before the triumph in his father's gaze. "I'll do what I can. If you will excuse me, sir..."

"Certainly. You've kept me long enough from important matters."

Unmoved by the hostile dismissal, Cranford bowed formally, and quietly let himself out of the room. Since his mother's death several years previously, he had spent a fair amount of time at Ashwicke Park, but it had not been largely pleasurable time. The house itself he loved, with its fourteenth-century fan vaulting and oak panelling. Nor could he fault his father for the care he took of the house and grounds. They were, in fact, an obsession with the older man. No incipient decay was left unattended; servants were dismissed preemptorily for any carelessness in their duties to maintain the ancient building. Granted to the Ashwicke family at the Dissolution, the old abbey had been successfully converted into a magnificent residence, and the current Lord Chessels was nagged only by the persistent belief that all of the former abbey grounds should be encompassed by his estate. But the king had seen fit in his wisdom to split the lands between the Storwoods and the Ashwickes, the latter gaining the more valuable property, and no subsequent families had intermarried to combine the two. Lord Chessels was determined to see this gross oversight corrected in his lifetime.

Cranford himself had no such desire, either to combine the lands or to marry the Storwood heiress. Both were matters of indifference to him, as were his father's wishes on the subject, but he could not be so sanguine in ignoring a match his mother had looked upon with favor. Of course, Trelenny had been only fifteen or sixteen when Lady Chessels had died, and his mother could not possibly have known what kind of young lady she would become. Her wish was based on the fondness she had for Trelenny as a child, as a younger friend for Clare, and also on her friendship of many years with Mrs. Storwood. It would be comforting to think that were she alive today, she would share his own dismay at Trelenny's behavior; unfortunately, he feared she would not.

Ashwicke Park was not the same without his mother and sister. The lifelong antagonism with his father now colored his stays there, unrelieved as they had been in the past by the loving concern of Lady Chessels and the charming enthusiasm of Clare. Cranford wandered into the drawing room and stood by the traceried gothic window, looking out over the park. Although he could easily envision Trelenny galloping about the estate, he could not summon an image of her presiding over the tea tray or seated at the Broadwood pianoforte. Not once had he heard her play, and he had a sinking feeling that she did not know how. His mother and Clare had entertained the family circle and guests alike with their delightful performances, leaving all (except the usually slumbering viscount) enchanted. Since these occasions were among the few pictures of domestic harmony which Cranford could call forth from his own memory, the fact that Trelenny did not fit into them was more than discouraging. It was depressing.

Impatiently he spun about and headed for the stables, where he learned that Wetherby had found an old saddle of Clare's stored in a little used cabinet under a variety of worn blankets. The groom watched him curiously as he studied the design of the horn, knee rest, fork base, and cantle. "Is someat wrong, sir?"

"Hmm. Certainly it is not a particularly safe or practical seat. Put it on Luckless if you will." Cranford ignored the groom's horrified expression and stood thoughtfully tapping his long fingers against a bench, his eyes unseeing but his mind rapidly considering and rejecting various innovations. When the groom called his attention to the fact that the horse awaited, Cranford nodded and, oblivious to the sensation he caused, swung himself onto the sidesaddle, muttering, "Damned awkward."

The stable staff watched with astonishment as he put

Luckless through his paces and eventually disappeared from their sight as he rode along a wooded path leading uphill. Although he did not return for half an hour, the men and boys made no comment and avoided one another's eyes as they went about their work. Definitely the young master had changed since his mother had died, but out of respect for their memory of him as a reckless youth they would not discuss the matter. If they could overlook his penchant for bringing home broken jars and muddy old coins, at his age, then they could try to overlook his riding out on a sidesaddle!

Even though he was an expert rider, Cranford found it difficult to adapt himself to the seat required by the saddle. Jumping was particularly difficult as his knees did not find the purchase they ordinarily had. Luckless, unused to the strange balance of the load he carried, attempted several times to unseat his rider, and very nearly succeeded when they jumped a low wall onto descending ground. Cranford returned to the stables more thoughtful than he had been when he left.

Unfortunately, Lord Chessels had tired of his work on the estate books and had determined to have a ride before dusk. He was just swinging himself up onto his bay stallion when his son rode into the stableyard. An angry red suffused his face to an accompanying roar. "What the hell do you think you're doing?"

"Attempting to assess the safety and practicality of a sidesaddle, sir."

"Don't you think perhaps you should be wearing a skirt?" his father asked in a voice laden with sarcasm.

Cranford considered the suggestion. "Yes, you are undoubtedly right, Father. It would be impossible to consider the safety without taking into consideration the wearing apparel used in conjunction with the sidesaddle."

Infuriated, Lord Chessels raised his whip, and, for the second time that day, Cranford automatically moved to protect himself. He twisted the whip from his father's grip and tossed it to the ground. The movement was unexpected, but Lord Chessels in his fury lashed his hand across the young man's face. Cranford sat perfectly still in the ridiculous saddle, the red of the handmark vivid against his white face. In a cold, detached voice he said, "You were always one to act without sufficient information. Miss Storwood complained of the insecurity of a sidesaddle in our rough part of the country. In an effort to ... accommodate her, I am endeavoring to work out a saddle with a better seat. I had hoped that she might be pleased with such a service on my part."

Lord Chessels merely sneered. "More fool she if anything you do pleases her."

"Doubtless it was a vain hope," Cranford replied stiffly. His voice dropped to a murmur. "I am sure you would prefer a daughter-in-law who rides astride."

The older man's eyes narrowed, but instead of replying he dug his heels into the bay and rode off at a gallop. When he was out of sight, Cranford dismounted but did not touch the whip which lay at his feet. Instead he allowed Wetherby to lead Luckless to his stall, instructing that the saddle be taken to the workshop. "Tell Gillray I will be by tomorrow morning to discuss some changes I wish him to make in the saddle. And have the chestnuts ready in half an hour. I'll be taking the phaeton."

"You be wantin' me to come with you?" Wetherby asked eagerly.

"No, not tonight."

The scene between father and son had been witnessed by all, and Cranford received encouraging smiles from the men he passed as he headed back toward the house. Without a glance, he avoided the whip where it lay in the dirt, and when he returned some time later, dressed in an elegant coat of navy with light gray pantaloons and Hessians, it was still there. Expressionlessly he climbed into the carriage and gathered the ribbons in his hands. The snapping of the whip under the wheels of the phaeton caused an audible sigh from the apparently occupied stable staff, but not a muscle moved in Cranford's impassive face.

Wetherby grunted as the phaeton gathered speed. "You seed him. And you heard him," he declared belligerently to no one in particular. "There's nothing amiss with young Mr. Ashwicke. He's a-fixin' the saddle for Miss Storwood. A man can't know what needs a-fixin' without he tries it hisself, by God. And I'm a-willin' to take on any man who thinks otherways. Just say one word agin him ..." Adopting the stance he considered most appropriate to a fighter, and looking for all the world like a bantam cock, Wetherby stared a challenge at his co-workers.

"Back down, big fellow," the coachman called jocularly. "Ain't a one of us thinks any different from you. He be worth a dozen of his pappy, and so I'd swear on a stack of Bibles. Only one of you tells his lordship I said so, and I'll break his neck, I will. Give over, Wetherby. Young master may be an an-tee-quary but he's a right-un."

Once the phaeton had gained the main road, which ran from Shap to Kendal, Cranford found himself caught up in the melancholy atmosphere of the chain of mountainous moors over which he passed. Darkness was falling, but the last rays of the setting sun touched on the uncultivated land with a mysterious light which never failed to fascinate the young man. It was at such times of day when he could most easily imagine those Roman settlements which had spread over Britain so long ago. Kendal itself might well have been the Roman station of Concangium, and Cranford had studied with avid curiosity the Roman inscriptions and altars that remained there, the urns found in the riverbank, and the stones and pieces of Roman bricks occasionally thrown up by the plow. Especially interesting to him were the coins and seals, particularly the one supposed to be Janus quadrifons and the medal of Faustina. After the disruptions of the day Cranford spent a pleasant hour lost in the mysteries of the past before he began the descent to Kendal, seated on the west bank of the river and flourishing with all the prosperity the changing times could muster for the mercers, sheermen, cordwainers, tanners, glovers, tailors, and pewterers who plied their trades there. Its two main streets, neatly paved, crossed each other and were lined with shops and manufactories. The knit stockings, Kendal cottons, and linsey woolsey the town was famous for could be the more easily forgotten at night when the darkness obscured the evidence of trade, and the warm glow of light issuing from the public rooms of the King's Arms invited the visitor to join the merriment within.

But it was not to the inn that Cranford directed his pair. He crossed the stone bridge leading out of town and continued a short distance along the main road. Though the light from the carriage lamp seemed feeble in the blackness, he had no difficulty in discerning the drive which gave onto the road from the left; he'd been this way before. There was nothing exceptional about the house he approached. It might have been any one of the modest homes of the wealthier tradesmen, a classic stone structure of a pleasing simplicity and symmetry with well-kept lawns and flower borders. The buildings were out of sight of the road, but no one in the neighborhood was unaware of their existence. And yet it was the best-kept secret in the north of England.

The groom who appeared at the sound of the approaching carriage lifted the lantern he carried close enough to allow him a careful look at Cranford, and his suspicious countenance softened into a welcoming smile. There was nothing tightfisted about Mr. Ashwicke; though it was evident that he was not one of your particularly well-heeled gentlemen, he never grudged a handsome gratuity for the care of his horses. "Fine night, sir. Shall I be giving them a good rub-down?"

"If you would, Will. Mrs. Reed is enjoying her usual good health, I presume."

"Never better, an' I'm any judge." The boy grinned. His employer held his devotion but hardly his awe.

"Excellent. Is there anyone here I am likely to know?"

"Aye, Mr. Rusholme and Mr. Bodford arrived not this half hour past."

"Tony must have made a recovery," Cranford murmured as he turned to leave.

The flambeaux on either side of the door lit the gravel path well enough to aid the visitor, and the flicker of candlelight from the first-floor drawing room gave the place a festive air which was not belied by entry into the hall. Ablaze with light and well supplied with liveried footmen, the hall had the atmosphere of a private party carried out to perfection. Entry was not by card, however, but by personal recommendation from a previous visitor, with Mrs. Reed having the final word on any newcomer. Cranford gave his hat and gloves to the footman and cast a hasty glance in the gilt-framed glass above the hall table. The black cravat he sported was rather a personal joke, poking fun at his own solemnity at those times when he discussed his researches on Roman ruins. His reflection assured him that there was nothing amiss with the folds of the cravat, or the straight black hair, but one of the high cheekbones retained a redness where his father's ringed hand had scraped the skin. With an impatient shrug, he turned aside to climb the finely carved oak staircase.

A dozen people stood about the room into which he was ushered, and all turned as he was announced. Mrs. Reed, a petite, aging beauty, tripped forward with outstretched hands. "Ah, Cranford, you have chosen to honor us with your presence. It's been some time and we thought you had forgotten us."

"Impossible," he retorted as he raised her hand to his lips. "You look as charming as ever, Sally. Am I in time for dinner?"

"That's all men ever think about," she admonished him.

"Hardly... in *your* house." His eyes strayed in turn to the five other women in the room, each elegantly dressed, all enchantingly beautiful. "I believe there has been an addition since last I was here."

"Margaret." Mrs. Reed motioned to a fiery-haired damsel as she spoke the name. "May I present Mr. Ashwicke to you, Margaret? He hasn't been here since you came, so we can surely accuse him of at least three months' neglect."

"I had to marshal my resources," he complained laughingly, "after that last foray into faro. Miss Margaret, I am charmed to make your acquaintance."

"The pleasure is mine, Mr. Ashwicke." The emerald-green eyes studied him frankly and a dimple appeared as she smiled. "Mr. Bodford has spoken of you."

"Has he now? And what could the bounder possibly have told you to call forth such a smile? I personally never believe a word he says."

"How unfair, Cranford!" declared a sturdily built young man who appeared at his elbow. "I need all the credibility I can muster with Miss Margaret and don't you go spoiling it. Told her nothing but that you were top of the trees, I promise."

"And that you collect broken tombstones," Margaret added, her eyes twinkling.

"I never!" Mr. Bodford protested. "You must be thinking of Rusholme. *He* is the one who thinks you're a ghoul, like Selwyn, but *I* have never known you to chase after funeral processions or frequent Tyburn. The man must have been dicked in the nob—Selwyn, I mean, not you, Cranford." Bodford eyed Margaret with mock reproach. "Now see what you've done, my dear. Gotten me all twisted up. Cranford is the best of fellows even if he does like to grub about in ruins. Just don't talk to him about old fortifications and you will find him a charming conversationalist. But be warned! One mention of the moldering past and he's off! I tell you only for your own protection, I assure you."

Cranford laughed. "It is no more than the truth, Miss Margaret. Once I get on my hobby horse, I am like to forget that my audience does not perhaps share my fascination with antiquities. Mrs. Reed has a habit of squelching my enthusiasm rather effectively, however."

Mrs. Reed regarded him affectionately. "You need do no more than call him 'Professor,' Margaret. It has the most wonderful effect on him."

The young woman dimpled again and said solemnly, "I shall remember."

"Come, Cranford," Mrs. Reed urged, linking her arm with his, "You've had no chance to speak with the others and it's nearly time for dinner."

chapter three

When the gong sounded, Cranford offered his arm to the young woman standing beside him, an elegantly tall, fair-haired beauty named Kitty. It was not the first time he had escorted her to dinner; in fact, when he came to Mrs. Reed's he invariably sought her out. There was a refinement about her wholly at odds with her way of life. Soft-spoken and surprisingly dignified, she was not the choice of most of the men who came, but she was a favorite of Mrs. Reed's because of her decided air of class. Mrs. Reed ran a very distinguished establishment and tolerated no ill-mannered ruffians amongst her guests, nor unseemly public behavior from her girls. Tuesdays, Thursdays, and Saturdays her doors were open to those privileged few whom she deemed worthy of entry; if any man dared treat her house as a common gaming house or brothel, he was quickly escorted from the premises and denied future entry. Her standards were high, and Miss Kitty, in her opinion, helped to set the tone of the house.

Lacking the vivacity of Margaret or Claudette, and, though well endowed, not nearly so provocative as Marie or Susan, Kitty yet had a fascination of her own for those who appreciated her calm personality and reserved demeanor. Mrs. Reed was protective of her prize asset, as one might expect, but Kitty's natural warmth stilled any resentment there might have been amongst the other girls. A shrewd businesswoman and a clever judge of character, Mrs. Reed had no girls who resented their way of life, even Kitty.

"Come and sit by me," Mrs. Reed urged Cranford as they entered the dining parlor, which sparkled with crystal and silver. "And Tony shall sit on Kitty's right to amuse her just in case you should backslide."

"Never fear. Between the two most beautiful women in the room I am more like to pour forth poetry," Cranford assured her. " 'Not marble, nor the gilded monuments, Of princes, shall outlive this powerful rhyme; But you shall shine more bright in these contents Than unswept stone, besmear'd with sluttish time.' "

Mrs. Reed pursed her lips. "I *think* that makes me feel old, Cranford, if nothing worse. How is your father?"

"Much as usual." Cranford unconsciously touched the scrape on his cheek.

"I've often thought it would be interesting to meet him. Have you been long at Ashwicke Park?"

"For the last few weeks. I spent several months at Coverly."

"That's your estate, is it not?"

"Yes, I inherited it from my mother."

Kitty asked gently, "And does it prosper, Mr. Ashwicke? You seemed troubled when you last spoke of it."

"I was concerned that an experiment I was trying might not prove successful, but it has exceeded my expectations."

Tony Bodford leaned forward to interject, "You don't say! You have the most incredible luck, Cranford. Who would have thought you could do a blessed thing with camomile? Surely there aren't that many people who drink the stuff as tea! Ugh!"

Cranford laughed. "Not only tea, Tony. It's used as medicine, too, and in warm fomentations. But it wasn't just the camomile. I've tried a new variety of sheep on the land. Smaller because the poorness of the soil won't support a larger breed. When next you buy Bagshot mutton in London, it may well come from Coverly and have that sweetness for which the sheep which graze on the heath are noted. Not that most of the Bagshot mutton is actually grazed there. Usually they come from the Hampshire downs."

"No doubt the viscount is delighted with your success," Tony said sardonically.

"He hasn't asked."

"You'd think he were run off his legs the way he cut you off when you inherited Coverly from your mother!" Tony blurted. "Whoever heard of such a thing? Rich as a nabob and he flings you off to make the best of a barren heath! Sometimes I think . . ."

Cranford flashed him a warning look and turned to Mrs. Reed. "Next time I'm in Surrey I'll have some of the mutton sent to you. I think you'll find it exceptionally good."

Though Kitty's gray eyes registered her surprise at the gratuitous information offered by Tony Bodford, she followed Cranford's lead and turned the subject to other matters. The table at the Cypress was no less extravagant than all its other claims on the gentlemen who came. No *haut ton* dinner party had a finer bill of fare; no gaming club in London was run with more finesse and order. The stakes were high but not exorbitant, and a table was often kept for more moderate plungers. Kitty sat quietly at Cranford's side as he played, smiling when he glanced at her and pleased when he rose early as a winner. As was the custom of the house, she left the room while he bade his friends good evening and made his farewells to Mrs. Reed.

Kitty's room was at the end of the west corridor and Cranford made his way there at a leisurely pace, quietly knocking on the panelled door to announce his arrival. When he entered he found her standing by the fire, its glow the only light in the room. He went to stand by her without speaking.

"Is what Mr. Bodford said true? Your father expects you to support yourself from a barren estate?"

"It's hardly barren," he said with amusement. "Tony disparages it because it bears no resemblance to his family's vast acreage. Admittedly it was not in good order when I inherited it. My father had made no attempt to keep it up, feeling much as Tony does and resenting the fact that my mother brought to the marriage only two relatively useless properties. My sister's husband is having the devil of a time doing anything with her inheritance, too."

"But your father doesn't support you, his heir?"

"No. He feels it will build my character to struggle under adversity," he replied ruefully as he stroked her hair. "And it was certainly an effective way to stop the spendthrift habits of my youth. My mother was forever purse-pinched from bailing me out of difficulties and when her allowance did not suffice . . . well, my father thinks of this as a way for me to repay him for his expenditures on my behalf."

Kitty touched the lines on his forehead with gentle fingers. "You make light of what cannot be a pleasant situation. What will happen when you wish to marry?"

"He'll make a handsome settlement on me—if I marry the lady of his choice."

"And has he chosen someone for you?"

"Oh, yes, there was never any question. He thinks when I tire of living hand to mouth I will marry and unite the two neighboring properties." Cranford traced the oval of her face and bent to kiss her.

After a while she asked, "And will you?"

"I suppose so, if Trelenny will have me, which is doubtful. But not because of my father."

"You love the lady?"

"Dear God, no. She's . . . no matter. There is another debt I owe. May I?" His hands rested on the buttons of her gown and when she nodded he began carefully to unfasten them, kissing the nape of her neck as he did so.

"And will you and your bride live with him?"

"He thinks so. I doubt he can imagine our living at Coverly, but he's wrong. I've spent as much as I dared in restoring the house there and it won't be long before it will be acceptable." As the gown fell unheeded to the floor he gathered her in his arms. "I'd like to have set you up somewhere this last year or so, Kitty. I couldn't afford to."

Her long fingers paused as she unbuttoned his coat. "I'm happy here, Cranford. It's lonely sitting in a house somewhere with no one about, waiting for your protector to come and visit you. You have no friends, no life outside those visits. Perhaps it would be different in London but London is so . . . rough. Don't be sorry you couldn't take me under your protection. I probably wouldn't have left here, anyhow."

"I see." He ran his hands gently down her slender body, aware that his touch quickly brought forth a response in her. "You wouldn't prefer . . . no, I won't ask that. You have the most beautiful body, Kitty. The gentle swell of your breasts, not like some ship's prow. And your hips—I should like to see you riding. You must be the most graceful rider imaginable."

Kitty smiled gently as he continued to stroke her body. "I don't know how to ride, Cranford, and I haven't the least desire to learn. You are quite a romantic, you know."

"Am I?" he asked, surprised. "I have always thought of myself as exceedingly mundane."

"You dream of ideals, I think. Oh, I like that. Shall I..."

Some time later she lay quietly in his arms as he traced a pattern on her naked body with a languid finger. "Will you be coming again soon?"

"I really don't know. I hope so. You really like it here?" he asked curiously.

"Yes. I like having friends around. Claudette keeps us laughing and Marie tells the most incredible stories. Mrs. Reed knows all the latest gossip and Susan is always ready to walk about the estate with me. I'm always warm, and full, and happy."

"But what of ... years from now?"

"Mrs. Reed puts aside money for us, and it's ours whenever we wish to leave."

"And that's enough?"

"We are handsomely paid. Oh, I see. Yes, that's enough." Kitty's gray eyes regarded him kindly. "You want there to be more. I'm sorry, Cranford, but there's not. You are idealizing again, you see. I don't support an aging mother or an invalid father or a dozen deserving brothers and sisters. There's only me, and I like to dress well and eat well and be warm and comfortable. I was not victimized by some lecherous man who robbed my virtue and started me on a life of degradation. I was not even wretchedly poor and abandoned. Some years ago I made a modest living as a seamstress to a very distinguished family. I saw how they lived and I wanted more. It's as simple as that. Now I have what I want. Does that shock you?"

"Yes." He sighed and then laughed. "You are right, dear lady. I build castles in the air. My mother was a dreamer; it was all she had. I wish ... well, perhaps I take after her. Which is not to say that my illusions are shattered! You are still the most desirable woman I've set eyes on in years, and I have every intention of returning as soon as may be." He kissed her and gently disengaged himself. "Sleep well, my lovely. I have a long drive ahead of me."

Trelenny, feeling reluctantly and belatedly guilty for the way she had treated poor, harmless Cranford the previous day, sat drowsing over his translations of Antoninus. It was remarkable to her how, when she had felt perfectly energetic before beginning her reading, only three pages of the unfamiliar names could make her feel overcome with the greatest lethargy imaginable. She had closed her eyes and her hand had slipped from the page when her mother's voice recalled her attention.

"Do you remember Cousin Filkins, Trelenny? I believe he's actually your father's second cousin by marriage. You must have met him, oh, perhaps five years ago when he came to visit."

"I remember him," Trelenny said dispiritedly as she stifled a yawn. "He kept telling me that freckles were the outward signs of sin and that if I did a good deed each day they would one by one disappear. I must be the most dastardly sinner, for I have more now than I did at thirteen."

"What nonsense! It is no such thing, my dear. Freckles have no relation whatsoever with your soul."

"Perhaps I could convince Cranford that they do," Trelenny said thoughtfully. "Surely such a righteous man would never consider a sinner for a bride."

"Trelenny! He is no more righteous than the next, I promise you. Why, I recall his mother telling me the most astonishing stories of the wild oats he was sowing. But pay no heed to me. I'm sure he is a very respectable fellow now and he doesn't mean to appear straitlaced. Has he scolded you about something?"

"Humph. He sets himself up as the model of every virtue," Trelenny said evasively. "Tell me what he did, Mama."

"That would be gossiping, my love, and you know I can't approve of gossip. But I was about to tell you that I have had a letter from Cousin Filkins. And can you imagine, he intends to visit us!"

"I can imagine."

"Not a rushed sort of visit, he says, but a good long stay to renew his old friendship with your Papa."

"I might have known."

"I wonder why he would come at this time of year?" Mrs. Storwood mused. "He must know that the weather is not at its best now. He should have come in the summer."

"He probably wasn't rolled-up then. Maybe he's had an

execution in his house," her daughter said hopefully. "I've never met anyone with his pockets to let before. Do you suppose he will borrow money from Papa to pay his debts?"

"Where *do* you learn these terms? It's vulgar to talk so, Trelenny, and we have no reason to believe that Cousin Filkins is financially embarrassed. Quite the contrary, in fact. He is coming post."

Trelenny sniffed. "It's all show, Mama. Probably Papa will have to pay the post boys to ransom him."

Mrs. Storwood rubbed her forehead; it was a common gesture she employed when her daughter wove some outrageous tale. Unfortunately she could not, as she wished to do, tell her daughter that Cousin Filkins was *not* financially embarrassed, because in all likelihood he was. But she had no intention of allowing Trelenny to spread such a rumor about the estate. "I think I will just take a small nap, dear. You're not expecting Cranford, are you?"

"Oh, no, you go right along, Mama. Does your head hurt? Shall I bring you something for it?"

"I only need to rest quietly for a while, dear. Perhaps a dish of tea, but nothing more."

When she had seen her mother laid down upon her bed, Trelenny returned to the Winter Parlor, and unenthusiastically picked up her former reading material, but her mind strayed. As though things weren't bad enough, now they had to sustain a visit from the most unappealing man imaginable. Although of considerable girth, Cousin Filkins considered himself of sartorial perfection. Spotted neckcloths and garishly striped waistcoats were his favorite attire, and his conversation consisted of little more than a catalogue of his wardrobe or the fallacies of others' dress. A self-confessed expert on feminine beauty, he had found fault with Trelenny's thirteen-year-old figure and her freckled face, producing a platitude to rectify each awkward point. It wouldn't do to have him about, pinching her cheeks and chucking her under the chin. She had a good mind to write and tell him she thought she was coming down with the scarlet fever, and the only thing that deterred her was a rather superstitious belief that she really might if she told such a lie. Although her father was not particularly fond of Cousin Filkins, he was unswerving in his family loyalties, and, for better or worse, Cousin Filkins was the last surviving relation he had, outside of his wife and daughter.

With the blasé incisiveness of youth, Trelenny determined that the most expedient solution would be for her father to send Cousin Filkins a supply of money that would enable him to rusticate at some watering hole and make it unnecessary for him to visit Sutton Hall. When she proposed this plan to her father, he regarded her dourly.

"Have you no sense of family feeling, Trelenny? Do you feel no obligation to anyone but yourself? It is by no means certain that Cousin Filkins is in need of money, and why you should distrust his motives in coming here is beyond me. I haven't seen my cousin in five years, nor he me. We will have a great deal of reminiscing to do."

"But, Papa, he only talks of clothes and you are not the least interested in fashion."

"Clothes? Whatever are you saying? Of course he talks of things other than clothes," her father said exasperatedly.

"Well, he never spoke of anything else to *me*. And I think he wears the most appalling outfits I have ever seen."

"You are in no position to stand in judgment of your elders, Trelenny. My cousin Filkins is coming to stay with us and I have every intention of enjoying his visit. I don't wish to hear any more on the matter, and I expect you to behave yourself while he's here." Her father made a gesture of dismissal.

"Yes, Papa."

It was difficult to argue with Papa because of his weak heart. Not that he precisely used his infirmity as an excuse to terminate any disagreeable discussion; he would probably have felt his authority sufficient to do so in any case. But there was always the fear of exciting him, and Dr. Moore had said most emphatically that he must never be disturbed by the emotional upheavals to which women were prone to subject men. Trelenny considered Dr. Moore an old fuddy-duddy, but she had herself seen her father suffer a spasm after an emotional scene and she did not wish to repeat the experience. Her Papa was the dearest, kindest man in the world despite his expectation of instant obedience from his daughter, which he seldom got, and he was also very indulgent of her. Clare Ashwicke had never been given the freedom by Viscount Chessels that Trelenny enjoyed under her father's benevolent reign, so she felt very lucky and found little cause to complain.

Another idea was forming in Trelenny's fertile brain. If

Cousin Filkins could not be pensioned off to a watering hole, perhaps she and her mother could go away. The more she thought of it, the more she could see that the plan had distinct possibilities. While Mrs. Storwood would never consider abandoning her husband to his own resources in order to go off galavanting with her daughter, here was the perfect opportunity to leave him in the care of his own cousin. What could be better? Mr. Storwood had ever intention of enjoying his cousin's visit (he had said so), and Trelenny considered it only fair that some use should be made of Cousin Filkins, since he was insisting on imposing on the hospitality of her family. It was the perfect chance to get to London at last—and perhaps the only chance she would ever have. Cousin Filkins' visit began to look like a blessing in disguise.

chapter four

"London?" Mrs. Storwood reached for her handkerchief and decided that either her nap had not been long enough, or that she should not have taken a nap at all, since obviously this pot had brewed while she so innocently slept. "Without your father? Darling, you are being unrealistic."

"But, Mama, it is the very best possible time to go, can't you see? Cousin Filkins will be here to keep Papa company. Just for a few weeks, Mama. It is not the season, but we would have a chance to see the shops, and perhaps one of your old friends would give a very *small* party for us. And we could go to the theatre..."

"No," Mrs. Storwood said firmly. "London is not simply an enlarged Kendal, Trelenny. It is a frightening city to be in without a male escort. My especial friends are not there now; Mrs. Waplington is in Bath and Lady Sandburn is at their seat. Have you considered the journey? No, no, it won't do. Highwaymen, footpads." She shuddered delicately. "I know it is very hard on you, dear, living secluded as we do. If you were to marry Cranford, I don't doubt you'd have a chance to see a bit more of the country, London..."

"Cranford again. How can you think I would marry him just so that I might have a chance to see London? What a despicable reason to marry someone."

"My dear, you misunderstand me. Of course you wouldn't marry him just to see London. I merely say that he would probably take you there one day."

"More like he would take me to see some Roman graveyard—on our honeymoon!" A strange light suddenly glistened in Trelenny's eyes, causing her mother to press the handkerchief once more against her lips. "If we had someone to escort us to London, could we go?"

"No my love. I'm sorry, but somehow I would feel disloyal to your father going to London without him. That is where we met, you know, and I could not bear to think of him here alone."

"With Cousin Filkins!"

"Thinking of me there amongst all that gaiety. No, no. It wouldn't be fair to him, Trelenny. He cannot make the journey with me, and I cannot go without him. Don't you see how unhappy it would make him? He frets enough that our life is restricted. You would not wish to add an extra burden. Think of what Dr. Moore said."

"Dr. Moore is an old woman. Oh, I know we mustn't upset Papa, but I can't imagine that he would be so alarmed at our going to London. Don't you think he would be happy for us? Glad that I would have a chance to get about a little?"

"Trelenny, I will not take you to London. Let's have no more discussion of the matter, and I strictly forbid you to broach the subject to your Papa. You must simply accept the situation, my dear." Mrs. Storwood regarded her daughter with sad eyes. "I don't know how to make it up to you, dear. Perhaps we could go to Kendal to buy some material for a new gown."

The girl bit her lip to still the rebellious reply that rose swiftly to mind. Not only would she not get a trip to London, but she would have to sustain a visit from the ludicrous Cousin Filkins as well. Swallowing painfully, she said, "I don't really need a new gown, Mama, but thank you. If you don't mind I think I shall go for a ride now. Is your head feeling better?"

"Much better," her mother lied gallantly.

Several days passed during which Trelenny did her best to hide her disappointment. Cranford did not come to visit her, and the arrival of her father's cousin was imminent. Surprisingly, it took her all that while to see that there was another avenue of escape. This time she did not precipitately reveal her thoughts to either of her parents, but spent several hours in the study going over travel books and guidebooks, as well as any of the antiquarian literature that might suit her purpose. She was browsing through the latter when there was a knock at the door. "Yes?"

A footman entered. "Mr. Ashwicke has called, Miss Storwood. He is with Mrs. Storwood in the Blue Drawing Room and your mother asked that you join them."

"Thank you, Hodges. I'll come directly." Before closing the book she held, Trelenny consigned the information on the page to memory. Drawing a deep, courage-engendering breath, she smoothed her dress and glanced in the glass to be sure that her blonde tresses had not come undone. She moistened a finger to rub away a smudge on her forehead and then, trying to remember all the lessons her mother had given her on deportment, walked as gracefully as she could to the drawing room. Her habit was to enter any room with more enthusiasm than poise, but today she forced herself to slip quietly through the door and wait until she was noticed.

"Ah, Trelenny, there you are. Look who has come to call," her mother said needlessly, a faint twitch of alarm stirring in her at the beatific smile her daughter wore.

"How kind of you to visit us, Cranford," Trelenny murmured as she extended her hand to him. A shadow of disappointment crossed her features when he merely shook it, but she persevered. "I hope you have not stayed away because I was cross the other day. Your visits are a bright spot on my horizons." There, that should do it, she thought, but she added the flutter of her eyelashes for good measure.

The corner of his mouth twitched but she did not see it, having demurely lowered her eyes. "Were you cross? I didn't notice, I assure you. A project I was working on took a great deal of my time. I had hoped you might come out riding with me this afternoon."

"Would that be all right, Mama?" When her mother nodded she said, "I won't be a moment changing, Cranford. Perhaps you would like a comfit? Mama brought me a box from Shap this morning."

Offering me treats, too, Cranford thought with amusement. What's the little devil up to now? "Thank you, no, Trelenny. I'll just talk with your mother while I wait."

The moment Trelenny was out the door she raced up the stairs calling frantically for her maid, who fortunately happened to be nearby. "Alice, could you do something with my hair? Right now? Something that would make me look older and more ladylike, perhaps?"

"It takes time to curl it, Miss Trelenny, and you seem in a powerful rush."

"Well, I can't keep him waiting long. Drat! Is there nothing you can do?"

Alice surveyed her critically. "We could take out the braids; they've probably left a little wave in it." Her fingers darted about, suiting the action to her words. "Hmm, not enough to dangle a curl here and there. If you want it different, it will have to be a bun at the back. Will that do?"

"I suppose so."

In her scarlet riding habit with the hat tilted slightly forward to accommodate the new bun, Trelenny presented herself breathlessly in the drawing room. Mrs. Storwood was saying, "We expect Cousin Filkins to make a good, long stay with us. I'm sure you will want to meet him. Perhaps we could have you and your father to dine. T-Trelenny?"

"Yes, Mama. Forgive me for taking so long, Cranford. We couldn't find the hat," she explained ingenuously to her mother.

"I . . . I see, dear."

"You look charming," Cranford assured her, "and well worth waiting for."

Trelenny bestowed another beatific smile on him. "I had hoped you would like it. The hat won't fit over my braids, you know, so I had put it in another closet, and just wore the black beaver. It seemed a shame, though, for I saw one very like it in *Le Beau Monde*, so it must be the height of fashion."

"It's delightful." He tucked her arm through his and said with suspicious gravity, "I do hope the feather won't make you sneeze."

"It is too long?" Trelenny turned anxiously to her mother. "I thought perhaps it was just supposed to brush my cheek, and not tickle my nose the way it does."

Mrs. Storwood suppressed the laugh which bubbled in her. "It's just that you have tilted the hat forward, which is very becoming. Here, we'll tuck the feather further into the band. That's perfect, my love. Have a nice ride."

The crisp fall day greeted them as they stepped out the

front door and Trelenny forgot for a moment her afternoon's goal. "I love this time of year. The air smells so good and the trees are glorious. Would you like to ride over to Lady Wood? The colors are spectacular just now, and the hills are gold and purple in the autumn light."

"The trail will be a bit hazardous after yesterday's rain."

"Yes, well, if you'd rather not."

"I didn't say I'd rather not. Actually, I think it might be a good idea."

Confused as to whether he wished her to break her neck or wanted to please her by accepting her suggestion, Trelenny abandoned the subject. "Mama told you that my father's cousin is coming."

"Yes. Do you like him?"

Trelenny wrinkled her nose distastefully. "He's ridiculous. I've never seen such a popinjay and he must be fifty if he's a day."

"Unfortunate," he murmured sympathetically.

"There is something I particularly wished to speak about with you, Cranford. You see, Papa will have company while he's here. That is, Mama won't ever leave Papa here alone, so naturally we never go anywhere. I can understand that, of course." She paused while Cranford gave instructions for the saddling of their mounts, and then smiled sweetly at him. "It's so comforting to have someone assume these little tasks for one."

He shook his head disbelievingly. "What is it you want, Trelenny?"

"Well, Mama won't take me to London because none of her friends are there right now, and we have no escort, and besides, she wouldn't feel right going there without papa. They met there, you know."

"I'd never thought about it."

"No, of course not, but they did, and she just can't bring herself to go there without him. But it does seem foolish to waste this perfectly providential opportunity, doesn't it?"

"Does it? What opportunity?"

"Cousin Filkins' being here. I mean, how often is there someone here to be with papa while we're away? But we couldn't go to London, so I thought... That's not my saddle. I've never seen anything like it."

"It's Clare's saddle and I brought it for you. I've done

some experimenting to give it a better seat. You're quite right that sidesaddles are not designed for our rough area. Will you try it?"

Trelenny blinked at him. "You did that for me?"

"Certainly. May I hand you up?"

Bemused, Trelenny nodded.

"Your left thigh goes under the crutch. When you jump, you need only raise your left heel and press in and up while you bring your right leg down tightly against the horn, gripping the two crutches. It should give you a three-point contact that is unshakable."

"Have you tried it?" she asked wonderingly.

"Yes." He watched her for signs of amusement, but there were none.

"I think perhaps that is the nicest thing anyone has ever done for me," she said softly. "Thank you, Cranford."

Just when he thought she could no longer surprise him, she did. "I enjoyed doing it. You'll see that I've also removed the knee rest to the right of the horn. It's a hazard if you fall and catch your skirt on it, but you may be used to it and feel less secure without it. If so, I can have it put back."

Unable to adequately express her gratitude, Trelenny merely nodded again and urged Stalwart forward. They rode in silence for some time as she accustomed herself to the new security of her seat. "May I jump now?" she asked at length.

"Whenever you're ready. I'd advise taking something easy at first."

She chose a low wall with secure ground on either side and set the mare to it. Never had it been so easy to maintain her seat, to feel at one with her horse. Her face was alight with enthusiasm when she returned to Cranford. "It's perfect. Almost as simple as riding astride, and I don't miss the knee rest, either. How can I thank you?"

"You have, Trelenny. I'm glad you're pleased with it." As they rode on toward the cataracts which coursed down the rocks and flowed into the small lake by Lady Wood, he watched her covertly. She made no attempt to reinitiate the conversation she had started before they reached the stables and his curiosity grew. "You were telling me of your plans to go away for a spell with your mother."

She flushed slightly. "Oh, no, well, I had thought of it, but it's not possible."

"But your Cousin Filkins would be here to stay with your father."

"I don't suppose Mama would really want to go when we have a guest, though I have always felt she disliked Cousin Filkins as much as I do."

"Then perhaps she would go. Is there some other problem?"

Trelenny's flush deepened. "Doubtless there are a dozen problems I have not even thought of. It was silly of me to mention the matter."

"If I hadn't worked on the saddle you would have told me. You are under no obligation to me, Trelenny. I appreciated the challenge."

"I was going to ask you to escort us to Bath," Trelenny confessed, idly toying with her reins. "Mama's friend Mrs. Waplington is there, and Mama could not have the same objections as she does to London. I know Bath is not so fashionable these days, but still there are assemblies and shops and the theatre and concerts. There were Roman baths there, you know. They called it Aquae Sulis and some years ago they found a gilded bronze head of Minerva. I read everything I could find on it, so that I could persuade you that you would be interested in going there."

"Persuade me," he urged, a smile playing about his lips.

"I know it was wrong of me to try to use you that way, but, oh Cranford, I want so much to go *somewhere*. You have never been restricted to one spot so I suppose you cannot understand. It's not that I don't love Sutton Hall and my parents, but I want to see what else there is. I want to meet some people of my own age and do the things other girls do."

"Not every girl gets out of the country."

"I know. You must think me very selfish to have such a desire, in my situation. Well, I *am* selfish. I don't think I'm mean-selfish, or inconsiderate-selfish or stomp-on-everyone-in-the-way-selfish, but I am selfish all the same. If I want something, then I try to get it. I want to go somewhere, and if I can't go to London, then I want to go to Bath. But I will not try to convince you to escort us because—well, because you have been very thoughtful, and, and that would be stomp-on-someone-selfish."

"Not if I wanted to go there."

"Yes, it would, because even if you wanted to go there you would not want the responsibility of looking out for Mama and me."

"I see. Let's leave the horses here. I'd like to see if there are fish in the lake." He came around to assist her to the ground and they walked to the small lake. As he skimmed a pebble across the water he asked, "What did you learn about Bath to convince me to take you?"

"They found the Minerva head in Stall Street in 1727 when they were digging a sewer. When the Duke of Kingston was building a new commercial bath in 1755 they found the remains of a large Roman bathing establishment. In 1790 they found sculptured stones from the temple pediment. Several monuments were found in Northgate in 1803."

He regarded her with astonishment as she mechanically rattled off the statistics she had committed to memory. "Good Lord! You must have been very determined, to go to so much trouble."

"The problem was finding the information; I never have any difficulty memorizing," she said simply.

"How long did you hope to be away?"

"Three or four weeks. I don't think Mama could bear to be away from Papa any longer than that."

"Very well, Trelenny, you may tell your mother that I would be pleased to escort the two of you to Bath."

Instead of the delight he had expected, she stared at her hands. "That's very kind of you, Cranford, but it was wrong of me to scheme so; and I would have to tell Mama what I had done, and she would not approve." She drew a line on the lake bank with the toe of her boot. "But if I don't scheme, if I sit around and wait for something to happen, I'll be here all my life."

"You don't have to be," he said meaningfully.

Her chin came up and she met his eyes defiantly. "Out of the frying pan into the fire? No, thank you. I'm not *that* grateful for a better sidesaddle."

"We're not talking about the sidesaddle!" Sparks of anger glinted in his eyes. "We are talking about your having a chance to see more of the world than this little backwater."

"No, Cranford, we are talking about my freedom or captivity. Let's not talk of it anymore. I'll show you a cave you may not have seen before. I only discovered it myself a few months ago." Without looking to see whether he followed, she skirted the lake and took a rough path through the wood until she came to a second fall of water.

As she crossed the stream, hopping from boulder to boulder, he said from behind her, "You'll get your habit wet."

"Oh, who cares? If you're concerned for your precious Hessians you need not come."

By the time he had crossed the stream, his boots were indeed soaked, as hers must have been, but neither of them commented on any discomfort. Trelenny continued on up the rise on the other side, pushing the shrubbery out of her way as she went and staying close to the water, which sprinkled on her from time to time as it cascaded over the rocks. The climb was steep and no evidence of the cave could be seen from below, but when Trelenny pushed aside some tangled vines, Cranford found himself at the entrance to a deep, well-defined space with jagged rock walls and ceiling.

"How did you find it?"

"There was a rock slide after a storm in July. Enough rocks came away from the entrance that I could see there was a cave, and I removed the rest. It took a few days, but isn't it wonderful? Much bigger than Greene Cave and there are some drawings on the wall that might interest you. I wish I'd thought to bring a lanthorn."

"Why didn't you tell me about it before?"

"Well, they're not *Roman* drawings, Cranford, or anything really *old*. Possibly from the time of the Abbey, but they have no distinctly religious flavor—no crosses or anything. Didn't the Abbey give sanctuary? Maybe they were drawn by some desperate fugitive who sought safety in the grounds. A hunted man who had ruthlessly murdered his employer or a jealous lover who had throttled his mistress to death."

Cranford cast his eyes heavenward. "Or some child caught out in a storm who whiled away the hours scratching pictures of his favorite puppy on the rock."

"You have no imagination, Cranford," Trelenny said dolefully. "You can't see them very well in this light. I made copies by lanthorn-light in my sketchbook. I'll show them to you." She attempted, unsuccessfully, to quell a sneeze.

"Not today, young lady. I'm taking you home so you can change into some dry clothing."

chapter five

Cousin Filkins arrived promptly on schedule, and Mr. Storwood indeed found it necessary to reimburse the post boys. "Temporary embarrassment," Cousin Filkins murmured as he descended in a lavender coat, red and white striped waistcoat, and green pantaloons. Trelenny tried to catch her mother's eye, but Mrs. Storwood would not look in her direction. "Dashed rough roads you have in this neighborhood. I think the set of my coat is permanently ruined." Trelenny tried to catch her father's eye, with no more success than she had had with her mother.

After Cousin Filkins had greeted her parents, he turned to Trelenny. "My, my, what a change there's been in you, my girl." He eyed her in such a way that the color rose to her cheeks. "Still have the freckles, I see. Not any better than you should be, ha ha. We'll have to have a cozy chat. You'll be wanting to know what the ladies are wearing in London." He pinched her cheek between his chubby fingers and turned to Mr. Storwood. "Fine-looking gel you have. Pity to keep her off in the wilds. You won't take offense if I just mention that knee breeches are out, will you? Even for evening wear, by Jove. Only the old fogies are wearing them to the balls and parties, and it's only a matter of time before you will see the Prince Regent himself in trousers, mark my words. If you will be so good as to show me my room," he continued, his bulging eyes now coming to focus once more on Trelenny, "I shall just refresh a bit and see what my man can do with this coat."

"Certainly, Cousin Filkins." As she led him through the hall and up the stairs she said, "I hope your journey has not been too trying. Sometimes the post boys go over the most hazardous roads at breakneck speed. You would think they would have more consideration for the horses."

"Wouldn't travel at all if I could avoid it," Cousin Filkins grumbled as he puffed up the stairs behind her.

"Well, you'll be settled here for a while now and I'm sure you will be comfortable. This is your room. I think you will find everything you need."

"And where is your room, young lady?" he asked with a jovial laugh.

"In the other wing, sir."

"This dress now," he said, reaching out to touch the lace at the neckline, "would not be worn so high in London. It would be cut much lower, about here."

Trelenny hastily stepped back to avoid his touch. "Clothing for the countryside is more practical, I think. Here's your man to see to you." Whereupon she fled.

The days took on an aura of unreality for Trelenny. Every vacant corridor became a potential meeting spot with Cousin Filkins. No matter that she had just left him with her parents in the drawing room, somehow he disengaged himself and appeared like a nightmare as she was turning the corner to her room, leering at her and making familiar comments under the guise of cousinly interest. Because of her disdainful comments on him before his arrival, she did not wish to go to her mother with tales of his behavior; and she would never have considered alarming her father with the story. Unschooled in how to handle such advances, she tried at first to placate him by turning the subject, and later by escaping by whatever means she could devise. The only place she was safe from him was when she rode, for the aging dandy would not come near a horse and never walked when he could be comfortably settled in a chair before a plate of biscuits.

But even if she had wished to, she could not ride all day, and her father admonished her for ignoring their guest when she absented herself for too long. On the night of his arrival Cousin Filkins had walked straight into her bedchamber as she was removing her shawl, laughed, and said, "Now how could I have made such a stupid mistake? I see your maid is not here. Can I help you with those buttons?" Fortunately her maid had appeared just then, and, not under the same restraints as Trelenny, harshly bade the old man remove himself immediately. Henceforth Trelenny had kept her door locked at all times.

Viscount Chessels and his son came to dine a few days after the visitor's arrival, and Cranford was surprised at Trelenny's lack of animation on the occasion. He had not expected her to show him any particular welcome, and she had not; but she was unusually subdued and started visibly when addressed by Cousin Filkins, who had come up behind the sofa on which she was seated. Cranford agreed with her assessment of her relation as ridiculous and found the evening in his father's company a trying duty. It was not until he lay restlessly in bed that night that a possible explanation for Trelenny's behavior occurred to him, and he set out for Sutton Hall directly after his breakfast the next morning.

As it was Cousin Filkins' habit to lie abed until an advanced hour of the morning, Trelenny escaped into the gardens as soon as she had finished her meal. If she rode now, she would not have an excuse for doing so when her father's cousin descended and tried to corner her in the study or the drawing room for a discussion of "fashion." She was pacing agitatedly along the gravel paths beside the hedges when the odious man himself appeared at her side.

"You startled me, Cousin Filkins. We are not used to seeing you abroad at this hour," she remarked as she tried to edge away from him into a more observable portion of the grounds.

"I saw you from my room, my dear, and could not bear to think of you alone on such a delightful morning. Have you no suitors who come to rhapsodize on your . . . charms?" His bulky form blocked her way into the lawn which sloped from her father's study, where they might have been under his watchful (though obviously benevolent) eye.

"I have no suitors at all, sir."

"What? You are teasing me, you naughty puss. I will not believe that there is no young man whose eye—" his own eyes rested hungrily on her ample bosom "—is not drawn by your beauty. Someone who does not slip his arm about you and give you a little pat on that saucy bottom of yours."

When he attempted to suit his action to the words, Trelenny smashed her elbow into his protruding stomach and dashed blindly away from him, only to run headlong into

Cranford, who had witnessed the whole scene as he approached. "Steady, now. Stay right where you are. I won't be a moment."

Shaking, she nodded miserably and watched as he approached the gasping Filkins. Although she could not hear the words which passed between them—or rather, which Cranford addressed to the older man, since cousin Filkins apparently had nothing to say—she saw the pudgy dandy blanch and step back as though struck. Cranford turned on his heel and rejoined her, pressing her arm under his for support. "He won't bother you again. Why did your father do nothing about this situation?"

"He doesn't know," Trelenny whispered.

"You should have told him."

"His heart..."

"Then you should have told your mother."

"Why are you angry with me? It wasn't my fault. I tried to stay away from him, to discourage him."

"But you didn't bother to tell your mother."

"How could I tell her? He is my father's cousin, for God's sake, and they expect me to treat him with the respect due a relative. They were both annoyed with me for making fun of him before he came. And what could mama do if I told her? She would be very upset, but she would not dare tell Papa."

"Of course she would. She would have to. Trelenny, your parents are there to protect you. Do you think they would have wanted this situation to continue?"

"No, but, Cranford, think how upsetting it would be to Papa. I could not do that."

"Then you should have spoken to me."

She darted a glance at his rigid face. "It never occurred to me. I wouldn't have thought you could do a thing about it."

Stung, he rasped, "Perhaps you like to have him ogle you."

The toe of her boot caught him sharply in the ankle. "How dare you say such a thing?"

"I'm sorry, he said stiffly. "I didn't mean that. But you are young and perhaps proud of your... womanhood, and there are few people to admire you."

"That's not admiration!" she exclaimed scornfully.

"That's... and I never asked for a large bosom! I don't like people to stare at me that way. It makes me feel wretched. Oh, go away, Cranford. You make me angry with your pious piddle." She pulled her arm from his and swung away from him. Belatedly she said over her shoulder, "Thank you for intervening."

"No, you don't, young lady." He grasped her hand firmly and headed for the house. "We are going to speak to your mother about this."

"Why?" she asked unhappily. "You said he wouldn't bother me again. There's no reason to upset Mama."

"There is every reason, Trelenny. Where are we likely to find her?"

"In the morning room."

Mrs. Storwood looked up from the list she was making when the young people entered the room. Cranford's grim expression and Trelenny's reluctant one immediately alarmed her. "Is something the matter?"

"Yes, ma'am. I just came upon your daughter in the garden with Mr. Filkins, who was attempting to make improper advances."

Although her face paled, Mrs. Storwood asked in a chilly voice, "I hope you are not suggesting that there was anything improper in Trelenny's conduct."

"No, of course not, but she is not worldly enough to know how to discourage such an old roué."

"He is undiscourageable," Mrs. Storwood answered, to their mutual surprise. Trelenny flung herself into her mother's open arms. "Forgive me, my love. I have been so distracted by him that I didn't even notice your distress. I thought if he was so persistent with me... but, there, that is no excuse. Your father will have to be told. He did not harm you, did he?"

"No, Mama."

"Thank God." An agonized sigh escaped her. "This will be very upsetting for your Papa. We will have to make light of it as much as we can and still insist that Mr. Filkins be sent about his business."

"Did he do this to you the last time he was here?" Trelenny asked.

"Well, yes, but he was not here for long then, though it seemed an eternity." She looked up at Cranford. "Thank you for your help. I'll see that matters are taken care of from here."

"Could I propose a solution which might save embarrassment to you and anguish to your husband, Mrs. Storwood?"

"Certainly."

"I gather that Mr. Filkins is financially embarrassed. No, Trelenny said nothing to me, ma'am. I have seen a score of Filkins' type, and I fear it would only put Mr. Storwood in a more difficult position to have to send the blighter away, and at the same time provide him with money, which he would doubtless feel obligated to do. Why not leave him here with your husband and go away yourselves? I have been considering a journey to Bath, a stay of perhaps three or four weeks, and I would be happy to escort you there. After such an annoying experience I dare say you and Trelenny would welcome the change."

"Go away? To Bath? But we have never been away."

"Surely this is the ideal time. Mr. Storwood need know nothing about these incidents, and I think it a fitting punishment to Mr. Filkins to leave him here without his prey. He has promised a long stay; let him be useful while he serves his time. Can you convince Mr. Storwood not to give him enough money to leave?"

"I . . . I suppose so," Mrs. Storwood said uncertainly.

"Of course you can, Mama," Trelenny urged enthusiastically. "You have only to tell Papa that you think it will do Cousin Filkins good to rusticate and keep him company while we are gone. And our odious cousin might just receive a whisper from Cranford that no mention will be made if he stays here until we return. *Then* of course he is to leave immediately and never come back. Oh, I think it a splendid idea, Mama. May we go?"

A dozen considerations flitted through Mrs. Storwood's mind: to spare her husband the upheaval such a disclosure would cause him; to avoid the unpleasant attentions of that disgusting man; to take her daughter out of his reach; yes, even to punish him for his horrid attentions to the two of them. And an opportunity to introduce Trelenny to just a taste of society. Perhaps then she would realize that Cranford was an unexceptionable match, that her exotic fantasies were merely a dream. "I think, my love, that we might. But, Cranford, I would hate to impose on you. I do have a friend in Bath just now, as it happens, but we would need your escort there and back."

"There is no imposition, Mrs. Storwood. Shall we plan to leave in the morning?"

"Tomorrow morning?" asked the poor woman.

"The sooner the better, I think. I'll just have a word with Mr. Filkins before I leave, with your permission."

"Yes, if you would. Can we be ready by tomorrow morning, Trelenny? What will your Papa say to such unseemly haste?"

"He will say that the sooner we leave, the sooner we shall return. I promise you I can have everything ready for the morning, Mama. You go speak with Papa and I'll see Cranford out." Trelenny smiled encouragement to her flustered parent, who rose to give her hand to Cranford before she hesitantly left the room.

When they were alone, Trelenny did not speak for a moment, could not even bring herself to look at him. "That was especially kind of you, Cranford. I . . . I'm sure I can never repay you, but I shall try. You won't mind going so very much, will you?"

"With all those antiquities to look forward to, how could I?" he asked ruefully.

"To be perfectly honest with you," she said miserably, "I am not sure where they may be found. That is, I could find no information on who has them now."

"Trust me, Trelenny. I shall find them."

She breathed a sigh of relief. "Well, I hope you may, Cranford, for I can see no other pleasure for you in Bath."

"Can't you? No, I suppose not. Never mind. I'll come at ten tomorrow if you can be ready by then."

"We'll be ready."

"Good. Now I'll just have a word with Mr. Filkins."

Relations between Cranford and his father had been cool, as might be expected, since the incident of the sidesaddle. No mention had been made of it, and the two men had frequently partaken of their meals together, when a desultory conversation ensued between them, but it was not the father's habit to apologize for his mistakes nor the son's to concern himself overmuch with being misunderstood. Lord Chessels had some stake in not antagonizing his son to the point where Cranford abandoned Ashwicke Park and his pursuit of Trelenny. For his part, Cranford had his own reasons for continuing his suit, and he was inured by past experience to his father's uncontrolled temper.

When Cranford returned to Ashwicke Park he sought an interview with Lord Chessels, who was perusing the *Shooting Directory* in the Lower Saloon, his feet propped up on a stool whose embroidered cover Cranford could remember his mother patiently laboring over.

"I wanted to let you know that I will be leaving tomorrow for Bath. I—"

Lord Chessels flung the magazine from him. "Damn you! You haven't made the least push to engage that girl's affections! Now you're wanting to run off and enjoy yourself at some mushroomy watering hole. Don't think I'll stand the blunt, my boy. Not a tuppence will you see from me."

"Sir, I am escorting Mrs. and Miss Storwood there, and I had not the least intention of asking you for money. You should not let this raise your hopes as to a match, however, as Miss Storwood has in effect told me that she won't have me. It is nonetheless an opportunity for us to become better acquainted, which may or may not prove beneficial." Cranford stooped to pick up the magazine which lay at his feet, and straightened it out before handing it to his father.

Lord Chessels grunted. "You should take the traveling carriage. If you go post you'll not have an opportunity to sit in the carriage with them now and again. It's well sprung; I had it worked over not six months past."

"I'll be gone a month."

"I won't be needing it. Take it, and the coachman, too. I'm not sure it's a good idea to let the chit see anything of the world, mind you. You'd do better to keep her here, but I suppose they would go without you. Bath. Hmm. Not likely to meet anyone interesting there. Place is filled with mushrooms and toad-eaters these days, not like it was when I first went there. Chits, the place is filled with them. At least it's not London. You can be grateful for that."

"I am."

"Yes, well, take the carriage and see you make a push for the girl."

"I will."

"You'll need to impress her. Make a bit of a splash. You can ask Jenkins for two hundred."

"Thank you, sir, but I won't need it. If you will excuse me, I must see to my packing."

Despite his curiosity as to how his son could afford such a trip, Lord Chessels refused to ask. His parting shot was, "Don't be boring them with your talk of ruins. Nobody's interested and nothing is surer to make the chit look around for a livelier companion!"

chapter six

As Mrs. Storwood had predicted, her husband was surprised by the haste with which his family intended to depart, but he was not averse to their going, especially when Mrs. Storwood exaggerated Cousin Filkins' thoughtfulness in staying to keep him company. "For you know, James, he said practically the minute he arrived that it was a shame that Trelenny could not see a bit of society. Is it not fortuitous that he should be here just when Cranford is planning a trip to Bath? I think it would be wrong of us to pass up this opportunity, don't you? Perhaps if Trelenny has the chance to see a bit of the world she will be more willing to settle down. It's not that I don't expect her to enjoy herself, you understand, but she will find that society is very restrictive and that marriage offers her more freedom than she expects. Shall we go, James? Will you be comfortable here with your cousin?"

"Of course you shall go. You know it is the bane of my life that my weakness keeps us here unendingly," he said sadly.

"Oh, James, don't be absurd. I have no desire to be anywhere but with you." She touched his cheek with gentle fingers. "But Trelenny—it's different for her. She feels that she's missing something, that there is a better life to be had elsewhere. I'm afraid she has a restless spirit, which is not to say I think that is wrong, but very unfortunate in our circumstances. Oh, I shall miss you, my love." She turned away to hide a trembling lip. "It frightens me a little, you know, after all these years to think of taking her to balls and parties. If it were not for Cranford escorting us, and Elsa Waplington being there . . ."

He took her in his arms and hugged her tightly. "Courage, my dear. I will only be happy knowing you are enjoying yourself."

Mrs. Storwood forced a tremulous smile. "I shall get my pleasure through Trelenny. She's so eager, so lively, so—"

"So incorrigible," he murmured with a crooked grin. "She'll be a handful, but I rely on Cranford to see she comes to no harm. He has never put his suit to the touch, has he?"

"No. Trelenny leads him a bit of a dance, James, and I cannot think he fully approves of her. This scheme may be his way of . . . oh, showing her how she should go on. You know I have tried."

"We have all tried, my love, but I have a great deal of faith in Cranford. For all her whimsical flights and her offhanded treatment of him, Trelenny has a measure of trust in him, which is not a bad starting point for a successful marriage. No, no, I won't say a word of the matter to her. You are quite right—pressure only makes her stubborn. Go and enjoy yourselves, and don't worry about me. Cousin Filkins and I will do famously."

So Mrs. Storwood had left to do her packing, her eyes moist and her throat aching, but with the knowledge that her husband need not suffer the agonies of hearing the truth about his despicable cousin. Trelenny was already in her mother's bedchamber directing her maid to have a small trunk sent up.

"We shan't want a great deal of luggage, Mama, for that would simply be a nuisance. Shall I help you choose what gowns to take?" Only when her mother came close did she notice the strangely sparkling eyes. "Oh, Mama, are you all right? If you don't wish to go, then we won't. I didn't know it would make you sad."

"Nonsense. I am just having my bout of homesickness before we leave, dearest. Your Papa is pleased for us, but I . . . I shall miss him dreadfully."

"Of course you will. But it is only a month, not so very long after all. Why, he will hardly notice we're gone, the time will pass so quickly. You do *want* to go, don't you?"

"Yes. I want you to see Bath and go to parties and have a little come-out of your own. I want Mrs. Waplington to meet you, and I want to see you stand up at the Assemblies."

Trelenny experienced a feeling of guilt. "And won't you be happy to see Mrs. Waplington again, Mama? And you shall dance at the Rooms, too."

"Silly girl. I'm far too old for such stuff."

"You're only eight and thirty!" her daughter protested. "I have every intention of cutting a dash at least until I'm forty. Papa would want you to dance, and I am sure all the older men will see that you are beautiful still. And I don't care if you cast me into the shade! I don't want to go if you're not going to have a good time."

Mrs. Storwood patted her cheek. "I have every intention of enjoying myself, Trelenny. Run along now and see to your own packing."

"Do you think Papa would let me have my quarter's allowance now? It's only a few weeks early."

"I wouldn't be surprised if he's arranging it at this very moment. Don't forget to thank him for giving his permission when you go to see him, and don't mention Cousin Filkins at all, or you are likely to say more than you intend."

"Yes, Mama, and *thank* you."

Trelenny carefully divided her money into two piles, slipping the smaller into her reticule and the rest into a leather draw-string pouch. From outside came the sounds of arrival, and she took one last hasty look about her bedchamber before closing the door behind her and hurrying down the stairs. Although Cousin Filkins stood in the hallway with her parents, she never gave him a thought as she came up to them, breathlessly exclaiming, "He's here! I heard the carriage."

As though summoned by her words, there was a rap at the door and Cranford, impeccably dressed in riding clothes, was shown in. "My father has offered us the use of his traveling carriage, so I hope you have not been too sparing in your luggage," he told Mrs. Storwood before he shook hands with her husband and offered a curt nod to Filkins, who had moved back from the group. With a practiced eye he took in Trelenny's carriage dress of green Merino and her cloak of a deeper green *gros de Berlin* lined with chinchilla. "Very sensible, Trelenny. We are likely to encounter some chill weather as we travel."

"That's why I wore it," she assured him pertly. "It had nothing to do with the fact that it is my most handsome carriage dress, or that I had a matching muff in which to keep my reticule. I wore it because it is comfortable and warm, and I knew you would approve." She thrust a toe forward from under her skirt. "I even wore my kid half-boots so my feet would be warm, too, and not because I love the chestnut color and they are spanking new."

Unperturbed by her sarcasm, Cranford merely nodded and turned to her father. "I will take good care of them, sir, and you should look for our return in about a month. A message sent care of the White Hart will reach me, though I may not stay there the entire time. There are usually houses to be had in Camden Place or Queen Square, but rest assured that I will find a suitable situation for the ladies. I have sent off an inquiry to a friend of mine who will have some information for us by the time we arrive, no doubt."

"I have every confidence in you, my boy," Mr. Storwood said as Trelenny stood staring at Cranford. "We'll just have their luggage put up and you may be off. Do you think you can make Preston tonight?"

Never once had it occurred to Trelenny that Cranford had been to Bath before. In her mind she had been offering him a treat, if a limited one, a chance to see some Roman antiquities, if he could find them, which were sure to be a source of interest. While the carriage was being loaded and her mother and father talked quietly to one side, she marched up to Cranford. "Why didn't you tell me?"

"Tell you what?"

"That you have been there before! Oh, you have spoiled everything!"

"You've lost me, Trelenny. What difference can it possibly make that I've been to Bath before?" He raised an impatient eyebrow as he watched the small trunk being strapped to the roof of the carriage.

"There is no reason at all for you to go, if you've seen all those old stones before."

"I didn't have time to look out antiquities when I was there previously. Do be a good girl and get in the carriage. I want to get started before your mother sheds any tears, and the longer we stay, the more likely that is." He watched nervously as Mrs. Storwood clung to her huband's arm with one hand and helplessly gripped a limp handkerchief in the other.

"Here." Trelenny thrust the leather pouch into his hands and left him with a swish of her skirts. The footman assisted her into the carriage and she called lightly to her mother, "We are ready to go, Mama. Goodbye, Papa. We will miss you."

Cranford absently stuck the pouch in the pocket of his coat and nodded his thanks to Trelenny, who glared at him in return. Lord, wasn't the girl ever pleased? Gently he disengaged Mrs. Storwood from her husband and handed her into the carriage, saying, "I shall ride for the first two stages, ma'am. If you need anything, have Trelenny call for me. There are warm bricks for your feet and a carriage rug," he instructed the maid, who was already seated across from the two ladies.

The coachman set his horses into motion at a signal from Cranford, and Mrs. Storwood waved until they were out of sight, whereupon she quietly wept into her handkerchief and Trelenny put her arm about her to comfort her. Cranford stayed to have a word with Mr. Storwood.

"Very good of you to take them with you, Cranford," the older man said gruffly. "I've made a rough reckoning what the trip will cost, and their lodgings, and doodahs and such, and it's all here in this purse. I hope you won't mind being Mrs. Storwood's banker, for she's a bit rusty at this sort of thing. You have only to write for more should this be insufficient. It's been so long since I've been away that I doubled what it would have been years ago, but that might not be enough. Trelenny has her own pocket money, of course, though I don't expect her to buy any new gowns out of it—there's hardly enough! But she's to have what she wants, provided her mother agrees. I just don't want her to have so much that it burns a hole in her pocket, so to speak."

"Well, she won't lose it, sir. She assured me once that she's never lost so much as a tuppence," Cranford replied with a rueful grin.

"She's not as shatterbrained as she sometimes appears, and she's a good-hearted girl, when all is said and done. Mind you, she's not been anywhere before, and her mother will tell her how to go on, but I depend on you to see that she gets in no trouble. It's a large responsibility, I know, but you aspire to her hand and it is in your own interest to see she behaves herself." He stared for a moment at the spot where the carriage had disappeared from view and then transferred his gaze to his companion. "Not with a heavy hand, Cranford. She's spirited and she resents being told what to do. If you explain *why* something is wrong, she is much more willing to listen. Will you remember that?"

"Yes, sir."

"Thank you. I won't keep you longer. My two most precious treasures are in your care, and I know you will justify my faith in you. God bless you, my boy."

If Lord Chessels had once in his life addressed himself in such a way to his son, Cranford could have forgotten all the verbal and physical abuse he had suffered under that tyrant. Pushing aside his regrets, he shook hands now with Trelenny's father as he said, "I'm honored by your trust, Mr. Storwood, and I'll do my best to see that the ladies enjoy themselves and have no worries. Take care of yourself, sir."

Not until Cranford had called a halt for refreshments in Burton, and he was overseeing the unharnessing of the horses and instructing that a new team be ready in an hour, did he remember the pouch that Trelenny had thrust upon him before their departure. He pulled it out now and counted fifteen guineas before replacing it in his pocket, surprised that she, too, apparently wished him to be her banker for the trip. As he entered the inn he was directed to a private parlor where he found her alone.

"Mama is just washing off some of the dust, Cranford. I have ordered a plate of meats and cheese, with some bread and tea. Will that do?"

"Certainly. One would think you have been traveling all your life," he teased her.

"It's not so very difficult, but Mama is a bit blue devilled, you see, and I didn't want her to have the bother."

Cranford jingled the pouch in his pocket, smiling. "I think you are wise to have me look after your allowance, Trelenny. I'll take care not to lose it."

Her brows drew together in a frown and she shook her head firmly. "No, that is money to pay for our posting charges. I know how you are situated, and this trip was my idea, so I am responsible for the extra expense to you. Papa will have given you money for our lodging, of course, but he thinks you intended to go to Bath and would have had that expense yourself. At least, I suppose that is how he would view the matter. I haven't enough to pay for your lodging in Bath, as I have to have some money for fripperies or Mama will wonder what I have done with my allowance, but I shall be able to repay you at Christmas."

One point in her whole recitation stood out in his mind above all the others. His angry eyes raked her face. "How do you know my circumstances?"

"Why, I heard Papa tell Mama years ago. Lord Chessels bragged of it, I think, but Papa was very upset and called it a dastardly thing to do. And I agree!"

"It is no concern of yours, Trelenny, and I don't want your money, or need it, for that matter." He set the pouch down on the table with a thump as Mrs. Storwood entered.

"Ah, Cranford. I hope you plan to ride in with us this afternoon, for your father's carriage is admirably sprung. Didn't you think so, Trelenny? My dear, you should not leave your money sitting about. It's not that I don't trust the servants (though it *is* a public inn and one can never be too careful), but you might forget it when we leave. Why don't you have Cranford keep it for you? That would be safest of all, I think."

"Yes, I will have Cranford keep it," Trelenny said with a demure glance in his direction. "You won't mind, will you, Cranford?"

"No." He pocketed the pouch once again, but after he had seated her mother and come around to hold a chair for her, he murmured in her ear, "It is *your* money. When you want it, just ask me for it."

Trelenny effected not to hear him but began to pour the tea, which had already arrived. "Would you prefer beer or wine, Cranford? I didn't know, so I just ordered the tea. Oh, good, here are the meat and cheese. I don't know how one can develop such an appetite simply sitting in a carriage all morning, but I'm famished." Throughout their meal she was particularly gay, cheering her mother with talk of the shops and assemblies in Bath, and teasing Cranford with made-up tales of careless Romans who mislaid their money, their baths, and most probably (she said) their wives.

When they resumed their journey Cranford had his revenge, or at least that is how Trelenny saw the matter. They sat side by side with their backs to the horses and once they were out of town he drew a book from a pocket on the wall.

The pocket on the opposite side, he assured her, contained a pistol which was loaded and primed in the event of an emergency. The book, however, proved to be the more powerful weapon, as it was purported to be a book of sermons that he suggested he read to them.

Even Mrs. Storwood gazed at him with astonishment, and Trelenny gasped, "You wouldn't!"

"No," he laughed, "I wouldn't. Really it's Fanny Burney's *Evelina*."

"That's an antiquarian's idea of a joke," Trelenny murmured scornfully to her mother. "And I've never heard of *Evelina*, either."

"Surely you must have," her mother protested. "It was written the year I was born but it was still the rage when I was young. How we loved it! It's the story of a young lady's entrance into society."

Trelenny eyed Cranford reproachfully. "So you are intent on schooling me, are you? A more palatable lesson than the sermons, perhaps, but a lesson all the same."

With an exasperated sigh, Mrs. Storwood said, "It's a delightful book, my dear, and very thoughtful of Cranford to have brought it."

"Yes, he might have brought Plutarch's *Lives*." But it took very little time for her to become engrossed in the story, though she told Cranford she thought Evelina a rather weak-spirited damsel and not quite so well possessed of understanding as the author seemed to imply. "*I* would never get in a carriage alone with the likes of Sir Clement. She might have known he would behave precisely as he did."

Fortunately Trelenny did not intercept the amused glance which passed between Mrs. Storwood and Cranford when the latter said, "I'm sure you would never do anything so improper." He replaced the book in its pocket. "The light is failing and we'll be in Preston soon, where we should be able to find accommodation at the Bull and Royal."

"We're stopping already?" Trelenny asked with astonishment. "But Preston cannot be more than sixty miles from home. At this rate it will take us forever to get to Bath."

"Four days," Cranford informed her.

"Oh, no! All of our time will be spent traveling! Surely it need not take so long. We could start earlier each day and not find an inn until well into the evening. Then it would be only three days and we would have a longer stay in town."

Cranford regarded her coldly. "I doubt your mother would appreciate our bumping along the roads for ten hours a day, Trelenny."

In the fading light of the carriage he could just barely perceive the blush which rose to her cheeks as she lowered her eyes to her hands. "No. No, of course not. And our journey can be interesting in itself, Mama, for I have brought some guidebooks on the counties we will pass through. Tomorrow I shall get them out and read to you about Lancashire and ... and any other counties we might reach during the day."

Mrs. Storwood regarded her daughter fondly. "That is thoughtful of you, my dear. I think we might plan to be on the road by nine tomorrow, Cranford, and decide as we see our progress where we might stay the night."

"As you wish, ma'am."

chapter seven

"There is room for you and Trelenny here, Mrs. Storwood," Cranford informed them when he emerged from the Bull and Royal, "but I shall have to find another hostelry. The innkeeper says the Castle is likely to have space for me, as it's not such a quality establishment as his." He grinned at the face Trelenny made, but was not so amused by Mrs. Storwood's look of concern. "There is nothing to worry you, ma'am. I promise you the Castle will be quite good enough for me, and you and Trelenny will be well looked after here. Shall I go ahead and make the arrangements?"

"Could we not all stay at the Castle?" Mrs. Storwood asked diffidently.

"You would not be so comfortable there as here."

Mrs. Storwood looked helplessly to her daughter for advice, not sure that she wished to be separated from the efficient escort he provided, and though Trelenny would have relished the opportunity to manage for the two of them, she felt sure her mother would be easier in Cranford's company. Trelenny said, "I'm sure we would do well to stay together, Cranford."

The Castle was a modest inn with but four rooms to let, and though these were clean, the furnishings had seen better days and they had never been more than serviceable. Mrs. Storwood bore this circumstance with equanimity, though she found the staff even less palatable than her surroundings. A surly innkeeper, a saucy maid, and a lazy ostler were their introduction to the Castle, and made her regret her decision to stay there, until Cranford, by a mere tone of voice, helped the staff summon up a due deference for their clientele. But nothing would induce Mrs. Storwood to sit in the cheerless parlor after they had finished their meal, and she retired with her daughter in attendance to the room they had chosen at the rear of the first-floor hall.

For Mrs. Storwood it had been an exhausting day and she allowed the maid to prepare her for bed without demur. When Alice had left, Trelenny kissed her mother's brow. "Go straight to bed, Mama. If you don't mind, I shall just sit up for a moment with the candle so I may look out our route on the map and have the right guidebooks available in the morning."

Within minutes Mrs. Storwood slept, and Trelenny considered the map on which Cranford had marked their route. She noted that he planned to follow the main mail coach road rather than the more direct road, which would take them to Lawton by way of Warrington instead of Manchester. As she debated the usefulness of arguing this point with him, she heard the sounds of arrival below in the hall and shortly thereafter footsteps along the passage which stopped at the door next to hers. The inn, as has been noted, was not a superior establishment and Trelenny could distinctly hear the murmur of voices through the walls. When the sound ceased, presumably after the landlord or maid had departed, the silence lasted only a short while before Trelenny could clearly hear the sounds of weeping from the next apartment. Nothing so easily stirred her ready sympathy as the thought of someone in distress. For several minutes she sat listening, but there was no abatement to the heartbroken sobbing and, after a glance assured her that her mother's peaceful sleep had not been disturbed by the sound, she crept to the door and cautiously opened it.

There was not a soul to be seen, and no way to tell whether Cranford was still downstairs or in his room at the head of the staircase. Trelenny tapped hesitantly at the next door and the muted sounds within stopped abruptly. A frightened female voice called, "Who is it?"

"Miss Storwood. I am in the room next to yours and I have come to see if I may be of any assistance."

"Thank you, no. I . . . that is, you are good to enquire."

"Might I just speak with you a moment? To assure myself there is not some service I might render?"

No answer came, but after a moment the door opened a crack and Trelenny could distinguish a pale face with masses of dark hair and large, moist dark eyes. The girl appeared to be about her own age, though slighter, and considerably agitated, her face streaked with tearstains and her eyes red from weeping. She seemed incapable of speaking, such was the despair under which she labored.

"I would like to help you," Trelenny whispered. "Are you being abducted to Gretna Green? You may take refuge with us, you know. My mother is very tenderhearted, and Cranford would see that the man did not make off with you."

A cold hand clasped hers and the girl silently pulled her into the room and closed the door. "How ... how did you know we were going to Gretna Green?"

Trelenny shrugged. "This is the road everyone uses. It passed right by our home and, when I was younger, I used to wave to everyone who went past and tried to determine if they were on their way there. Will you let us help you?"

"You ... you don't understand. I *wish* to go to Gretna Green with Robert, but everything has gone awry. All my jewelry and his money were stolen by a highwayman today—when it was hardly dark!—and we haven't enough between the two of us to pay for my room here tonight. I don't know what to do!" The girl wrung her hands as two tears spilled over and ran unheeded down her cheeks. "We can't apply to either of our families since they are nowhere nearby, and besides, my family has forbidden our marriage. And I am so afraid, so afraid."

Trelenny put her arm about the girl and wiped away the tears with a lawn handkerchief. "Come now, my dear. I can give you money to pay your shot; Cranford is holding some for me, more than enough to get you to Gretna Green if that is what you wish, and I know he won't accept it in the end, so I might as well have it now. Shall I go and ask him for it?"

Dumbfounded, the girl protested, "But you don't even know me. I can't take your money. Not that it would not be repaid! If we get out of this mess we shall manage very well and be able to repay you the very second we return to Hampshire."

"Then it's settled, and I wish you will dry your tears, for you haven't a thing to worry about."

"But I do." A fresh spurt of tears coursed down her cheeks. "Robert was so desperate, I am afraid for him, afraid he will do something foolish."

"What?" Trelenny asked sharply.

"He went away saying he would find some money... had to find some money. I am so afraid he will rob someone."

"Surely not!" Trelenny objected.

"He could not bear me to suffer the mortification of being unable to pay for my room in the morning. I told him I didn't need a room but he insisted. I would have slept in a barn or a meadow!"

"Where has your Robert gone? We need only find him and tell him there is no need to do anything foolish."

"But I don't *know* where he's gone. And I don't know what he may do. Oh, he will surely be killed!"

"Come now, it is no such thing. We have only to find him before he does anything unwise. I know, we'll ask Cranford to find him." She tugged at the despondent girl's hand. "Take heart, miss." Gently she urged the girl out of her room and down the corridor to Cranford's, where she tapped lightly. When there was no response she repeated her summons with more energy, but there was still no answer. "Now where can he have gotten to? We planned an early start in the morning. Well, never mind. I shall go down and ask after him. Tell me Robert's name and what he looks like."

"Robert Laytham. He's very tall and has curly blond hair."

"What's he wearing?"

"A blue coat and buff pantaloons, and Hessians with little gold tassels."

"Very well. Wait for me in your room." Trelenny watched as the girl scurried away, and then she proceeded down the stairs. The door to the public room stood open and the sounds of male merriment assailed her ears, but she was loath to go close enough to see if Cranford was one of the occupants. Instead she turned toward the kitchen, where she was sure to find a servant to deliver a message to him if he were in the house.

In the ill-lit passage she failed to notice a door open behind her until her arm was caught by someone who reeked of liquor. "Ho, what have we here? You've mistaken your way, my girl. You'll be wanting to join our little private party."

Trelenny shook off his hand with an angry gesture. "How dare you touch me?" she cried in her loftiest manner. "I should have you horse-whipped! Innkeeper!"

When Trelenny desired to be heard, there was no denying her. Not the softest-voiced girl to start with, she had a truly magnificent range when she chose. The man who had accosted her shrank back and, as several doors opened in answer to her cry, made a wild dash for the rear door, stumbling in his eagerness to be away. Satisfied, Trelenny surveyed the new arrivals, picked the landlord from amongst them, and said, "That rogue had the temerity to address me, sir. It had best not happen again."

"No, miss, but if I might be wondering as to why you was down here in the first place..." he said with mingled servility and insinuation.

"It is not your business to wonder at anything I do, my man," she declared regally. "However, since I have unearthed some assistance at last, I will inform you that I wish to learn the whereabouts of Mr. Ashwicke, our escort, as a problem has arisen which only he can handle... for my mother," she added as an afterthought.

"You might have rung," he retorted sulkily.

"And so I might, were the bell-cords of your establishment in operation."

"Weren't a thing wrong with the bell-cord in your room when last I looked."

"Then you had best look again, hadn't you?" she asked placidly. "But this is all far from the point, sir. Will you convey my message to Mr. Ashwicke?"

"I can't do that, miss." He smiled broadly. "He went out some little time ago."

"Very well. The matter will have to wait until morning." She turned abruptly from him and headed back down the passage, the object of a variety of amused eyes.

When Trelenny informed her new friend of her devastating news, the girl cried, "Now we won't be able to save him! It's not your fault! You have done everything imaginable, and for a pitiful stranger. But I have just thought of the simplest thing, and I could die that I didn't think of it before he went off. We could sell our clothes." She opened a modest valise which stood beside the bed. "You see? Of course there is only one change for each of us because eloping is a very delicate undertaking. One cannot walk out of the house with a bulging portmanteau and half a dozen band boxes! Robert thought we should have less trouble sharing a case. But he has all his clothes made by Weston and surely they would bring us something. And I wouldn't mind parting with my dress. If only I had *thought* before he left!"

Trelenny was considering the contents of the valise with a speculative eye. There was nothing for it but to go looking for Mr. Laytham herself, she decided reluctantly, and it would be far safer to do so dressed as a man. Perhaps if he was a great deal taller than she, her decidedly feminine figure would be enveloped by his coat. "What's your name?" she asked abruptly.

"Oh, Lord, have I not even introduced myself?" The girl ran a distraught hand over her eyes. "Caroline Moreby. I'm from Bath."

Momentarily distracted from her mission, Trelenny asked curiously, "You've come from Bath? How long did it take you to get there?"

The girl opened her eyes wide with astonishment. "How long? Why, we've been traveling since very early yesterday morning. I crept out of the house before dawn and we didn't stop last night until very late. Are you worried that someone is following us? I can't believe so, for we planned our departure when my stepfather and stepbrother were from home. They aren't due back until tomorrow, and I do not believe Mama could have gotten a message to them soon enough to make their arrival more prompt."

"Miss Moreby, I have a mind to go in search of Mr. Laytham, but I think it would be wise for me to dress as a man. Would you be willing to let me borrow his clothes?"

"Go out? At night? Alone? You would not do anything so dangerous, surely!"

"I can think of no other way to prevent your young man getting himself into mischief. He *is* young, isn't he?" Trelenny asked, suddenly wary.

"Robert will be nineteen come November."

Trelenny breathed a sigh of relief. "I'm glad to hear it. They get more pompous as they get older, you know. Cranford is quite unbearably high in the instep now, but Mama says he didn't use to be so stuffy. And you are not to worry about me going out. I shall love the adventure and, as I shall be dressed as a man, no one will accost me." Her eyes twinkled with amusement. "I have a very effective weapon, too."

"You . . . you wouldn't carry a pistol?"

"No, no. I was speaking of my voice," Trelenny confessed modestly. "I'll just take these clothes along to my room and change."

"Oh, I wish you wouldn't, Miss Storwood," the girl begged. "Possibly Robert will think of selling the clothes himself. You don't think he will try to find the highwayman, do you? He . . . he was very upset at being forced to give over everything. You know what men are! He felt he should be protecting me, and though I assured him there was not a thing he could have done, still he lamented his impotence in the matter. He is so very proud! I think he would have gone after the fellow if it had not meant leaving me with just the postillions."

"I can't see the slightest chance of his finding the highwayman, Miss Moreby, so be easy in your mind." Trelenny edged toward the door, clutching the unknown gentleman's clothing under her arm. "When I return, I will come to see you, no matter what success I've had."

Without allowing the girl another protest, Trelenny slipped out the door, though she hesitated in the corridor for a moment. It would not do to have her mother waken and see her dressing in a man's clothing, so she knocked once again at Cranford's door, and when there was no response she tried the brass handle. So he has not enough faith in the hostelry to leave the door unlocked, she thought indignantly, but he would go off and leave us here alone. She stalked to her own room.

Through the whole dressing her mother slept peacefully but Trelenny hastened as best she could, tugging the cravat into the semblance of a fashionable knot. Her reflection indicated that there was a great deal wanting in the completed toilette, but she was convinced there was no reason anyone should suspect her disguise. When she had waited at the head of the stairs until a servant in the lower hall had disappeared toward the rear, she quickly made her way down and out the front door. All was darkness in the street except for the light issuing from the public rooms at the inn. The sounds of voices dwindled as she strolled off toward the Bull and Royal, attempting to make her stride as long as her legs could manage.

Although there was no reason to suppose that Mr. Laytham was in the Bull and Royal, seeing as he possessed no money, Cranford might be there; and Trelenny crept cautiously to one of the lit windows for a view into the room.

The scene within was quiet and several men sat about talking, but Cranford was not one of them, nor was there a tall blond man. Still Trelenny contemplated the scene, never having been so near a male retreat, and her eyes widened when she witnessed the liberties the serving girl allowed the customers. One pinched her bottom, and she only laughed good-naturedly as she thumped another mug onto the table. Engrossed by the view within, Trelenny was so startled by a rough hand laid on her shoulder that she very nearly screamed as she was swung about.

chapter eight

"And what be you doin', young sir?" a gruff voice asked her as she regarded the man with terrified eyes.

"I be . . . I mean, I was looking for my brother."

"How I'da thought you'da just gone right in, like most bodies." He regarded her with not unfriendly eyes, and the strong smell of horses that pervaded his vicinity led her to believe that he worked in the stables.

"Well, as to that, Cranford does not allow me to go into public rooms, you see." She attempted a tone of indignation. "He says I am not old enough."

The man peered more keenly at her face and laughed immoderately. "Maybe he's right, at that. Ain't got a whisker about you yet." He ran a hand through his grizzled hair as he cocked his head to study her glaring eyes. "Now there, young sir, I remember well how it is. Tell you what. There's no need to go in; I've a bottle of the best in the stables. You just come along with me and have a swig before you trot on home. No one will be the wiser."

Unable to find a way to deter the well-intentioned fellow from urging her toward the stables, Trelenny murmured in her most husky voice, "That's kind of you, sir." She was led around to the rear and through a low door into a tack room where the man drew up two stools and dug behind some horse blankets to produce a bottle of dark liquid, which he uncorked with his teeth. He took a healthy swig straight from the bottle and then to her horror, handed it to her. There was no way to refuse without absolute churlishness, so she awkwardly lifted the bottle and took a very small sip, which burned all the way down her throat.

Again the man roared with laughter. "That be no way to drink, young sir. You gotta grab that bottle like you mean business, throw ya head back and slug it down. Watch me carefullike."

His demonstration made Trelenny feel weak with despair, for he consumed a quarter of the contents before he thrust the bottle at her once again. Only because he watched her with such kindly interest did she manage not to fling the bottle from her. In imitation of his bold method, she clutched the neck and bravely brought it to her lips once more, though the angle she chose allowed a great deal more of the brandy to course down her throat than she could handle. In a moment she was gasping and sputtering as the man pounded her on the back and cried, "Heigh ho! Not so bad, young sir. Gotta learn to swallow just right, don't'ee see?"

"I . . . I think perhaps if I don't go now, Cranford will discover I've gone out," she croaked, wiping the droplets of liquor from her chin with the back of her hand.

"Onct more, young sir. You be close to havin' it right." He smiled encouragement as she queasily eyed the hated bottle. "Give 'er one more try."

Reluctantly, Trelenny raised the bottle and managed to down a sufficient quantity to satisfy her tutor. Immediately she struggled to her feet, sick, and gulped, "I must go. Thank you!" Digging in her coat pocket for the coins she had put there, she tossed him one. "Buy yourself another bottle on me, sir."

On unsteady legs she made her way out of the stable and down the lane to the main street. Her purpose in being abroad had escaped her and nothing seemed important but that she return to her room with all possible speed. The churning of her stomach alarmed her and she could feel her throat constricting with the taste of bile. Again and again she swallowed frantically to keep down the wretched stuff long enough to reach her room. Too sick to be aware of her surroundings, she did not notice the two men who came out of the Bull and Royal and followed her irregular route to the Castle.

Her *chapeau bra* tilted crazily over one eye and the cravat stained with brandy, she made a sorry sight when she stumbled over a rut in the road just as Cranford and his companion came abreast of her. Shaking his head disapprovingly, Cranford caught her arm to steady her and somehow, even without seeing her face clearly, he was aware that it was Trelenny. Regardless of his companion, he cried, "Damnit, what the devil are you doing out in the street in the middle of the night dressed like that?"

"I'm sick, Cranford," she whispered.

The brandy fumes assailed him when she spoke, inciting him to still greater wrath. "You'll be a lot sicker when I get through with you, my girl. I've a good mind to turn you over my knee and beat you."

Trelenny attempted unsuccessfully to pull her arm from his firm grasp. "You're just like your father," she mumbled derisively. "Everything will be solved by violence."

Abruptly he released her arm and drew back from her as though struck. "Occasionally there is good reason for physical discipline."

"I am going to be sick," was her only reply as she stumbled to the grassy verge of the street. Cranford immediately took hold of her shoulders and held her while she retched, violently, for several minutes. Although she heard him speak to his companion, she was too ill to pay any heed. His cool hand soothed her brow and, when she had ridded herself of the brandy, and almost everything else in her, he wiped her face with his handkerchief.

"Are you all right now?"

"Yes, I think so, but I want a glass of water. Will you take me back to the inn?" she asked humbly.

"Of course. Laytham, take her other arm, will you? And try to keep her from being recognized."

Trelenny gazed confusedly from one man to the other, finally focusing her eyes with difficulty on Cranford. "You found him, then? But I don't remember asking you. You weren't in your room when I tapped and I could not see you in the Bull and Royal. And I am positive that I stopped nowhere when I left the stable before you found me." Her face contorted with the effort to recall any further happenings during the evening. "Well, of course I didn't find you, because just now you were very angry to see me and talked of beating me. How did you know I was trying to find Mr. Laytham?"

"I didn't, Trelenny, but I would like very much to know why you were," Cranford said, his countenance grim, as he and his companion urged her forward.

"I had to tell him not to rob anyone, you know. Miss Moreby was very upset that he might, and she did not think until afterwards that they could sell their clothes. Not that he will be able to do so now." Trelenny's face crumpled with dismay. "I have gotten brandy on the cravat, I fear, and perhaps worse on the coat and pantaloons. But you are not to be concerned, Mr. Laytham, for I shall pay to have them cleaned, and I had already promised to lend Miss Moreby the money you will need to get to . . . where you are going. Cranford won't let me pay for the post horses in the end, anyway, so there is no reason you should not have the money. You will give it to him, won't you, Cranford? If you have decided that I may pay for the horses, then I shall pay you from what I have kept. It is not as much, to be sure, but I can pay you the rest later, or borrow some from Mama."

Cranford frowned. "Dear God, your mother doesn't know you've gone out, does she?"

"Well, of course not. Did you think I would wake her to see how I looked in Mr. Laytham's clothes? I think you've been drinking yourself, Cranford. Oh, do you know what I saw a man do to the serving girl in the Bull and Royal?"

"No, and I don't wish to know," he replied sternly. "How did you get so drunk?"

"The stableman found me looking in the window, and he thought I wouldn't go in because my brother didn't allow me. So we went to the tack room and he taught me to drink like a man. Disgusting! Do you drink like that, Cranford?"

"I haven't the slightest idea how he taught you to drink."

"You grab the bottle round the neck and just swill it down." Trelenny wrinkled her nose with distaste. "Now what is the use of drinking in that manner? The liquor pours down your throat so fast you can get no pleasure from it, and I dare say one may pick up all sorts of diseases from sharing a bottle."

They had arrived at the Castle and Cranford motioned Laytham forward to open the door and see that no one was in the hall. Before Trelenny knew what was happening, Cranford had cautioned, "Not a word," and she found herself lifted clean from the floor and transported up the stairs at lightning speed. In the upper hall she was deposited unceremoniously by Cranford's door.

"Which is Miss Moreby's room?" Laytham asked anxiously. When Trelenny had pointed to it with an unsteady finger, he grasped her hand and shook it. "You are an angel to have taken so much trouble for a stranger, Miss. I should never have left her in such disquiet. Forgive me for being the author of your unpleasant adventure, and know that I am forever beholden to you. If you will excuse me, I will just see if I may put all her fears to rest."

"But the money—"

"Mr. Ashwicke has already made me a loan."

Trelenny watched as he tapped at the door and softly called to Miss Moreby. Her view of the very affecting scene that followed was rudely interrupted by her being drawn precipitately into Cranford's room. She backed against the closed door and said frantically, "I shall scream if you touch me."

"For God's sake, what's gotten into you?" he demanded irritably as he tossed his hat on a flimsy table by the bed. "I am not your Cousin Filkins."

"He is my father's cousin. And I won't let you beat me, Cranford. If . . . if Mama thinks I should be beaten, then—"

"Your mother will not be told of this escapade, Trelenny. I will not have her upset by your stupid, improper conduct. Oh, don't tell me you went out on a mission of mercy. A shilling in the bootboy's palm would have had him scour the town for me, and you may be sure he would have found me even in a private parlor at the Bull and Royal were he promised another if successful."

She turned aside from his glaring eyes and lifted her chin. "I never thought of that."

"Then you'd best think, my girl, for I am not disposed to treat you with the kid gloves your parents do. On this trip my word is law and my will is obeyed, or you will find yourself back at Sutton Hall before you have time to blink. Do you understand me?"

"Y . . . Yes. Could I have a glass of water?"

"Please."

Her eyes dropped before his. "Please."

The ewer paused in midair as he turned to her and asked, "Have you any idea what might have happened to you tonight? Don't you care? Did you give one thought to how your parents would feel if you were raped or killed?"

Trelenny shuddered but said nothing.

With calm deliberation he filled a glass and walked toward her. "Your father put you and your mother under my protection. I dare say that is a meaningless phrase to you,

Trelenny, but you will take my word for it that it is very significant to me. Do you think those ill-fitting clothes would have concealed your identity in any well-lit room? Or that Providence would look over when you fell down drunk in the road and your hat slipped off, with those long blonde tresses exposed? If no one accidentally rode over you, you may be sure some drunken lout would have carted such a prize off to his room."

"I wouldn't have had to go out if you had been here to 'protect' us," she retorted stubbornly.

"I see. You would like me to feel the burden of leaving you here alone to face such a crisis unassisted. Tell me, Trelenny, did Miss Moreby encourage your folly?"

Silently she took the glass as she shook her head, which was beginning to ache.

"I did not intend to leave the inn, but I, too, saw an emergency arise. Foolishly believing that you and your mother were reasonably safe for the night, I scarcely hesitated when I saw Mr. Laytham fling out of here in despair.

"By the time I had gained a bit of his confidence, we were at the Bull and Royal and I desired a private parlor there to discuss his ... problems. I should like to know how you thought you would find him by yourself in a strange town at night."

"I ... could we talk of this another time, Cranford? I feel awful." Her head was spinning and the small amount of water she had been able to sip only made her feel nauseated.

"Are you going to be sick again?" When her face crumpled and she began to gag, he dashed for the basin and held it for her just in time to prevent yet a worse disaster. Patiently he held her and stroked the hair back from her pale face until she no longer needed the basin, but she remained dizzy and he lowered her gently into a chair. "Poor child. You'll feel better if I can get you to bed. I daren't call for your maid, Trelenny, or this whole mess will be common knowledge. Is your room unlocked?"

"Yes."

"Then with your permission I will slip in and bring you your night clothes. You can change into them while I wait in the hall. Will that do?"

She attempted a smile, but it went awry. "Yes."

There was a light tap at the door, which caused him a

moment's alarm until the visitor identified himself as Laytham. Cranford opened the door a crack and asked, "Is everything well?"

"Yes, thanks to you and your friend. Miss Moreby was exhausted and I stayed until she slept, but I'll go now to the room you've spoken for me at the Bull and Royal. I have no idea how to express my gratitude, Mr. Ashwicke. Only know that I will return your money as soon as possible and repay my debt to you whenever you may call on me to do so. I am yours to command."

"Just take care of the young lady. I cannot condone an elopement in the ordinary course of events, but I wish you well." The two men shook hands and Cranford watched until Laytham had descended the stairs. Without a glance at Trelenny he proceeded to her room and, feeling every kind of fool, opened the door and let himself in. What would poor Mrs. Storwood think if she woke to find him there? Not desiring to find out, Cranford quickly scooped up the nightdress and dressing gown set out on her bed.

On regaining his own room, he closed the door softly behind him and said, "I have your night clothes, Trelenny." Only then did he realize that the girl was asleep, and he found, on attempting to waken her, that it was no ordinary sleep, but one of intoxication and weakness from which he could not draw her. Although she mumbled occasionally at his persistence, there was no bringing her to consciousness.

"Oh, Lord." Cranford regarded her with exasperation, and something akin to despair. "Now what?" There was only one solution, of course, but for some time he refused to accept it. He contemplated waking Mrs. Storwood or Miss Moreby, even calling for the Storwoods' maid, but he knew very well that he would not. Mrs. Storwood would be horrified, Miss Moreby he could not bring himself to disturb after her traumatic day, and the maid—well, Cranford was not willing to trust to the discretion of her tongue. He rose at length and made one final, unsuccessful, attempt to awaken Trelenny.

Now it might be possible to accomplish some tasks with one's eyes closed, but undressing and redressing an unresponsive body is not one of them. Feeling himself honorbound to view as little of her nakedness as possible, Cranford kept his eyes averted when he could, but it only made the process take longer and finally, in desperation, he decided that, given a preference, which she wasn't, Trelenny would prefer to have the business completed as quickly as possible. Consequently, he stripped her naked and swiftly pulled the nightdress over her head, patiently worked her arms through the sleeves, and at last covered the rest of her body from his sight. Despite his resolution, he was shaken.

Upbraiding himself for his failure to view his undertaking with the proper detachment, he peeked into the hall to make sure all was quiet and returned to lift her in his arms, tuck the clothes under his elbow and carry her to her room, where he settled her in a chair before releasing any remaining pins from her hair. Did she sleep with it loose? It waved softly about her face and came nearly to her waist and, as he lifted her once again to convey her to the bed, he could feel the silkiness of it against his chin.

As he settled her on the bed, she mumbled something incoherent and he put a finger against her lips to still her voice. Unconsciously she kissed the finger and he regarded her perplexedly as he pulled the bedclothes over her, unaccountably bending down to kiss her forehead before he withdrew. Surely he had been in scrapes enough that he should sympathize with Trelenny for her absurd adventures; and he would have, perhaps, if she were merely a friend. In a potential wife it was another matter altogether.

chapter nine

Trelenny awoke in the morning when Alice entered with a tea tray, and for a moment she could not imagine why she felt so decidedly ill. On the other bed her mother moved to a sitting position for Alice to set her tray on her lap, then she turned to smile at her daughter. "For all it is not the best inn I have ever visited, I must say I have seldom had a better night away from home. And you, my love? You know, Trelenny, you are looking a bit peaked. Do you feel well? I hope you aren't coming down with something," she said anxiously.

"No, no. I fear I did not sleep as well as you, Mama." Trelenny glanced down at her nightdress and touched the hair that lay about her shoulders. It was not her habit to loose her hair at night, but to braid it and then brush it out in the morning. A deep flush rose in her cheeks. "I . . . I have not spent a night away from home in ages, since you and Papa took me to York years ago, and the unfamiliarity—"

Her mother smiled. "Your color is better now, I think, love. You'll get used to sleeping in strange beds and eating in strange places. It's all a part of traveling."

"Yes." The tea tray was set on her lap and she busied herself in adding milk and sugar. "But you say you slept well, Mama? Nothing disturbed your rest?"

"Not a thing, dearest. Could you hear noise from the public rooms? I feared this inn would attract a rowdy bunch of men of an evening. Cranford didn't really want us to stay here, I think, but I hated to be at a different inn from his. Tonight we will find a more peaceful spot so that you can get your proper rest."

"Oh, I shall sleep in the carriage, no doubt. Don't give a thought to me."

But Trelenny's own thoughts were scurrying frantically to and fro as she sipped at her tea. Cranford had undressed her! He must have, for she would never have undone her own hair. No, perhaps Miss Moreby had done it. Obviously her mother knew nothing of the previous night's adventures, and there was no sign that Alice was hiding some deep secret as she went about laying out their clothing for the day. Oh, please, please, let it have been Miss Moreby. But how was she to ask her? Even if they saw her she could not let on that they had met, since that would require an explanation to her mother. And could she possibly ask Cranford? Her heart sank at the very thought.

As it turned out, it was unnecessary to ask him. From the very way he avoided her eyes, she knew, as certainly as though she had put the question directly to him. Trelenny instinctively realized that he had harmed her in no way, had taken no advantage of her indisposed condition. He would not have been Cranford if he could do such a thing. But there could have been no way for him to avoid seeing her naked. She was unable to eat more than a slice of toast, and that only because of her mother's concerned eyes.

Unaware of any tension between her two companions, Mrs. Storwood chatted cheerfully to Cranford, detailing her delight in having spent a restful night. "I fear Trelenny did not fare so well, however. Another time I will not insist on staying at the same inn, if it means our staying where there are disturbances to keep her awake."

At Cranford's inquiring look, she continued, "The public rooms, you know. I think the noise made sleep difficult for her."

"I'm sure it was just the strange bed," her daughter protested, unable to meet Cranford's eyes. "Tonight I'll have no trouble at all, I promise you."

"I hope that will prove to be the case," he returned blandly as he ushered the ladies to the waiting carriage.

When Cranford climbed in to sit beside her, Trelenny uneasily shifted further into the corner away from him, and he pretended not to notice. He could see not only the signs of embarrassment but of headache and mawkishness as well. "Would you like me to read some more of *Evelina*, Trelenny?"

"No, thank you. I think I will try to sleep for a while." So saying, she drew the carriage rug more closely about her lap and proceeded to fall asleep, undisturbed by the sway of the carriage and unconscious that her head had fallen against Cranford's shoulder. Not until they halted at midday did she awaken, and she sat abruptly upright, casting a suspicious glance at Cranford which made him shake his head ruefully. "I feel a great deal better now, Mama. Are we stopping for luncheon? I'm famished."

"She must be better," Mrs. Storwood confessed to Cranford. "Ever since she was small, she never had the least appetite when she was ill."

After doing justice to a good serving of pigeon pie, apples, and cheese, Trelenny was feeling almost normal again, until Cranford suggested that she ride for a stage with him. It seemed to her that it was more of a command than a suggestion, and she would have plead renewed illness except for not wishing to alarm her mother. Her fervent prayer, that they would not have two hacks available, or have no sidesaddle, was not answered and she soon found herself riding beside Cranford some distance behind the carriage so they would not be covered by its dust.

"You might like to know that our new friends got an early start this morning," Cranford offered conversationally.

"Did . . . you restore Mr. Laytham's clothes?" She kept her eyes straight ahead.

"Yes. I gave him one of my cravats to replace the soiled one. Trelenny, I'm sorry I had to undress you. I couldn't wake your mother, and Miss Moreby was already asleep."

She asked in a strangled voice, "Will I have to marry you?"

"For God's sake, you don't think I touched you!"

"No. I know you never would, but . . . am I not compromised?"

"I suppose so, technically, but only the two of us know, so it cannot matter. I thought of telling you that Miss Moreby had done it, but I couldn't lie to you. You were so overtaken that it was impossible to wake you. I had hoped you might think you'd done it yourself in your intoxication."

"I don't loosen my hair at night."

"Did your mother notice?"

"No, she was only concerned with my feeling unwell."

Trelenny agitatedly thumped a hand down on her thigh. "I can't *bear* to think of your seeing me!"

"Discard it from your mind, as I have from mine," he suggested with more gallantry than truth.

"Oh, I believe you could, you unfeeling bookworm! Don't you see that makes it all the worse? Treating me like some cold marble statue of a Roman maiden, probably calculating my imperfections in comparison! I can see your wretched detachment now. No, she would not make a good tombstone, even with a concealing toga."

"God help me, Trelenny, what do you want? Are you disappointed that I didn't rape you?"

"Oh, shut up. You shouldn't have done it."

"I had no choice. You put yourself in an awkward position and I felt it my duty to extricate you by the only means at hand." He studied her seriously for a moment. "If I *hadn't* done it, Trelenny, you might have been forced to marry me. Your mother would not see the incident as lightly as you do. Her mortification at your wandering around town in men's clothes, and being seen by me in them would likely have urged immediate action on her. She has a fine sense of propriety and could only consider you compromised by such behavior. Let's have no more of your missish rantings, my girl; they ill suit you."

His harsh words, carefully calculated to sting her out of her embarrassment, accomplished their purpose only too well. With flashing eyes but a grimly set face, she retorted, "You have done everything for my good! How very thoughtful of you, you great brute. You surprise me, Cranford. I should have thought you would welcome the opportunity to force me into marriage with you. Did you not do so with poor Clare to your best friend? Do you think I don't know she had fallen in love with someone else?" Trelenny clamped a horrified hand over her mouth. The secret had slipped from her without thought in her anger and she urged her horse to gallop to avoid his startled eyes. Not even to her mother had she so much as hinted at her knowledge, the cause of her anxiety over her friend's marriage. She had been sworn to secrecy by Clare's letter, and she had honored that pledge for the last year and more without fail. To have let it slip in a moment of unguarded hostility chastened and alarmed her.

Before she had time to collect her thoughts she found

Cranford alongside her, intent on hearing more of her knowledge. "What did you mean just now, Trelenny?"

"Nothing."

"Don't be absurd. What fairy tale have you concocted in your mind to account for your imperfect understanding of Clare's situation?"

Trelenny rode in silence for several minutes before answering. Then, with a resolution which cost her a great deal of courage, she looked Cranford directly in the eye and said, "If you will forget what I said, I will forgive you for ... undressing me."

Although Cranford did not feel the need for her forgiveness, being convinced that he had acted from the purest of motives, he understood what she was saying, and he realized that it cost her a great deal to say it. She would will herself to act with him as she had before the incident, not shunning his company or seething with indignation, and he respected her determination. There was also the matter of her obvious regret that she had allowed her wayward tongue to let escape a drop of sacred intelligence which she wished she could recall. Despite his very real desire to learn what she knew of his sister's situation and what she surmised, he said gently, "Very well, Trelenny. Both matters are closed."

"Thank you, Cranford." She extended her hand and he shook it solemnly. "I'm sorry if I called you names. You're not such a bad fellow after all."

"You flatter me," he returned wryly.

" 'I have time for no more; the chaise now waits which is to conduct me to dear Berry Hill, and to the arms of the best of men. Evelina.' Well, Trelenny what did you think of it?" Cranford asked.

"If you wish me to say I loved it, I must disappoint you," she said with a grin at her mother. "And I would point out to you that she got in a great deal more trouble trying to behave as she ought, than she probably would have if she had just followed her inclination."

Mrs. Storwood sighed. "How you can so easily dispose of poor Evelina is beyond me, my dear. Doesn't it warm your heart that all came out well for her after all the adversities she endured? Doesn't her virtue shine through all her misadventures?"

"I made most note of all the tears she shed," Trelenny admitted sacrilegiously. "She must have filled buckets and soiled any number of handkerchiefs. What a lot of work she gave the laundry maids!"

"You're incorrigible," Mrs. Storwood groaned with a doleful shake of her head. To her the journey had sped by with the reading of her beloved book, the care Cranford took of them, and the comfort of the carriage. She was not so sanguine about the relationship between her daughter and their escort; they seemed, if anything, to be further apart than ever, with Trelenny constantly teasing him about Evelina's righteousness and Cranford berating her for her lack of proper feeling. Had she known of the contretemps between them, however, she would have been amazed by the ease with which they resettled into their former raillery, perhaps even encouraged by the lighter vein in which they pinched at one another. Their shared secret had forced an understanding between them which brought them closer and made them more dependent on one another.

"Oh, look!" Trelenny exclaimed as her first view of Bath impressed itself on her. "Why, no drawing I have ever seen does it the least justice! What a beautiful town. Where is the Pump Room? Isn't the Abbey magnificent? Do you suppose it will take us long to find lodgings? Shall we spend the night at the White Hart? Will Mrs. Waplington have had your letter by now, Mama? Is it too late to walk about the town a bit before dinner? Will we wait until tomorrow to send Mrs. Waplington a message? What nights are the Assemblies, Cranford?" Bombarded by her questions, and touched by her pathetic eagerness, Cranford tried patiently to answer each one before yet another escaped her.

Accommodations had been arranged by post at the White Hart and while Mrs. Storwood settled into her delightful suite, Cranford agreed to walk with Trelenny until the dinner they had bespoken was prepared.

"The ladies look so fine in their French bonnets and cornettes. Will I be out of fashion, Cranford?"

He cocked his head to study her circular hat with its plume of quadrille feathers and satin ribbon ending in bows at her waist. "I think not. Your mother has always kept up with the latest fashions, whether you paid the least attention or not. You look presentable, but you might try to do something about those freckles."

"I shall long for the day when you don't pay me a backhanded compliment," she retorted. "Why I should think you would know the first thing about fashion... Oh, Cranford, have you ever seen a shop with so many ribbons? I think they sell nothing else."

"Shall I give you some of your money now we are in town?"

"No, I don't need it, and I wish you would keep it as I asked, for if you lent money to Mr. Laytham, you're sure to be short."

"Allow me to worry about my own finances, if you please," he said coolly.

"As you wish, Golden Ball. I'm sure I don't care a fig if you find yourself at point non plus. Is that a sedan chair? Shall I ride in one? Won't Mama look elegant carried about in such a way? Oh, I wish Papa could be here to see."

A thousand questions sprang to her lips as they retraced their direction to the hotel but Trelenny observed a bursting silence, while Cranford pointed out sights of interest in an amused voice. Under cover of his discourse Trelenny surreptitiously watched the passersby, wondering if she would subsequently meet the pretty young ladies and the smart young men. She drew more than one appreciative glance from the latter, but one man in particular she noticed, for he started at the sight of her and moved as though to approach before retreating to his former position at a printshop window. Not a young man (Trelenny judged him to be five and forty or so), he was distinguished looking and had an air of assurance which was only slightly marred by his puzzled expression. Obviously he found it difficult to take his eyes from her but was conscious of the impropriety of staring, and, when they had passed him, Trelenny glanced back to see that he watched as they entered the White Hart.

"Did you know that man, Trelenny?" Cranford asked sternly.

"No, of course not."

"Then you shouldn't encourage him to stare at you. If you so openly show your appreciation of a man's interest, he will think you fast. You will have to adapt to town ways, Trelenny. This is, in effect, your come-out and girls your age are expected to show a becoming modesty and shyness. Your bold behavior of the countryside will not do here, my girl, unless you are in search of rakes and adventurers or wish to be mistaken for something your mother would blush for. You don't go out unescorted, you listen to your mother's advice on whom you accept as partners at the assemblies, you try for a little decorum, and, most of all, you continue to accept my authority if you don't wish to set off immediately for Sutton Hall."

"You are an insufferable tyrant, Cranford. The man was old enough to be my father."

"His age makes not the least difference. Girls your age are married to men of his years every day, and frequently a great deal older."

"Well, I think that's disgusting!"

Cranford relaxed his severity for a moment to grin. "I do, too, my dear, but ambition makes for some very strange matches. Now don't attempt to rescue every girl you find engaged to some old cadger; for all you know, she may be perfectly in agreement with the arrangement."

"I doubt I would have enough sympathy for such a lady to wish to help her," Trelenny retorted.

They returned to find Mrs. Storwood with a guest, and Trelenny recognized her immediately as the woman they had passed in the sedan chair, a well-dressed matron with a few extra pounds to her credit and a cheerful, beaming countenance. Mrs. Storwood had been informed of all the discomfort she would suffer in searching for a lodging of her own and the distraction of choosing adequate servants, but it was mostly for her daughter's ease in being made known to Bath society that she had accepted Mrs. Waplington's pressing offer to stay with her. By the time Trelenny arrived all that remained to be done was to introduce the newcomers and set a time for the Storwoods to present themselves in Henrietta Street the next morning. When Mrs. Waplington had hugged Trelenny to her like a long-lost daughter, she drew her wrap about her ample frame and allowed Cranford to lead her down to her waiting chair.

"I hope I have done the right thing," Mrs. Storwood said anxiously. "You don't think your Papa would object, do you? Mr. Waplington himself instructed the White Hart to let them know the moment we arrived so they could invite us."

"Papa would want you to do just what would make you comfortable, Mama. And Cranford didn't raise a brow, so he must consider your acceptance not the least objectionable. Of course if *he* had thought it wrong, we would not have done it."

Totally missing her daughter's irony, Mrs. Storwood sighed. "No, of course not. We should be very grateful for Cranford's guidance."

"Indeed."

chapter ten

The Waplingtons' house in Henrietta Street was a fine example of classic architecture, gracefully relieved by fluted pilasters and a broken pediment. Trelenny marveled at the various rooms through which they were conducted by an enthusiastic Mrs. Waplington, who seemed unconscious of the overcrowded furniture and the wall space completely taken over by family and historical paintings. There was very little room to move about in the dining room, library, or drawing room, crowded as they were with tables, chairs, desks, stands, and musical instruments of all descriptions. No surface was unrelieved by some bowl or candlestick, figurine or silver box. Where they had apparently run out of portraits or pastoral scenes, mirrors of all sizes and shapes filled in the empty spaces, as though Mrs. Waplington could not bear to see the damask wall coverings beneath. The busy designs of the Axminster carpets gave a kaleidoscopic effect which caused Trelenny to press her lips together as her mother politely proclaimed the elegance of each room in turn. When applied to for her proficiency on one of the musical instruments, however, Trelenny's amusement quickly faded.

"I fear Mama has not succeeded in teaching me to play the pianoforte passably, ma'am, and I beg you will not call on me to entertain, for I would surely disgrace myself. Years ago we ascertained that I had no talent, as I was even less successful with the harp than the pianoforte."

Mrs. Waplington gave vent to a rumbling chuckle. "Now there is a girl after my own heart, Maria. I cannot tell you, my dear, what agonies I used to suffer when my mother would insist on my performing. Have no fear, Trelenny; I would not inflict such a trial on anyone."

"Thank you, Mrs. Waplington. I am extremely grateful."

Cranford's fears confirmed, he made no comment, but Trelenny noted, when she glanced at him, that his face was set with disapproval; and she remembered the delightful times she had spent with his mother and sister around the pianoforte. Well, there, she thought, with less satisfaction than she would formerly have gained, he has yet another reason to leave off his useless pursuit of me. I have absolutely none of the qualities he wishes in a wife and, she reiterated firmly to herself, he has none I wish in a husband. The matter should not have occurred to her at all, perhaps, at such a time, but she was oblivious to the anomaly.

Cranford excused himself before they were shown their rooms, and Mrs. Waplington watched him depart with a sigh. "Such an elegant young man. Would that I had had a son! But with such a shatterbrain for a mother he would not possess near the air or address of Mr. Ashwicke, I fear. I think there is nothing so delightful as an attentive, gentle manner, do you, Maria?"

She opened the door of a bedchamber done in green— the sofa, the chairs, the draperies, the carpet, the wallpaper, the bedcover all in various shades—and announced, "Maria, this is the room you shall have. I call it the Garden Bedchamber and have only recently redone it. Do you think perhaps you will need another chair and table? I have a kidney-shaped gueridon in the attic, but I had hoped to have it regilded before using it."

"Please don't think of it! How very charming! Not a thing is needed, I promise you." Mrs. Storwood took in the vases full of fall flowers and the paintings of gardens and still lifes of blooms of all varieties. "I have never seen anything half so ... fascinating. Is it your own idea?"

"Yes," Mrs. Waplington admitted proudly. "I do not at all favor the Egyptian craze—so very heavy, you know. And in town I am apt to miss my extensive gardens, so I specially designed this room to my own taste. You will be the first to occupy it, my dear. I've put Trelenny next to you," she said as she opened the interconnecting door. "Now here, I fear, Andrew has insisted on a more masculine setting, for he says he won't have the whole house full of female fripperies when his friends come to stay. A trifle sparsely furnished, I fear, and rather austere, but there, men have such simple tastes."

Since the furniture in the room consisted of a circular rosewood table, a pair of bronze lampstands, an enormous armchair, a smaller chair, a settee, a folding card table, and a *secretaire* in addition to a dressing table with washstand, to say nothing of a wardrobe and a four-poster bed, Trelenny could only regard her hostess with astonishment. It was perhaps the only room in the house where the wall color could be seen, since there were only two pictures on each wall, and they were Rowlandson prints that bordered on the risqué.

When Mrs. Waplington noticed the direction of Trelenny's eyes, she exclaimed, "I had forgotten those! Andrew will have his little joke. Never mind, I shall replace them for your stay, my dear. Let's see. Eight. Yes, I am certain I have at least half a dozen paintings of dogs. Do you like dogs? There may be eight. Or there are a dozen views of Somerset stored in the attics, by the most remarkable painter. Have I told you of him, Maria? It is all the fashion to have an artistic protégé, you will find, and I congratulate myself on finding this particular fellow, for he is undoubedly talented. Yes, you will doubtless prefer the landscapes. Not that I don't appreciate the robust humor of Mr. Rowlandson's prints, you understand, but they are hardly proper material for a girl of Trelenny's age to meditate on. And landscapes are so uplifting, don't you think?"

"Indeed I shall be enchanted to have them," Trelenny assured her politely, "and I find the room delightful."

"Splendid. I will leave you and your mother to unpack and rest, my dear, but I hope you will join me in the drawing room when you wish." She squeezed Trelenny's hand affectionately. "Where is my mind wandering? I have forgotten to tell you that I have invited a few very close friends to dine with us this evening. Mr. Ashwicke is included, of course, but I fear you will find most of them rather elderly. Still, I cannot think but that you will feel the more comfortable for knowing a few people when you go to the Pump Room in the morning."

Mrs. Storwood expressed her appreciation and Trelenny's eyes danced with sheer good spirits. Her very first social occasion away from home! It mattered little what it was. She was in Bath, and her introduction to the world was about to begin.

It came as no surprise to Maria Storwood that the "small dinner party" turned out to consist of twenty guests, who were seated at one enormous table in the vast dining hall from which several superfluous items of furniture had been removed for their accommodation. Even in their youth Elsa Waplington had shown a tendency to entertain in accordance with her flamboyant personality—everything on a grand scale, with the best food, the best dinner service, the best people. And yet there was a lack of pretension for all this extravagant manner which endeared Mrs. Waplington to her friends, among whom Mrs. Storwood had been numbered for better than twenty years, maintained without their seeing each other even once, through the medium of letters. Over the years Mrs. Waplington had imparted news of all their acquaintances in a voluminous running journal, while Maria Storwood had written of her husband and child, feeling sadly deficient as a correspondent and frequently wondering whether she had anything to say that would be of interest to Elsa. Had she but known that Elsa lived parenthood vicariously through her, she would not have worried, and would rather have been pleased that she could give so much pleasure with so little effort.

As she dressed for dinner, Mrs. Storwood gazed anxiously in the glass, aware of a nervousness that she had not experienced since she was Trelenny's age. Mysteriously secretive on who was to be at the gathering, Elsa had hinted that her friend would meet several old acquaintances, but she had such a wicked twinkle in her eyes that Maria's heart nearly failed her as she settled a blue silk shawl about her shoulders. She turned to the maid to ask, "Is Trelenny ready?"

"Yes, ma'am. Shall I have her come to you?"

"If you would." She felt an unusual burst of pride when her daughter glided into the room in a white crape frock over a primrose sarcenet slip, the bodice ornamented with deep vandykes of primrose velvet. Her headdress was of three folds of primrose *crêpe lisse*, with rows of pearls beneath, placed between large bows of her silken blonde hair, which was arranged in festoons of plaits on the left, and a single bow on the right fastened by a pearled comb. "You ... look beautiful, my love. Never say Alice did your hair!"

"Mrs. Waplington sent her dresser round to do something special. Do you like it?"

"It's delightful."

"Yes," Trelenny said thoughtfully, "I think it makes me look a bit older, don't you? I'll have Alice peek at the guests so she can experiment with some new styles for me. Isn't it exciting, Mama, to be here at last?"

"It is, love. I hope you are not in agonies over your introduction to a lot of stangers. How well I remember my own first formal party. My hands were like ice and I hadn't the least color in my cheeks." She took her daughter's hands and found them a great deal warmer than her own. "Your cheeks are not so rosy as usual, Trelenny."

Her daughter grinned. "Mrs. Waplington's dresser thought a touch of powder would disguise the freckles."

"Oh."

"Shall I wash it off?" Trelenny asked anxiously. "The freckles don't seem half so prominent as usual, anyway, for the days we spent in the carriage."

"No, love, you look wonderful just as you are. Pray pay no heed to me. I own I am a great deal more nervous than you appear to be." With a puzzled shake of her head, she linked her arm with her daughter's. What Trelenny lacked in an air of modesty and a retiring deportment she would fully make up for in her natural enthusiasm, Mrs. Storwood decided with confidence. Refusing to allow herself any misgivings on this head, she proceeded with her daughter to the drawing room, where she presented Trelenny to Mr. Waplington, who had regrettably been kept from home the whole of the day.

Andrew Waplington was half a head shorter than his wife, and a wiry, energetic man of forty. "Maria, forgive my not being here to welcome you. A matter of business, and most pressing. Miss Storwood, an honor to meet you. The image of your mother, as Elsa told me. Is your room comfortable?"

Since Mrs. Waplington had forgotten to have the prints removed and replaced, Trelenny's eyes sparkled with mischief as she assured him, "It is more than comfortable, sir, and we are very sensible of your kindness in taking us into your home."

Mrs. Storwood watched fascinated as he conversed with

Trelenny in a sort of rapid firing of questions, followed by the most profound attention to her answers. No shyness inhibited her daughter from answering with frankness his inquiries as to her home, her father, her education, and her hopes for her visit to Bath. As the first guest was announced he turned to Mrs. Storwood and pronounced judgment. "You've raised a very lively girl, Maria, and I congratulate you. No retiring flower here, by God, and I'm pleased to see it, if you want the truth of the matter. Bless me if you don't find a parcel of milk-and-water misses at this watering hole, and nothing could be more boring than a chit who's afraid to open her mouth for fear of putting herself forward unbecomingly. What's that, my dear?" he asked as his wife recalled his attention.

"Our guests," Mrs. Waplington scolded with a touch of her painted gauze fan to his arm.

Although her courage was reinforced by Mr. Waplington's favorable opinion of Trelenny, Maria Storwood nevertheless felt grateful that Cranford was among the first to arrive. There were other familiar faces, of course, but it was in most cases more of a strain than a pleasure to renew old acquaintances. Too often she was conscious of the enormous gap in time that separated her from this fashionable gathering. Did they pity her for her years of retirement away from the social scene? Would they accept Trelenny, with her open countenance and exuberance—and her freckles? She glanced over to see her daughter, under Cranford's watchful eye, greet each newcomer with lowered eyes and an expression of her extreme pleasure at the honor done her. And she heard Cranford murmur, "Well done, Trelenny. I hope the strain will not prove too much for you."

"If it does, I shall faint dead away on some sofa and declare I am so overcome with such disginguished notice that I am unable to bear my joy," her daughter retorted in an undervoice, all the while smiling shyly at him.

"You won't like it if they burn feathers under your nose."

But Mrs. Storwood entirely lost the rest of their good-natured bickering. A voice at her elbow, a voice that had once been very familiar, startled her so badly that her fan dropped unnoticed from her nerveless hands. The gentleman who retrieved it smiled bemusedly at her. "I should have known. First, I saw this young lady," indicating Trelenny "yesterday and then I received an indubitably provocative invitation from Elsa. Her note said that although my acceptance would give her great pleasure, she thought my pleasure would be greater." He lifted her icy hand to his lips. "Maria Champion... Storwood, after all these years. My good fortune overwhelms me."

"Mr. Wheldrake," she replied breathlessly, accepting her fan without noticing, and promptly dropping it again. "Elsa did not mention you were in town. Thank you. May I present you to my daughter, Trelenny Storwood?"

He turned to the girl with an apologetic smile. "You will forgive me staring at you yesterday, I hope. I thought for a moment I had suffered some sort of attack or had been illogically transported back in time. Is this your first stay in Bath?"

"Yes, sir, we only arrived yesterday, shortly before we saw you in the street. May I present Mr. Ashwicke, our neighbor and escort?" Trelenny observed the older man's easy grace in acknowledging the introduction, and his equal ease in returning to conversation with her mother, whom he soon maneuvered out of the growing crowd of guests to a retired seat in the corner.

"I don't see Mr. Storwood here. Did he not accompany you?"

"No, he doesn't travel owing to a weak heart," Mrs. Storwood replied. "Elsa wrote some years ago that your wife had died. I am so sorry for you."

"Thank you."

His head bowed slightly at her remark and she noticed the silvering at his temples. How very many years had passed, and yet the graying was the only significant sign of his aging. "You have children of your own, I believe."

The solemnity vanished from his face to be replaced by an engaging animation. "Two boys, slightly younger than your daughter, I should say. They're at Harrow just now, and kicking up every sort of lark. I expect them to be sent down at any time," he said ruefully.

"Sometimes I think we should have sent Trelenny to school. Not that she isn't well read, for her father took a hand in her education and she is very quick. She lacks the ... restraint one sees in young ladies educated away from home, though." She lifted her eyes from her hands. "She is the dearest girl, you understand, and I would far rather she not suffer from the shyness which so distresses me, but—"

"I thought her very properly reserved."

"She's just behaving that way to taunt Cranford," Mrs. Storwood confessed. "They are forever at loggerheads, and largely over this very matter. Listen to me going on about my concerns as though they could be of the least interest to anyone else. Do forgive me."

"Not at all. I'm honored with your confidence after all these years." He shook his head wonderingly as he smiled gently at her. "You are still as lovely as ever, Maria."

Two flushed spots appeared in her cheeks. Just as though I were a girl of Trelenny's age, she thought in confusion. "You flatter me, Mr. Wheldrake." In attempting to fan her warm face, she once again dropped the fan, and stared at it helplessly.

Mr. Wheldrake retrieved it for the third time and tucked it in his pocket. "I've always thought ivory too slippery a material to use for fans. Will you be going to London with your daughter?"

"No, we can only be away for a few weeks. This is all the come-out Trelenny will have, so I am intent on seeing she enjoys herself to the fullest. She's never been to a ball or an assembly, not even to a dinner party so large as this. I really shouldn't leave her."

"Of course not." He rose and walked with her toward Trelenny and Cranford. "I hope you will allow me to assist Mr. Ashwicke in escorting you about town. He probably has friends of his own with whom he will wish to spend time, and I promise you I am entirely at your disposal."

Mrs. Storwood found it difficult to meet his hopeful gaze. "I have worried about that. It seems wrong to tie up all his time and yet . . ."

"You had no one else to serve you, but now you have. I could ask for no greater pleasure than to be called upon."

"Thank you, Mr. Wheldrake. I have no right to ask such a favor of you."

"You have every right, and you used to call me Frederick."

"That was a very long time ago," she said faintly.

"In years, perhaps, but not in memory."

His gray eyes sought to hold hers, but she quickly looked toward her daughter with a fond smile. "Have you met everyone, dear?"

"Yes, but I am quite at a loss to remember half their names, Mama," Trelenny whispered.

"Repeat them as you are introduced, and as often as you can in conversation without sounding forced, love. We're going in to dinner now. I'm sure Cranford will take you."

"I . . . think he'd rather not. He's met an old friend," Trelenny said forlornly.

chapter eleven

Cranford had, in fact, met several old friends. As he stood beside Trelenny and was introduced to their fellow guests his eyes wandered to the door where Lord and Lady Babthorpe were entering; he a man of sixty-odd and she a lady of perhaps five-and-twenty. It was just the sort of match Trelenny had deplored the previous day and as they approached she pinched Cranford's finger and murmured, "A gray-beard with a youthful maiden." She was considerably surprised, therefore, when Cranford greeted them as previous acquaintances.

"Lady Babthorpe, Lord Babthorpe, a pleasure to see you again. May I introduce Miss Storwood? She and her mother are neighbors in Westmorland."

Owing to his reduced financial circumstances, Cranford had not been about town much in the previous two years, but his acquaintance with the couple went back some time before that, and though his knowledge of Lord Babthorpe was slight, his acquaintance with his lady greatly exceeded it. Lady Babthorpe had an air of provocativeness which was proclaimed in her slightly pouting lips, her loosely flowing black hair, and her sleepy eyes as well as her alluring figure. "Ah, Mr. Ashwicke. I can see Bath holds more interest than I had thought this year."

Her husband, who came to Bath for the waters, drew himself up like a bantam cock (which he greatly resembled, to Trelenny's mind) and glared at the younger man. "Bath is of all places the most tiresome. No variety compared to London, and a batch of loose hangers-on into the bargain. We come only for its health-restoring properties and have little time for social intercourse."

"One doesn't, of course, refuse an invitation from Mrs. Waplington or any other of equal importance," Lady Babthorpe said with a speaking look at Cranford that very nearly caused Trelenny to blush.

"It would be a great deal too bad to see such a charming lady retired from society," Cranford replied with practiced gallantry.

"She is much in *my* society," Lord Babthorpe retorted, "and that is just as it should be. *You* are not likely to see much of her."

"*Quel dommage*," Cranford murmured, before turning the conversation. "Miss Storwood has not been to Bath previously, and has yet to sample the waters."

"They have a frightful taste," Lady Babthorpe informed Trelenny negligently, "but I dare say you will journey regularly to the Pump Room with all the other misses on their daily round."

Her condescension pricked Trelenny, whose eyes flashed with annoyance. Very likely she would have retorted had she not seen Cranford slightly shake his head at her. "I suppose I shall, ma'am."

"I can't see the fascination country people find in drinking nasty-tasting water and fatiguing themselves strolling along the promenades," Lady Babthorpe commented with a nod of dismissal to Trelenny and one last intriguing smile at Cranford before she continued her progress with her insistent husband.

Since her mother was not at hand, Trelenny was strongly tempted to tell Cranford exactly what she thought of his friends, but he watched the anger boiling up in her and said firmly, "Mind your tongue, Trelenny."

Resentfully she bit back a stinging epithet she had devised and said, with a sweet smile at him, "They are well suited."

Cranford was genuinely amused, and might have let her know it, but for the arrival of yet another acquaintance of his. "Now here is someone you will enjoy meeting, Trelenny, and might do well to pattern yourself after." Too late he realized he could have said nothing which would more likely put up her back and rule out any possibility of friendship between the two ladies. "I don't mean that as I said it. Lady Jane does not deserve your antagonism for my blunder."

"I shall try to keep an open mind," Trelenny assured him as she offered a smile to the tall woman who approached. Lady Jane, for all her unusual height, carried herself with an unconscious elegance which made her appear more attractive than her less-than-classical features would otherwise have allowed. Her pleasure at seeing Cranford was evidenced by a warm smile which lit her entire face, making the hazel eyes shine.

"Dear Lord, it's been years, Cranford! You remember my father, Lord Barlow."

"Of course. How do you do, sir? I read your speech in the House some months past and would have written to tell you of my enthusiastic agreement if I had not feared you would think me presumptuous."

"I always defended your intelligence, Ashwicke, no matter what I might have thought of your occasional folly," the older man replied wryly as they shook hands.

When Cranford had presented Trelenny, the four stood chatting for a while before Lord Barlow was called away. At the time, Lady Jane and Cranford had moved slightly aside so that their reminiscences would not disturb the others, and Trelenny found herself a bit discomposed, not wishing to interrupt the obviously enjoyable tête à tête by inserting her presence. At that uncomfortable moment her mother had arrived to spare her, and for the first time Trelenny realized that not everything would be perfect, even now that she had achieved her goal of being in Bath. Somehow it seemed to her that if she could just *get* there, the rest would take care of itself. She was taken in to dinner by Mr. Wheldrake, as Mr. Waplington took her mother and Cranford took Lady Jane. Mrs. Waplington believed in preference above precedence.

Seated between Mr. Wheldrake and Cranford, Trelenny once again found herself in an unenviable position. Although both men, out of simple good manners, conversed with her during the meal, it was evident to her that each was more interested in talking with the lady on his other side—in Cranford's case Lady Jane, and in Mr. Wheldrake's Mrs. Storwood. And when they did speak with her, it was generally of episodes with which she was unfamiliar.

Witness Mr. Wheldrake: "I remember when your mother made her début in London, Miss Storwood. Long before I ever met her I had heard her praises sung in Brooks, but I hardly credited the truth of such dazzling rumors until the night of Lady Knavesmire's ball. Was there ever such a night? Tom Whimple broke his leg climbing over a sofa to reach your mother before anyone else did, and Charlotte Lawrence cried all night because Henry Lambert asked your mother for a dance before he asked her. The men were three-deep around her and I didn't have a chance to dance with her until at least two weeks later." Etc., etc., etc.

Cranford was, if anything, worse: "Did I ever tell you that it was Lady Jane who first interested me in antiquities, Trelenny? She had been with her family to Rome and Athens at the time of the Treaty of Amiens when she was but a child, and Lord Barlow knew Lord Elgin very well, so she had seen the marbles any number of times before I met her. When I proposed an excursion one day, she suggested we see the marbles, and I thought she must be quizzing me." He glanced fondly at Lady Jane, who was in animated conversation with a gentleman whose name Trelenny could no longer remember. "They are enough to fire anyone's imagination, those marbles, and Lady Jane knew the stories they depicted. Imagine my surprise at finding the expedition I had expected to be a dead bore turn into a fascinating journey into the past! Do you know what Centaurs are? Well..." Etc., etc., etc.

Before dinner was concluded, Trelenny was suffering from the headache and worse was to come. When the ladies retired, Lady Jane made a point of speaking with her, and, assuming that she shared Cranford's interest in Bath's Roman history, owing to her polite attention at dinner, Lady Jane kindly imparted what information she could on the subject, and she was very knowledgeable. Aware of her intended thoughtfulness, Trelenny was forced to smile encouragement, and only after a lengthy dissertation was she able to change the course of their talk.

"Do you come often to Bath?" she asked in desperation.

"Perhaps two or three times a year, for a retreat from the estate. And my father suffers from the gout occasionally; he finds the baths soothing."

"Just the two of you come?"

"Yes, my mother is dead and my brothers and sisters are all married."

"Have you a lot of brothers and sisters?" Trelenny asked wistfully.

"Two of each." Lady Jane smiled. "That's how I originally met Cranford, you know. He was an especially close friend of my second brother, Geoffrey, and he ran tame in our town house in London during the season. My older brother, Samuel, kept complaining to my father that Cranford was a bad influence on Geoffrey, and in some ways I suppose he was, in those days, but Geoffrey took no permanent harm."

Trelenny's eyes lit at the possibility of learning about Cranford's obscure past. "What did he do? Cranford, I mean."

"Oh, just the sort of thing all restless fellows do before they find something better to occupy their time."

Disappointed, Trelenny tried again. "Like drinking, and gambling, and . . . women?"

Lady Jane's gaze drifted to where Lady Babthorpe sat with another rather dashing young matron. "Yes, that sort of thing," she replied vaguely, and finally.

"Cranford's sister Clare was my best friend. I miss her dreadfully. Do you know Lord Hinton?"

"Very well, and I met Clare when she was in town." A shadow crossed her face so briefly that Trelenny could not be sure it had been there. "Do you hear from them?"

"Sometimes, but they haven't come to Ashwicke Park since they've been married. Cranford went to visit them. You know how brothers are, I suppose. I haven't any myself, but he couldn't even remember if her hair was still short or whether she had said anything that would be of particular interest to me. I don't see why they can't settle at Lord Hinton's seat in Derbyshire," Trelenny suggested questioningly.

Lady Jane only smiled softly. "Newlyweds like to be away from familiar places and faces, I think. They need time to really get to know one another."

Of course she would never have asked, but Trelenny would have liked to know how Lady Jane arrived at such a conclusion, since she was herself obviously still unmarried, and not in her first blush of youth either. Why, she can't be a day younger than Lady Babthorpe, Trelenny decided, and felt a moment's pity for the older woman. But she flushed at the thought, realizing that it was as condescending as Lady

Babthorpe's previous remarks on country people, and Trelenny would have had no difficulty in recognizing Lady Jane's quality and worth, even if Cranford had not rashly suggested that she pattern herself after the lady. If he thinks she's such a paragon, Trelenny thought mutinously, why doesn't he marry *her* and leave me alone? The question seemed superfluous, however, since he seemed to be doing a very good job of leaving her alone that evening.

Among the first of the men to drift in from the dining hall, Cranford joined them immediately, commenting, "I'm glad you two are getting to know one another. This is Trelenny's first visit to Bath, Lady Jane, and she is all eagerness to plunge into the social whirl. It occurs to me, Trelenny, that you probably don't know how to waltz."

Chagrined, Trelenny shook her head. "No, Clare was to teach me when she returned from London, but then she got married."

"Do you know of a dancing master here, Lady Jane?" Cranford asked.

"Several, but that's such a dreary way to learn. Who wants to whirl around with a stately fop who bounces about on tiptoe all the time? Might I suggest something?"

"Certainly."

"Bring Miss Storwood to Queen Square tomorrow morning, and I shall play for you while you teach her. That's how we all did it when it first became the rage, do you remember? We had more fun, I swear, during those morning practice sessions than ever we did at the balls where everyone had an eye on us."

"Cranford teach me?" Trelenny gasped, unable to even imagine him in a ballroom.

Lady Jane regarded her with surprise. "Why, he's one of the most accomplished dancers I know, Miss Storwood."

The corners of Cranford's lips twitched suspiciously. "Trelenny tends to view me rather sternly, Lady Jane, and to believe that I have no social graces whatsoever. Not that I blame her, you understand, as she has never seen any exhibited, I dare say."

"You are very polite to Mama," Trelenny offered generously. Lady Jane and Cranford shared an amused glance which made Trelenny bite her lip. "Do you *want* to teach me, Cranford? Mama could arrange for a dancing master."

"I'll be pleased to teach you, Trelenny. Shall we accept Lady Jane's kind offer?"

"Yes, thank you very much," she replied automatically, unable to meet either of their eyes and feeling that they were laughing at her.

Impulsively Lady Jane pressed her hand. "We'll have a lovely time, Miss Storwood. There is nothing so comfortable as learning something new when there are no critical eyes to alarm you."

"Cranford is always critical of me."

When Lady Jane lifted a questioning brow at him, Cranford shrugged helplessly. At this silent acknowledgment of the truth of Trelenny's statement, Lady Jane said, "I'm surprised to hear it. When I think of the mischief he and Geoffrey got into. Perhaps I should tell you about the time they—"

"That's blackmail" Cranford protested, laughing. "Very well, Lady Jane, I'll try not to be too severe with Trelenny. I am only thinking of her own good."

"People always say that," Trelenny scoffed, "and it usually means they are thinking of their own convenience."

"Touché." Lady Jane chuckled. "Just remember, Miss Storwood, that I have a whole warehouse full of wonderful anecdotes about Cranford, and, if you feel he is unjustly censorious, I might be bribed to tell you one or two."

Quickly warming to the older woman, Trelenny smiled her thanks. "I'll remember."

"No doubt I'll live to rue the day the two of you were introduced," Cranford complained with mock despair, though in actual fact he *was* disgruntled by the confederacy between the two ladies. Not that he supposed Lady Jane would purposely undermine any little authority he had with Trelenny. His respect for the lady was too great to believe her imprudent, and she could not help but see that Trelenny needed a guiding hand. Still, Trelenny could be an engaging little thing, and any hint of previous misadventures of his wheedled from Lady Jane would be blown out of all proportion in her active, nay fantastic, mind.

Mrs. Waplington interrupted them to ask Lady Jane to play for the company, a request she graciously agreed to after ascertaining that Trelenny had no desire to perform. There was a magic in her fingers and all but the most obtuse sat spellbound during her recital. Trelenny, whose appreciation far outstripped her patience to work at such an accomplishment, felt transported to those days with Lady Chessels and Clare around their pianoforte. A curious glance at Cranford assured her that he, too, if he was not recalling those days, was at least mesmerized by the music. Even Lady Babthorpe contributed to the entertainment by singing a ballad of unrequited love in a rich, husky voice which filled the room with sensuous overtones, her husband preening himself on his wife's accomplishments while that lady's eyes were locked on Cranford.

Tables were then set out for cards, and the company settled to indulge themselves in modest stakes and good-natured ranglings over whether each hand had been played to its fullest potential. Trelenny found herself partnered by Lord Babthorpe at the start of the evening, and though she was an excellent player, he insisted on blaming his own errors on her in a loud, obnoxious way which made her blush for his rudeness, and squirm in her desire to answer him back.

Cranford looked over at the commotion from where he sat talking with Lady Jane on a sofa and immediately assessed the situation. "Would you mind . . . ?"

"Not at all," she replied mischievously. "I have undertaken just such a task with his lordship before and it gives me infinite pleasure."

Almost before she realized what was happening, Trelenny found herself replaced at the table by Lady Jane. Her relief was profound and she smiled uncertainly at Cranford. "I can't think what I did to upset him, for it was his own mistakes which caused our downfall, I feel certain. Unless Papa has taught me incorrectly . . ."

"Hush a moment. I know you play very well. Watch how Lady Jane handles him."

It was not uncommon for Lord Babthorpe to spend too long at the dining table over his port, with a consequent fuzziness about his mind for the remainder of the evening. He became argumentative or indolent, and frequently shifted from one extreme to the other. Possibly he was not aware that his partner had been switched, for he continued to harangue at length after Lady Jane was seated, thumping a gnarled hand on the table to emphasize each point.

Lady Jane paid not the least heed to him. First she turned to the lady on her right and commented on the continuing warm weather. Next she informed the gentleman on her left that she had seen the most remarkable print in Milsom Street and wondered if he had possibly noted it. Her inattention to Lord Babthorpe incensed him still further until he roared, "You are not listening to me!"

Slowly turning her gaze in his direction she asked, "Did you speak, sir? I fear I did not notice."

"I was speaking directly to you," he growled.

"Oh, no, sir, you could not have been. *No one* speaks to *me* that way."

Scattered titters about the room indicated that there were any number of auditors to this scene, and Lord Babthorpe, red faced, tossed the new hand he had been dealt onto the table. "I think I won't play another hand, if you will excuse me." With a glowering countenance he withdrew to a far corner of the room, dropped onto a chair, and promptly fell asleep.

During the commotion Lady Babthorpe maintained an uninterested calm and followed her husband's retreat with scornful eyes. Her apparent disregard of any feelings of either mortification or shame, let alone concern or compassion, shocked Trelenny in spite of Lord Babthorpe's extraordinary behavior. In a whisper to Cranford she asked, "I know he is a hideous man, but why did she marry him if she hated him?"

"For his wealth, for his title. It's the way of the world, Trelenny."

"I don't feel very well. Do you think Mrs. Waplington would mind if I retired?"

"I'll make your excuses. It's been a busy day for you." He touched her pale cheek with a gentle finger. "It's not all ugliness, you know. Don't be discouraged."

"Of course not," she said stoutly. "Good night, Cranford."

Standing in front of the glass in her room, she pulled the headdress apart with impatient fingers as Alice unfastened her gown. What high hopes she had had for the evening! Before going downstairs she had thought herself looking prettier than she ever had before, and she had expected to have a very gay time meeting new people and getting her first taste of polite circles. The event had proved otherwise. Her reception had been indifferent, and she had made no acquaintance she wished to pursue, with the possible exception of Lady Jane, who was, after all, Cranford's friend. Trelenny allowed Alice's chatter to wash over her, not caring what headdresses and styles would most become her for future occasions; not caring, in her disappointment, if there *were* future occasions.

chapter twelve

The resiliency of youth and Trelenny's natural optimism asserted themselves overnight and she woke to a cloudless day, full of enthusiasm for exploring the city and making the most of her precious time. Less than three weeks remained to them, and Trelenny considered it her duty to squeeze every drop of enjoyment out of that period. There were the Pump Room, the libraries, the shops to be visited, assemblies in the Upper and Lower Rooms, card assemblies, concerts, the theatre, Sydney Gardens, the Abbey. Never had so much entertainment been at her fingertips, and she laughed aloud to think she had been feeling low the previous evening. A Rowlandson print entitled *Exhibition Stare Case* caught her eye with its lively satire on the gentry's avid interest in art, and she scrambled out of bed determined to ignore the failings of human nature and glory in its finer achievements—such as Bath.

On days after she had entertained, Mrs. Waplington kept her room until an advanced hour of the morning, but Trelenny found her mother already in the breakfast parlor when she descended.

"I came to your room when Cranford told me you weren't feeling well, my love, but you were already sound asleep. Has your indisposition passed? You look blooming."

"I feel marvelous. Was it all right that I left the party? My head was aching abominably."

"No wonder," Mrs. Storwood replied with asperity. "Lord Babthorpe should be ashamed of such behavior, and it astonished me to hear from Elsa that it is not uncommon. We perfectly understood your retiring, my dear."

"May we go to the Pump Room, Mama? Now, I mean? Later Cranford is to take me to Queen Square to visit Lady Jane Reedness, Lord Barlow's daughter. They are going to teach me to dance the waltz." A grin lit her features. "Would you like to come and learn?"

"Thank you, no. I'm too old for such frivolity. Do they dance the waltz at the Assembly Rooms?"

"I don't know, but they are sure to do so at private parties. You don't object to my learning, do you?"

"Of course not. I would be hideously old-fashioned to frown on the waltz, though it does seem a peculiarly *intimate* form of dancing, and I would hope you would choose your partners with special care," Mrs. Storwood urged with an anxious frown.

"Oh, Mama, you are the dearest person there ever was." Trelenny dropped the piece of muffin she was eating and hugged her mother. "Did you enjoy yourself last night?"

"Yes, but it was strange to see so many people I had known years ago. You can tell they are aging, and you know you must be, too, but you don't *feel* as though you are. It rather underscored the years." She sighed and patted her daughter's hand. "You'll meet more young people in the days to come."

Trelenny regarded her impishly. "I might meet some right now if we go to the Pump Room."

"Oh, get your hat, you little beggar. Shall we walk?"

While Mrs. Storwood entered their names in the Subscription Book, Trelenny surveyed the company with eager attention. In spite of a preponderance of older people, there were clusters of young ladies chattering and young men indolently sauntering about. Nor was the gathering wholly genteel, as ever and again a raucous laugh or an indiscreetly raised voice caused the more refined to shudder and turn aside from the offender. Trelenny undertook the mental exercise of deciding to which social sphere the various members of the group belonged.

A demure miss closely attached to a woman dressed in a gown of virulent purple was newly released from a boarding school, she surmised, while her mother had social pretensions beyond her beginnings, a conclusion Trelenny reached largely because the matron strongly resembled a cook they had had at Sutton Hall some years previously. Her enthusiasm for her game was undaunted even when Mrs. Storwood was hailed by the woman, who turned out to be from one of the first families in Kent. The girl *had* been to boarding school, it developed, though she was not recently released, as she had been married these two years past.

Although Mrs. Avening, on closer observation, still appeared more a schoolgirl than the wife of an M.P., Trelenny would have been perfectly willing to make a friend of her, had the young lady not suffered from acute shyness, which even several years of marriage and a life in political as well as social circles had not reversed. To each of Trelenny's eager questions she replied in a voice so soft that, the noise level of the Pump Room being what it was with conversation and music everywhere, Trelenny was hard pressed to hear her answers. After several attempts, Trelenny, as much for the girl's sake as for her own, abandoned the effort and stood patiently listening while her mother reminisced with her old friend. Trelenny was not unaware, however, of having attracted the attention of a young man dressed in the first style of fashion who lounged with several friends near the entry door.

Half an hour passed before Mrs. Storwood, in her progress around the room, came into conversation with someone from whom the young man felt he could inveigle an introduction to the newcomers. His arrival caused Trelenny no surprise, as she had noted his continued observance of their movements, and her only wonder was that he had not approached sooner. Already she had been made known to several gentlemen, as well as a number of ladies, whom she had cause to expect she would meet that evening at the Upper Rooms, but none of these new acquaintances, to be sure, had quite the air of gallantry or of mystery with which Mr. Rowle was invested. There was a brooding light in the green eyes, a lurking hint of recklessness in his smile, and, at least to Trelenny's mind, an aura of adventure about his person. Obviously he was a favorite of the lady who undertook his presentation, for, though in her middle years, she fluttered like a maiden when he kissed her hand and tapped him playfully with her ever-present fan.

"Here you have a very dangerous fellow," the lady opined to Mrs. Storwood, "for I swear he has stolen the hearts of half the young ladies in Bath. Have a care, Mr. Rowle! Miss Storwood is a newcomer to our city and unfamiliar with the likes of such dashing young gentlemen as yourself, I'll be bound."

"Miss Storwood has not the least thing to fear from me, I assure you," he replied with an engaging grin. "One does not trample the fairest blossoms underfoot but takes care they shall be preserved in all their splendor for the world to admire. I hardly credit my good fortune. Miss Storwood, it is an honor to meet you."

Despite the florid extravagance of his rhetoric, he left Trelenny in no doubt that he was teasing her, not unkindly but as though he had identified her as a kindred spirit through all the trappings of social *politesse*. Her response was typically impulsive. "You are too, too kind, Mr. Rowle, and too, too ridiculous," she laughed.

"I beg you won't think me so! How can I repair this distressing misapprehension?" He turned pleading eyes on Mrs. Storwood. "Is there some service I can render you? Perhaps I might procure a glass of the waters or ask the musicians to play a particular song? I am at your command."

Such easy familiarity did not recommend itself to Mrs. Storwood. "Thank you, no, Mr. Rowle. We are in need of nothing."

Instantly perceiving his mistake, the young man dropped his bantering tone and adopted a formality which would have done credit to the occasion of a court presentation. His discourse on the lesser-known attractions of Bath and its vicinity could not help but lift him in Mrs. Storwood's estimation, though she could not altogether approve of the ease with which he adapted himself to her obvious displeasure. Trelenny found the incident amusing and regretted that he soon took his leave of them, with the fervently expressed hope that they would meet again. She secretly shared his hope, feeling that here at last was someone out of the ordinary, someone whose soul was not earthbound and mundane, someone who knew that the world held excitement for those who dared to claim it. Of course nothing of this flight of fancy was shared with her mother on their return to Henrietta Street; Trelenny's love of her mother was not blind to the fact that Mrs. Storwood's was not an adventurous soul.

Ever prompt, Cranford had arrived at the Walpingtons' shortly prior to their return. Mrs. Storwood was all apologies for their tardiness. "We've been to the Pump Room and I fear we allowed ourselves to forget the time. I knew several people, and they were so obliging as to introduce us to others until... well, I hope you will forgive us for not returning when you were due."

"Oh, Cranford won't mind," Trelenny assured her. "He has allowed half an hour for us to reach Queen Square, and I dare say we shall need no more than twenty minutes."

"I only arrived a moment past," Cranford said, ignoring Trelenny's interpolation. "There were two letters for you at the inn, and I've brought them with me."

The sight of her husband's handwriting powerfuly affected Mrs. Storwood and she acceded to Cranford's wish that she would not hesitate to read them in his presence. Hardly had she broken the seal than she cried, "Dear God!"

"Oh, Mama, there is nothing wrong is there? Is Papa all right?"

"Yes, yes, my love, perfectly all right." Her concerned eyes lifted to Cranford's. "All our subterfuge is for naught. Mr. Storwood discovered his Cousin Filkins imposing himself on the housemaid." She read further. "He has sent his cousin off with a flea in his ear and banned him from Sutton Hall in future. Oh, dear, now he will be alone, and this is bound to upset him, no matter what he says."

"What does he say, Mama?"

"Only that we are not to think of returning on his account, and that he would never have expected such disgraceful behavior in one so closely related to him."

"Closely! Why the man is no more—"

Cranford gave her a sharp glance. "Let your mother finish her letter, Trelenny."

"Your father sends his love, dear, and hopes that you are enjoying your holiday." Mrs. Storwood set aside the first letter and broke the seal on the second. "Strange that two of them would arrive at the same time. Oh, Lord."

Silently crossing her fingers, Trelenny tried to await bad news with fortitude. Cranford, standing behind her chair, put a firm hand on her shoulder and said nothing.

"It occurred to Mr. Storwood only after sending off his letter that perhaps Cousin Filkins had misbehaved toward us. Oh, I can just hear his anguish in the words he writes. He called together the female staff and questioned them minutely on his cousin's conduct toward them and anything they might have seen concerning us." A tear spilled over and dropped onto the sheet. "Cook had seen that wretched man with you in the garden, love, and Betty once came into the parlor when he tried to kiss me. Oh, I cannot bear to think of James' agony. He asks me why I didn't tell him of these matters and then blames himself for 'his foolish blindness and his stupid weakness,' which obviously prevented our disclosing the whole to him." Mrs. Storwood was weeping openly now and before Cranford could move to give her his handkerchief, Trelenny was on her knees before her mother's chair, wiping away the tears.

"Don't cry, Mama. We can leave today and be back with him in a very short time if we take the mail coach. Isn't that so, Cranford? They travel at night, too, and though it will be uncomfortable for you, just knowing how fast we are traveling back to him will make you forget any inconvenience. Cranford can see to our booking while Alice and I pack the portmanteaux. Shall I bring you some hartshorn and water?"

Struggling desperately to overcome her upset, Mrs. Storwood shook her head and blew her nose. "No, no, my dear. Your father expressly forbids our coming home. See for yourself. He will not be the cause of both our running off and our rushing back, he says. You are to have your come-out here and he will send more money so that we can stay longer if we wish, and if it is convenient for Cranford. I think if you and Cranford will just go along to Lady Jane's now, I would like to be alone for a moment."

Trelenny looked helplessly at Cranford, and after a moment's hesitation he nodded. "Very well, Mama. I'll just see you to your room and have Alice come to you." She picked up the two letters and linked her arm with her mother's. "You will want to write Papa a letter, of course, and explain that we would rather be with him, and that we will await his permission to return. Tell him there is not so much to do in Bath and that we will be bored beyond description by the time your letter reaches him and we receive his in reply. That won't take so very long, you'll see." As she left the room, she turned to Cranford briefly to say, "I'll only be a moment, if you won't mind waiting."

"There's no hurry, Trelenny."

Left alone, he wandered about the room, his thoughts on the impression she had unconsciously made on him. No, she wasn't mean-selfish, or inconsiderate-selfish, or stomp-on-everyone-in-the-way-selfish. More than anything in the world she had wanted this opportunity to get away from home and see something of the world, and yet she was ready, more than ready, to abandon the scheme when she had finally achieved it, out of her devotion to her parents. There was no hesitating, no weighing of her own desires, just a simple heart-felt response to the distress of others. Cranford had been amused by her persistent determination to reach her goal, and alarmed by her rash behavior in Preston, but he was touched by her readiness to accommodate herself to a situation totally opposed to her own wishes. Surely she deserved that he be more accepting of her, less stern and judgmental. She was, after all, only a child, and he of all people should hardly blame her for her occasional unruly behavior. Too often he had been guilty of the same in the past. But she wasn't completely a child. Physically she was a woman, and a highly desirable woman, he finally admitted to himself, even as he tried to erase the image of her body from his mind. Because he was unsuccessful, and because the image persisted when she reentered the room, he said more stiffly than he had intended, "Is your mother all right? Do you think you should go out when she's upset?"

"She needs to have some time to herself right now. In private she can cry until the ache eases. Poor Mama. It's difficult for her to be so far from my father when she should be there to comfort him. Were we wrong to keep it a secret? Dr. Moore is forever prating on about our not upsetting him, but I think sometimes that Papa would rather know. I realize he would be upset, but this way he feels that his incapacity is a double burden." Her skirt had become rumpled from the careless way she crushed it while she gave vent to her agitated thoughts, and now she smoothed it down. "Mama would like me to go ahead to Lady Jane's, but if you think I shouldn't . . ."

"It will only distress her further, I suppose, to think that you have stayed on her account," he conceded gruffly. "Trelenny, I . . . Straighten your hair before we leave, please."

She made a face at him but went to the glass and tucked in the wisps of blonde hair which had escaped their pins and replaced the hat she had discarded when they returned home. Unaware that she observed him in the mirror, he clenched his hands in impotent frustration at finding himself unable to tell her that he sympathized with her own worries and respected her unselfish actions. Trelenny sighed at what she could only imagine to be anger with herself, and turned unhappily to face him. "What have I done now, Cranford? No, don't tell me. I have had enough upsets for one morning." Despondently she untied the ribbons and removed her hat, allowing it to fall unheeded to the floor. "Make my excuse to Lady Jane, will you? I feel sure she will understand."

In two hasty strides he had reached her and snatched up the hat. "Don't be a goose. I'm not angry with you, and I have every intention of taking you to Queen Square." While she stood meekly before him, he carefully smoothed the silken hair, placed the hat upon it, and tied the ribbons under her chin. For a long moment they regarded one another without speaking, then he traced the sprinkle of dots across her cheeks. "I wouldn't worry about the freckles. They're like the spots on a lady's slipper orchid."

A strange sensation assailed her at his touch. Confused, she laughed uncertainly, and bent to get her reticule. "The powder only made it look as though I were trying to conceal a communicable disease, anyway."

"You looked very pretty last night."

Trelenny regarded him speculatively. "Are you feeling sorry for me, Cranford? I promise you there is no need. I've suffered disappointments before, and I shall again, no doubt. Right now I have a few days reprieve and I had hoped to make the most of them, but if you are going to stand there all morning I might as well return to my room."

When she reached up to untie the ribbons once again, he stayed her hand with a firm grip. "If you muss your hair a third time, my girl, you can be sure I won't take you. We're leaving right now."

Back on their old footing, they passed from Henrietta Street into Laura Place and over Great Pultney as far as the High Street. Trelenny caught glimpses of various goods in the shop windows, but Cranford had set an ambitious pace owing to their lateness, and she refused to ask him to pause. "Could we stop at a circulating library on our return? At the Pump Room someone mentioned a book I should like to read."

"Something edifying, I presume."

"I'm not sure. It's called *Emma* and it sounded more—oh—realistic, I guess, than *Evelina*."

"There's a library adjoining the Pump Room, or Duffield's in Milsom Street. Did you meet many people this morning?"

"Quite a few. Mama saw several ladies she remembered from London. Do you think you can tell much about people by their appearance, Cranford?"

"No." He laughed at her disappointed expression. "Don't tell me you have discovered a highwayman or a marchioness in disguise. Are you already building fairy tales about the Bath beaux?"

"I think you can tell a great deal. Of course, I was very wrong about Mrs. Avening, but that is not so very strange. She whispers and is as meek as a mouse, and her mother wears the most startling clothing. But I had a very definite *feeling* about Mr. Rowle."

Cranford's gaze sharpened. "What sort of feeling? Was his name familiar to you?"

"No, I'd never heard it before. But there is a decided air of adventure about him, as though he lives a more exciting life than everyone around him."

Cautiously Cranford suggested, "Usually you find that men with an air of adventure about them are adventurers, Trelenny, not the romantic heroes you envision, but a rather base sort of villain on the look-out for his own advantage."

"Do you know Mr. Rowle?" she asked suspiciously.

"I'm sure I've never met the fellow; I merely offer you a word of advice." Which was all wholly true, if it was not the whole truth. Cranford had *heard* the name before, but he did not wish to indulge in Trelenny's own habit of leaping to conclusions. Although not a particularly common name, it was certainly possible that more than one man in Bath possessed it, but Cranford had the sinking feeling that, given Trelenny's penchant for scrapes, she could be trusted to have met just the man whose name had so recently come to his attention. Her father's words occurred to him now: "not with a heavy hand." Cranford knew very well that Trelenny resented being told what to do, and he had no intention of spurring her in the wrong direction by his carelessness. "Probably your new friend is the most amiable of fellows, Trelenny, and merely spirited and lively as you are. I presume your parents' influence has taught you well enough how to judge the worthy and the worthless. You don't need my opinion on the subject."

Having worked herself up to a denunciation of his aspersions, Trelenny felt severely deflated by this amendment to his previous statement. Somehow he had managed to tarnish a little of Mr. Rowle's magic, and she felt rather annoyed with Cranford for his reasonableness. "Do you know, you spoil everything, Cranford?" she complained as they approached Queen Square.

He shook his head ruefully. "I had no idea, my dear."

chapter thirteen

After carefully rereading every word of her husband's letters, Mrs. Storwood had a good cry and felt the better for it. She was not a woman whose face became puffy or whose eyes reddened unbecomingly, so she had no hesitation in descending to the front parlor to write a voluminous letter to Mr. Storwood, in which she tried to explain her reasons for dissembling, attempted to minimize the annoyance of Cousin Filkins, and praised their daughter's readiness to leave for Sutton Hall on the next mail coach. "You must know that I am severely tempted to do exactly that, my love, but for your forbidding it and for Trelenny's sake, of course. We owe her this opportunity, I think, to see that her happiness does not depend on where she is, or on anything, really, but her own determination to lead a wholesome, fulfilling life. She does not appear to get along any better with Cranford, I fear, though they have a better understanding, one of the other, since they have spent so much time together. I am determined that I will get her out more in Westmorland when we return so that she doesn't feel imprisoned. Trelenny suggested I write for your permission to return now but, if you will bear with us, I think we should stay for our three weeks—and not a moment longer! I cannot tell you how much I miss you, dear James."

Pursuing that line of thought was too upsetting at the moment, and she turned to a description of their situation and their activities since they had arrived. As she dipped the quill, a footman arrived to inform her that Mr. Wheldrake had called and begged a moment of her time. She knew a slight hesitation, thinking irrationally that she had no chaperone, a woman of eight and thirty, she scolded herself. "Yes, you may show him in."

In his morning dress Frederick Wheldrake looked no less distinguished than he had the previous evening. "Forgive me for calling so early, Maria, but I have always entertained the suspicion that you were an early riser, and I see I am not mistaken."

"We've already been to the Pump Room and back this age," she admitted as he took possession of her hand and held it for a long moment. "Won't you sit down?"

"Am I interrupting you?" he asked with a glance at the pages scattered on the *escritoire*.

"I was writing my husband. Before I finish I will want Trelenny to add a line, so there is no hurry."

"Is she out?"

"Yes, she and Cranford have gone to Lady Jane Reedness' for a lesson in waltzing. Trelenny doesn't know how."

"Then I presume her mother doesn't either."

Mrs. Storwood seated herself before she answered. "No. Shap is a very remote town, without an assembly to its name, and with very few gatherings of any description. We've never even seen it danced."

His regard was teasing. "Oh, it will shock you, my dear lady, and you will wonder whatever is becoming of the younger generation. Boys embracing girls on the dance floor! Who would credit it!" He smiled and withdrew an enameled snuffbox from his coat pocket, deftly flicking it open to retrieve a pinch. "It's a very graceful dance, you know, with none of the posturing so agreeable to our aging dandies. Granted, there is more physical contact than heretofore, but somehow I don't think it will lead to a breakdown of society's moral standards."

"Of course not." She smiled at his mockery. "I suppose I do worry about such things, Mr. Wheldrake; it's having a daughter, I guess, and one who has not been raised in society. We live very retired."

"With her mama's example she can hardly go wrong."

"Her temperament is very unlike mine. There is no caution or timidity to restrain her exuberant spirits, but she is an obliging girl."

"Would you give me permission to keep an eye on her? I

assume Mr. Ashwicke does, but it could do no harm to have two men checking her liveliness when necessary."

"You are kind to offer, Mr. Wheldrake, and I confess I would be grateful, but Trelenny is no more likely to accept your authority than Cranford's. Perhaps you would let me know if you perceive any problem."

"With pleasure." He replaced the snuffbox and withdrew an ivory fan, smiling as he did so. "I could have returned this last night, of course, but it provided me with an excuse to call this morning, and I felt sure you wouldn't lay a complaint against me."

"I had completely forgotten it," Mrs. Storwood admitted, grasping it firmly so she would not once again allow it to slide to the floor.

"How disappointing, when I treasured it so for the brief period it was in my possession."

She was unable to meet his eyes, half mocking, half serious as they were. Memories of her youth flooded in, taking hold of her mind for an unconscious minute. There had been several suitors for her hand, and she had begun to consider the place Frederick Wheldrake held in her affections when she met James Storwood. Unlike his rival, he aspired to no social position, viewed the London scene with indifference, and was, in addition, a rather serious, studious young man. But her heart was captured by his gentleness and integrity, by his goodness and intelligence. She cherished the very absent-mindedness which made him forget social engagements, the disinterest which led to his being jokingly voted the worst-dressed member of Brooks. Her parents, she recalled with a tender smile, had thought her deranged to have settled on such a strange fellow, but they had not objected. His breeding, his fortune, even his person, could not be faulted. And Maria Storwood, for all her retirement from society, for all the problems that her husband's weak heart entailed, had never once regretted her decision.

Her preoccupation afforded Mr. Wheldrake an opportunity to study her unobserved. The shining serenity which had always so greatly enhanced her beauty was still present, though he had sensed she was upset when he arrived. He suspected that her daughter was the cause of her distress; concern for that damsel was frequently on her lips. His own memories he forced back in his determination to see that her special calm was restored. "May I escort you and your daughter to the Upper Rooms this evening?"

Startled from her reverie, she regarded him blankly for a moment. "Why, I suppose we *should* plan to go. Trelenny will wish to attend an assembly, but I have not spoken with Cranford."

"Allow me to make the arrangements, then Mr. Ashwicke may accompany us or not as he pleases."

Mrs. Storwood, realizing that she and her daughter had absorbed a great deal of Cranford's time in the last week, agreed. "Provided," she said seriously, "that you will not expect me to dance. It is too many years since I took any part in such youthful pastimes, and I would only make a figure of myself."

"Bath is full of gouty old gentlemen and decrepit old ladies who step out eagerly with all the rest to point a toe. But I will not press you. I only beg that you will not reject the possibility out of hand, my dear Maria. None was ever so graceful as you on the ballroom floor."

Her daughter, at that very moment, was attempting to follow Cranford's lead as Lady Jane played for them, but the waltz, so different from the dances she had previously learned, was incomprehensible to her, and Cranford's hand at her waist was disturbing. Lady Jane paused for a moment when Cranford exasperatedly said, "You are paying no attention to the music, Trelenny."

Although it seemed unlikely, a thought occurred to Lady Jane. "Have you never seen the waltz danced, Miss Storwood?"

Trelenny bit her lip. "No, ma'am."

"Well, Cranford, how can you expect her to understand if she doesn't know what she is about?" Lady Jane asked with a laugh. "We will show you, my dear. Come, you shall play for us."

"I don't play at all well," Trelenny admitted softly.

"No matter. I can hum." She rose from the pianoforte bench and smiled at Cranford. "It's a pity we can't show Miss Storwood how wretched we were in those early days. Do you know, I remember your tripping me twice in one morning so that I not only landed on the floor but had to have my dress rehemmed."

"You're thinking of someone else," he protested, his eyes

twinkling, as he encircled her with his arm. "I'm sure I don't recall ever doing such an ungracious thing as tripping a lovely lady."

She broke the rhythm of her humming to say, "You did though. I wrote it in my journal, and had a bruise on my hip for a week to remember you by. And Mr. Bodford was no better with Nancy; she had a sprained ankle for close on a month."

Forgotten, Trelenny stood beside the pianoforte and watched the couple whirl about the floor, gracefully gliding to Lady Jane's faint hum. They made a handsome pair, the lady's height dwindling beside her even taller partner, her lively eyes and quick smile bringing forth an answering response from him. Cranford is very attractive when he's enjoying himself, Trelenny thought mournfully as she toyed with the ribbon on her dress, untying the bow with her unthinking fingers.

When they stopped before her, Lady Jane lifted a quizzical brow. "Does that help you get a feeling for the waltz, Miss Storwood?"

"Yes, thank you. I did not realize one moved about so. Don't you bump into other couples?"

"Only if your partner is careless." Lady Jane reseated herself on the bench. "You won't have that difficulty with Cranford."

Trelenny had given him her hand in preparation for another attempt at the dance, but he noticed the untied ribbon and, with deft fingers, he secured it in a bow, making her feel a child before the friendly eyes of Lady Jane. "You could have called it to my attention," she informed him in a fierce whisper. "I'm not a child in need of being—" Her face suffused with a painful flush and she turned from him.

"Lady Jane is waiting," he told her back in a neutral tone.

It required every ounce of her resolve to face him and allow him to take her in his arms. She kept her gaze rivetted on the top button of his coat and stiffly moved about as he dictated, oblivious to the strains of the pianoforte, but all too aware of his contact. Under cover of the music he murmured, "Remember our agreement, Trelenny. The incident is forgotten. Relax. Listen to the music. Has your imagination deserted you? Can you not picture yourself at Almack's dancing with someone entirely different? Lady Jersey has introduced you to one of the lesser princes of Bavaria, a madly wicked fellow with a romantic scar and a dazzling smile. You are the envy of all the other ladies as he guides you about the floor, telling you he wrote the music for you alone."

Despite her amusement, Trelenny grumbled, "That's not the sort of thing I imagine."

"Isn't it?" He could feel the tension desert her and grinned when she stole a peek at him. "Well, perhaps you are sailing to Greece and the captain, a dashing, daredevil sort, points out that the night is balmy and the decks of his ship quite suitable as a dance floor. He calls to a sailor, who, as it happens, is accomplished on the fiddle, and under the black skies with their glittering silver stars you float together, waltzing as though there were no tomorrow, as though the pirate ship in the distance had not the least intention of attacking within the hour."

"You should write romances instead of antiquarian tracts, Cranford."

"Certainly they'd have a larger audience." He laughed.

Lady Jane concluded the piece and smiled at Trelenny. "You are astonishingly quick to learn, Miss Storwood. I think you have nothing to fear at any dance, but I will be happy to play another song if you wish."

"Thank you, no. You are kindness itself to devote so much of your time to my instruction, Lady Jane. I think we should not stay longer."

"Would you mind my showing Cranford a Roman wine cup my father has acquired? I think it would be of interest to him."

"Of course it will," Trelenny agreed, careful to keep the amusement out of her voice.

"I won't be a moment," Lady Jane promised.

Left alone with Cranford, Trelenny absently picked out the tune her hostess had just played. She did not refer to the music but hummed as she worked her way through it, her brow contracting in concentration.

"It's easier to read the music," he suggested helpfully.

"Not for me."

"Why not?"

"Because all those little dots are confusing, with their wispy tails and strange lines. I can play a song if I hear it, not if I see it, and I think that is perfectly logical."

"Expedient, perhaps, for you. The truth of the matter is that you haven't the patience to learn to do it right."

Trelenny brought her hands down on the keyboard in a discordant thump just as Lady Jane reentered. Their hostess chuckled as she handed the wine cup to Cranford. "If that is a sample of your skill, Miss Storwood, I must admit that you *don't* play at all well. Have you no interest in learning?"

"None," Trelenny said with a defiant glare at Cranford.

Her annoyance was lost on him, unfortunately, since he was studying the cup with a connoisseur's appreciation. "I've rarely seen one in such perfect condition, Lady Jane. Augustan, I would judge, though the design is slightly unusual."

The conversation which ensued was infinitely boring to Trelenny, though obviously far from it for the two participants. They shared an enthusiasm which she found unnerving, and she dared not even ask the simple questions the sight of the ancient object inspired in her—such as how did they know it was a wine cup at all? There was a vase at Sutton Hall remarkabily like it in shape, in which she frequently arranged calceolaria with scarlet geraniums and blue lobelias from the ribbon borders. Trelenny gave no hint of her restlessness but politely appeared to attend to the two of them while she secretly planned a little joke on Cranford.

When Trelenny had once again expressed her thanks to Lady Jane and they were walking toward Milsom Street, she said, "You have read *Emma*, then?"

"No." His brow quirked in perplexity. "Why should you think I had?"

"The stories you told while we were dancing. Isn't there a wicked Bavarian prince in the book? And doesn't the heroine journey to Greece on a ship with a daredevil captain?"

"I have no idea, Trelenny. I tell you I haven't read it."

She drew her arm from his and frowned. "You are very wrong not to confess your mistake, Cranford. Certainly there is nothing amiss in weaving a fantasy from someone else's tale (I would be the first to admit that, you know), but to persist in denying your knowledge is, I fear, reprehensible."

"Don't be absurd, child. If I had read it, I would say so."

Trelenny sighed unhappily. "Mama will be so very disappointed when I tell her."

"When you tell her what?" Cranford demanded, mostly exasperated but ever so slightly alarmed.

"Well, you see, Cranford, she thinks of you as a virtuous person and I feel it would be wrong for me to conceal this fallacy in you. Lying about little things has a way of getting out of hand. The clergyman at Shap has made that the subject of his sermons ever so many times. Do you think his wife lies to him?"

"No, I don't! And that has no bearing on what we were discussing. I have not told you a lie, Trelenny, and I cannot imagine how you have discerned my lack of veracity on a subject you know nothing about. *You* haven't read the book."

"No," she said sadly, her dejected eyes lowered to her hands. "And I think perhaps I shouldn't. There are few things more disheartening than finding that someone you respected would deliberately tell you an untruth."

"You most certainly *will* read the book," Cranford retorted hotly, all the while resisting a strong urge to shake her. "If there are Bavarian princes and daredevil captains sailing to Greece I will be monstrously surprised."

"No, I couldn't bear to be so disillusioned about you, Cranford," Her face set stubbornly. "No matter what anyone says, I will be able to champion your truthfulness if I do not read the book. Don't you see? If I do not confirm the fact myself, I am quite at liberty to deny any allegations of your dishonesty. Yes, that will be much the best thing to do. We needn't stop at the circulating library, after all." Trelenny abruptly turned on her heel and headed back down the street, but she had not gotten more than a few feet when she felt Cranford's hands on her shoulders.

Much to the amusement of several passers-by, he swung her about to face him, his brows drawn low over his eyes. "You will march yourself directly into the library and get that book, my girl. Enough of your foolishness. If I *ever* hear you call me dishonest again, I'll . . ."

"Beat me?" she asked sweetly.

"I'll abandon you to your wretched fate. Nothing I could do to you would be more ghastly than you are determined to do to yourself. What well-bred young lady would wander about a town dressed as a man in the dead of night? You put me out of all patience, Trelenny."

"Of course I do, and you are determined to throw all my past indiscretions in my face to obscure the issue. For shame,

Cranford. You are to see me home this very moment." She tapped an indignant foot while he struggled for composure. Let him see how it felt to be upbraided for the smallest thing; it would do him the world of good. He might, it was true, find out that *Emma* was a very domestic novel which took place almost entirely in one small English village but then, she had never claimed to have read it (since she hadn't) but only to have heard it spoken of in the Pump Room (which she had). She had not precisely said that there were princes and captains in it, either. "Well?"

After one last, longing look at Duffield's, Cranford shrugged helplessly. "I'll take you home now." They were the last words he spoke until he bid her farewell at the Waplingtons' house in Henrietta Street.

chapter fourteen

In all likelihood Trelenny had no idea what she was talking about, Cranford decided as he stalked away from the house. Far from ever having read the book she talked of, he had never even heard of it. His irritation at her believing him incapable of weaving a tale of his own came close to eclipsing his indignation that she could believe him capable of subterfuge. She could be the most infuriating girl, with that stubborn little chin defiantly set and those perfectly arched brows haughtily raised. And for all her pert frankness, she had an uncomfortable way of wounding him to the quick. Nothing was more repugnant to Cranford than being compared to his father, unless it might be calling him to account for his neglect of his mother and sister. Trelenny, with her imperfect understanding of the situation at Ashwicke Park, was yet able to touch him on the raw at times as few others knew how or dared to do.

Although Cranford was paying little attention to his direction, so engrossed was he in his thoughts, he soon found himself once again in Milsom Street approaching Duffields. It aggravated him to think that he would have to read the book, probably a fanciful romance of incredible improbability, in order to prove his point. Not once did it occur to him that Trelenny herself had done a certain amount of reading on his account, nor that she had not suggested that he do so in this instance. Oblivious to the fashionably dressed ladies and gentlemen who frequented the shop, he paid a subscription fee and inquired for the book with no suspicion of being thwarted in his aim.

"We haven't a volume in just now, sir," the young man

informed him politely, "though we do have a different work by the same lady. Would you care to see it?"

"You don't have *Emma* in?" Cranford asked, astonished. "Is it so popular then?"

"In the last week or so there have been several ladies ask for it. I dare say it's been moldering on the shelves for some time, but once a book is touted in the Pump Room suddenly everyone wants to have it. The interest quickly dies. Probably I will have it here again next week to be unclaimed for months. Shall I show you another of the lady's works?"

"Thank you, no. I was only interested in *Emma*," Cranford admitted, his annoyance roused but kept well under control as he turned away.

"Were you not interested in Drucilla, then?" Lady Babthorpe murmured. She had seen Cranford enter and had inobtrusively worked her way toward him until she stood at his elbow when he finished speaking with the clerk.

Her eyes conveyed the same message they had the previous evening, an invitation not unmixed with challenge. Cranford regarded her with faint amusement. "One would have to be blind to make so rash a statement, Lady Babthorpe. Does your husband attend you?"

"My lord would rather be found dead than in a circulating library. He considers it his greatest achievement of the past five years that he has not once opened the cover of a book." Her nostrils flared with disdain. "My maid accompanies me."

"Perhaps I could have the honor of seeing you home?"

She pursed her provocative lips thoughtfully. "I had intended to take a stroll in the Sydney Gardens before returning to Laura Place."

"You will certainly need my protection then, Lady Babthorpe. Your maid would be insufficient discouragement, I fear, for the young sparks who would be drawn to your flame."

Lady Babthorpe smiled appreciatively. "Ah, yes, the labyrinth and the grottoes are too secluded to traverse alone. One needs a trustworthy companion, even in the daytime."

"I believe I may be trusted to see to your ladyship's ease of mind."

"Do you think so? I'm sure you are mistaken, Mr. Ashwicke, and I would be very pleased to have your company." With an arch look, she took his arm, issued a peremptory command to the maid to follow with her books, and allowed Cranford to lead her from the building into Milsom Street. "I was surprised to see you at Mrs. Waplington's last night. You have scarce shown your face this last year or so."

"There has been a great deal to do at Coverly."

"And you are escorting that buxom maiden I met you with?"

"Miss Storwood. Yes, I have brought her and her mother to Bath from Westmorland. Mr. Storwood is an invalid of sorts and Trelenny was anxious to see something of the world."

"I would have thought seeing you was quite enough for any young lady," she retorted.

"Trelenny finds me a dull stick."

Lady Babthorpe gave a tinkling laugh. "In the dining parlor, perhaps, when you are engrossed in your antiquities, but in the boudoir . . ."

"You flatter me, Drucilla. I hope Lord Babthorpe made no difficulties for you."

"Alfred is a swaggering fool. Had he found us in the bed itself, rather than my parlor, he would have done no more than rant and rave. Come to that, it might have been better if he had. Perhaps an apoplexy would have carried him off."

"Goutish men have a way of turning nasty. I wouldn't push him too far."

"Pooh. I can twist him around my little finger, the old lecher. He very nearly died of ecstasy on our wedding night."

Uncomfortably Cranford turned the subject. "Have you read this book *Emma?*"

"I heard of it, and read some three pages before I threw it down. Very mundane stuff, Cranford. I wouldn't bother with it."

"Are there Bavarian princes and daredevil captains in it?"

"How should *I* know? I told you I only read a few pages, but I shouldn't think so. You'd do better to read one of Fielding's," she suggested with a speaking glance.

"No, it's *Emma* I have to read. Have you a copy of it?"

She made a wry face. "I suppose it is somewhere around.

Mr. Kelston bought it for me, though I can't think why he would think I'd enjoy such stuff."

"Mr. Kelston?"

"One of my admirers here in Bath. I have them everywhere I go, you know. This one is a young cub with a spotty face who can't put two words together in my presence but writes voluminous letters and poetry that's enough to curdle your insides. I stopped reading them after he compared me to a pineapple."

In spite of himself, Cranford laughed. "It's better than a turnip."

A tiny frown wrinkled her brow. "I'm not at all sure he didn't try that metaphor as well, though I was not altogether positive, for he had such a superfluity of flowers and crops in his 'Ode to Persephone' that I could never be sure that it was not the meadowlark or the gentian which was supposed to represent me. It might be that the turnips and swedes were only put there for a little earthiness."

"At least he was on the right road," Cranford said approvingly. "There is a decided earthiness to you, Drucilla."

"I hope you mean that as a compliment, my dear sir, for I intend to take it as such."

"I hate to see all the earthiness bred out of a woman. It leaves only an artificial shell surrounding emptiness. On the other hand—"

"Don't tell me," she protested, lifting an admonitory finger. "Are you not going to get me a chair, Cranford?"

The thought had not once occurred to him; Trelenny would have spurned the very suggestion of a chair for such a paltry distance. Ever gallant, however, Cranford apologized and motioned to the two men standing nearby with their sedan chair, which had seen better days. Lady Babthorpe wrinkled her nose delicately as she allowed Cranford to hand her in, and made no attempt to converse with him during their progress to the gardens where she arrived in high good humor, taking little notice of her maid's breathless condition. In fact, it suited her very well. Sit here, Clothilde, and rest yourself until my return."

Although it had been no problem for Cranford to keep up with the hurrying chairmen, the girl was another matter and she nodded her head and murmured, "Yes, my lady."

There were tree-lined walks by artificial waterfalls, grottoes, thatched pavilions, and a sham castle among the attractions of the Gardens, in addition to two iron bridges in the Chinese style over the canal and a charming rotunda at the far end, but Lady Babthorpe's goal was the labyrinth. From past experience she knew an ideal spot in it where one might count on no interruptions, since attaining it meant making almost every conceivable wrong turn in the maze. For the weary or discouraged there was a rustic bench to which she soon led her escort, though she was far from weary and quite the opposite of discouraged.

Cranford was amused by her determination but wary of her intentions. Years ago it had seemed nothing but a lark to be her lover, to cuckold that irascible old man who was her husband. Not that she was any less desirable today than she had been then; the violet eyes were still sleepily provocative, the sensual lips begged to be kissed, and she had a way of tucking her lawn handkerchief down the cunningly low front of her walking dress which made him long to retrieve it. Languidly she tapped the place beside her and eyed him with raised brows.

When he hesitated, she said, "No one ever strays this far afield, Cranford. Have you lost your nerve? You surprise me. Or perhaps I've grown haggard this last year and not noticed." The full red lips pouted invitingly.

"You know you haven't, Drucilla." Unsmiling, he took the seat beside her, calmly draping one leg over the other. "When I was younger I *had* no nerves, nor any prudence either. I have developed great stores of both these last years. Don't mistake me, Drucilla. You are as desirable now as you were then and I'd as lief take up where we left off as not, if it weren't for this confounded sense of responsibility I now labor under."

"Hogwash! You haven't a fiber of morality in your body, Cranford; I should know." Her eyes sparked with anger. "Who was it who led young Reedness to every gambling hell in London though he couldn't for his very soul keep himself sober enough to know what he was doing? Who was the fire-eater who nearly fought a duel over the right to see me, a married lady, home?" Her tone became strident for her *coup de grâce*. "Who was the man who lay in my arms the night he was supposed to be at Ashwicke Park, the night his mother died?"

Cranford's face set in cold, hard lines, and a muscle in his cheek twitched. "I didn't know she was dying."

"You had faithfully promised to be there. I saw you write the letter at my *escritoire*."

"I should have been, God help me. Things have been different since then."

"Men don't change, Cranford. That streak of wild abandonment is there just beneath your polished exterior, waiting for a chance to escape. Do you think I didn't see the way you looked at me just now? Were you remembering those nights? There was an added thrill to think of Alfred in his room down the hall, snoring loud enough to wake the dead, drunk as a wheelbarrow. Admit it, Cranford. You loved every minute of it." When he said nothing, merely met her eyes with an indecipherable gaze, she shook her head and said softly, "I don't blame you for adopting this prudish air, just don't think you can fool me by it. I know you too well. You'll go on better in society acting just as you do; no more mothers will protect their daughters from your rakish advances, and no more fathers will protest their sons' keeping company with you. But you needn't maintain such virtue in private, my dear. Bath can be very dull for the virtuous, and releasing a little pent-up mischief will only help you maintain your image. I can be very discreet, as you well know."

"Yes." He withdrew his gaze from her face and contemplated the gravel walk absently for several minutes, almost unaware of her presence. Possibly she was right, but he thought not. His dissipated youth he had seen for some time as a rebellion against his father's tyranny. Life at Ashwicke Park had not been easy for him and his inability to make the positions of his mother and sister easier had driven him in frustration to London. Not that he had thought of them much when he was there. It was all too easy to forget their uncomfortable plight under that petty dictator when one threw oneself into the frenzy of town life. All too easy to become enmeshed in gambling debts and sordid love affairs, which merely made life more difficult at the Park, but he was not there to suffer for his dissolution. Lady Chessels and Clare were the ones to send him what money they could from their allowances, and beg any necessary additional from his father. Even now he cringed to think of those years, and Lady Babthorpe was inextricably linked in his mind with that past.

Cranford was realistic enough to acknowledge her sexual appeal for him and yet determined that he was not willing to become involved yet again in such a situation. There was always Kitty in Kendal to satisfy his desires; he wouldn't be in Bath that long. The wild rage in him which had exhibited itself in those London years was spent, or under control. If Drucilla was right—that it was just under the surface—he did not want her to call it forth.

He allowed his gaze to alight on her bosom, where the edge of the handkerchief just barely showed and he smiled regretfully. "You're an enchantress, Drucilla, but I cannot afford to be enchanted just now. I've given my word to take care of the two Storwood ladies; and, believe me, the daughter takes a bit of looking after."

Flattered by his praise, but disgruntled by his rejection, Lady Babthorpe pouted. "Is she an heiress then? And you mean to have her?"

"We're neighbors and here on holiday," Cranford answered noncommittally. "I'll be expected to chaperone them to assemblies and parties."

"I'll be bound Mr. Wheldrake would willingly stand in for you."

Cranford raised a questioning brow. The previous evening had seen him too occupied with old acquaintances to take note of Mrs. Storwood and Mr. Wheldrake.

"He's a widower now and methinks with a lively eye for your neighbor's wife. You could easily leave the escort duties to him."

"I doubt that would overly please Mr. Storwood."

"But it might please his wife. I know what it's like to have a sick old man for a husband.

"Mr. Storwood is young enough to be Lord Babthorpe's son." Cranford rose and extended his hand to raise her. When she hesitated, an angry flush on her cheeks, he conciliated her by stooping to raise her hand to his lips and kiss it lingeringly. "I had no notion I would find you here in Bath, or I might have thought twice before arriving here encumbered. And I haven't the least desire to make any of your admirers jealous, Drucilla. Do you remember Sir Lowell? He very nearly had me impressed into the Navy!"

Reluctantly she laughed. "You would have been if you hadn't spouted Latin at that gang. Oh, Cranford, we had such a lovely time."

"Yes." He ran a finger around the oval of her face. "It's not an easy life for you, Drucilla, but you chose it with your eyes open."

She shrugged a negligent shoulder. "Is has its compensations."

"I'm glad to hear it." She had risen and he placed her hand on his arm. "I'll take you home. Shall I get you a chair?"

"No, it's only a step. Have you heard what happened to Sir Lowell? He's the most incomprehensible fellow."

They strolled back through the walks in reasonable charity with one another, picking up the maid as they left the gardens and progressed along Great Pultney Street. Lady Babthorpe was not pleased with the result of their interview, but she did not despair of bringing Cranford to heel. Her vanity did not allow for the disenchantment of her former slaves, and in his eyes and his touch she divined a reawakened interest. She enlivened their walk with a bright, sophisticated chatter interspersed with sultry glances and the sensuous play of her fingers on his arm. Amused, but not altogether unaffected by her presence, Cranford nearly forgot his mission.

The laughing, victorious sparkle in her eyes stayed him at her door. "Are you not forgetting something, Cranford?"

With the promptness of someone recollecting a face thought unfamiliar at first glance he replied, "The novel I wished to borrow."

"Wait here, I don't think my lord would appreciate your coming in. I'll have Clothilde bring you the volumes."

"Thank you, Lady Babthorpe," he said for the benefit of the footman who opened the door to her. "I trust the walk has not tired you."

"Not at all. I feel quite rejuvenated." She flashed him a brilliant smile before disappearing into the townhouse.

Cranford was left to amuse himself on the stoop for an unconscionable period of time, during which he counted two curricles, three phaetons, and a barouche pass by, in addition to nine groups of strollers. He was about to depart, thinking she was toying with him, when the maid at last appeared at the door and delivered several volumes into his hands. "My lady hopes you will enjoy the book, sir," the girl murmured, swiftly glancing about her, "and most especially the contents of Chapter Three."

Irritated by the air of intrigue with which this was

delivered, Cranford tucked the books under his arm and replied only, "I shall return the volumes as soon as possible."

Being around the corner from Mrs. Waplington's house, he had a good mind to take *Emma* directly to Trelenny and insist that she read it herself, but thought better of the plan. He refused, also, to look up at the window above him as he walked away, sure that Drucilla was there expecting him to do precisely that. Devil take the both of them, he thought, chagrined. Women are a plague bent on destroying the sanity of mankind. Cranford absently made the turn into High Street, where he accidentally brushed against a young man coming from the opposite direction. "My apologies, sir."

"Ashwicke? What the hell has brought you to Bath? When I saw you at Sally's I thought you were ensconced at the Park for the autumn!" the fellow ejaculated.

"Tony Bodford! Lord, the place is crawling with familiar faces. What brings you here?"

"Royal command. The old man sent me down to find him lodgings for the winter, says he couldn't last it out if it's like the last few years." At his companion's look of concern, he laughed. "Oh, it's just a whim of his. Really, I've not seen him in finer fettle in years. Where are you putting up?"

"At the White Hart, though Rissington has offered me a room in his place here in High Street. I've escorted some neighbors here. The Storwoods. Do you know them?"

Tony shook his head. "I don't believe so. Staying long?"

"I hardly know. A few weeks, a few days. It may be necessary for the Storwoods to return sooner than expected. Join me for a glass, Tony. I should send a note off to Mrs. Storwood and I can pen it while they bring up a bottle."

When they reached his room Canford tossed his hat on a table and carelessly discarded the volumes of *Emma* beside it while he waved his friend to a chair. "I won't be a moment. Help yourself when they bring the Lisbon." He broke the seal of a letter handed to him on entering to find that his friend, Lord Rissington, insisted on his removing himself to High Street without delay. "Tony, Rissington has found a place for the Storwoods, but they're staying with Mrs. Waplington. Maybe it would do for your father. Here, see what he has to say about it." Handing over the letter, he seated himself at the desk and pulled forth a sheet on which he quickly penned a note to Mrs. Storwood asking if he might escort them somewhere that evening. If their stay was to be short, Trelenny certainly deserved to do as much as possible before they left.

In the hours which followed, Cranford visited with his friend Tony and removed his belongings to High Street, where he took dinner with Lord Rissington and received a note from Mrs. Storwood (thanking him for his thoughtfulness and saying that she felt quite up to going to the Upper Rooms if he would be so good as to accompany them). Not once did he glance at the volumes of *Emma* which he had brought with him and, since he had to hurry in dressing, he completely forgot that there was doubtless a message from Lady Babthorpe inserted in Chapter Three.

chapter fifteen

The Upper Rooms were crowded by the time the Storwoods arrived. Trelenny had never seen so many people in one place in her life, and she shrank closer to her mother as they entered the long room with its Corinthian columns and fireplaces, brilliant chandeliers and musicians' cove. There were so many people that it was difficult to move about, and the sea of faces contained no familiar one for Trelenny, outside of their party, which consisted of the Waplingtons, Mr. Wheldrake, and Cranford. Mrs. Waplington seldom attended the assemblies, which had become, so she said, "infested with the common folk, and far too crowded for real enjoyment," but her cheerful demeanor belied any negative feelings she might have. She knew everyone, or so it seemed to Trelenny, who was introduced to dozens of people whose names she could not catch in the constant roar of voices, and whose faces soon merged in her mind with one another.

Helplessly she looked to Cranford for encouragement, since her mother's attention was claimed by Mr. Wheldrake; but he was acting distant with her because of the morning's contretemps and she gave a resigned sigh, feeling very much on her own. Mr. Waplington soon deserted them for the card room and, after one set with her, Cranford stood back with a detached expression on his face as if to say, "Well, get on with it. Let's see what you can make of yourself."

The smile remained frozen on Trelenny's face as young men were presented to her and led her off for the country dances. She was not used to the stilted conversation which the movement of the dance necessitated, but she refused to be tongue-tied under Cranford's critical eyes. Several times she attempted remarks on riding and life in the country, but her partners seemed surprised and not altogether pleased. When they spoke of prominent figures in the *ton* she could do little more than disguise her ignorance. The evening began to stretch out to uncomfortable lengths.

And then Mr. Rowle appeared with his mysterious eyes and adventurous air. He was elegantly dressed in a coat of blue superfine, which set his athletic figure off to advantage, for though he was not a tall man like Cranford he had a set of broad shoulders and a well-turned leg which could evoke only admiration. Mr. Rowle came first to Mrs. Storwood to make his bow, reminding her solemnly that they had met that morning in the Pump Room. Had he assumed that she would have remembered him, she would probably have been less pleased at his appearance, but he presented to her a very proper diffidence which she found altogether acceptable. He was unknown to Mrs. Waplington, and on being presented was highly respectful, though he soon made her laugh with his clever observations on the company. Cranford regarded him impassively and Mr. Wheldrake with no more than ordinary interest, but Trelenny waited impatiently for the moment he would turn to her and request the honor of a dance.

"I had not looked for an opportunity to meet with you again so soon, Miss Storwood. Dare I tell you how charming you look? Or will you tell me I am ridiculous?" His eyes danced with amusement.

"I find it is all the rage here to lavish compliments like so many raindrops," Trelenny replied mischievously, a dimple appearing in her cheek. "One would think all the ladies were parched and in need of such refreshment. But I believe the gentlemen are mistaken, you know. Such praise loses its efficacy in a downpour. A daily sprinkling is so much more beneficial."

"Then I shall hope to have the opportunity of regularly showering upon such a rare flower. May I have this set?"

Mrs. Storwood, looking on complacently as they found their places in the dance, failed to notice the frown which had gathered on Cranford's brow. Perhaps it did occur to her that it was strange that Elsa Waplington did not know the young man, but her friend had been charmed by his careful attentions and quick wit, so she felt no stirring of unease. Mr. Wheldrake had honored his promise not to press her to dance and she was taken by surprise when Cranford himself urged her to join Trelenny's set with him. After his many thoughtful kindnesses of the past few days, she did not have the heart to turn down his earnest request, and they positioned themselves two couples away from Trelenny, who smiled approvingly at her mother's advent.

Despite the music and the conversation of the other dancers, Trelenny found no difficulty in attending to her partner. His clear accents made it not impossible for Cranford to overhear them as well.

"Is this your first visit to Bath, Miss Storwood?"

"Yes, we've come for a short stay."

"It can't be that you need the waters. I've never seen a healthier-looking lady in my life. I'd take my oath you spend a great deal of time outdoors. Do you ride?"

The question rather surprised Trelenny. Didn't everyone ride? She cocked her head, brows raised and eyes dancing. "On every possible occasion, in any available manner."

Cranford stiffened and cast her a withering glance which she did not intercept, mainly because she had to concentrate on the steps of the dance, whose intricacies she had forgotten in her delight at feeling free to converse uninhibitedly with her partner.

Puzzled but encouraged by her obvious teasing, Mr. Rowle adapted his tone to hers. "Bath itself is poor sport, but I have a vast knowledge of the countryside. Perhaps you would ride with me one day."

Uncertain as to whether it would be proper to ride alone with him, but suspecting it would not, Trelenny asked, "Do you live here, Mr. Rowle? In Bath, I mean."

"I do. You see before you a native of the city, Miss Storwood, and you should congratulate yourself on such a find. What with the half-pay officers, and retired men of the cloth, to say nothing of the ailing aristocracy, you would be hard pressed to come upon someone who was born and bred here. You have found yourself the perfect guide, I assure you. Who else could so easily recommend the best stables, tell you the history of the Abbey, inform you of the exact shop in which to purchase lavender *gros de Naples,* or take you over every inch of the Sydney Gardens? But that's nothing! I can show you the precise spot where Sheridan had his duel with Major Matthews or the house where Beau Nash lived. I keep a copy of Anstey's *New Bath Guide* for very special visitors. It's old now, of course, but for those who would appreciate it, I am never loath to lend it, and I suspect, Miss Storwood, that *you* would find it vastly amusing."

This was delivered as a compliment of the highest order with a comical quirk given to his brows which made her laugh. "Then I should very much like to read it, Mr. Rowle. I had intended to do some other reading," she commented with a reproachful glance down the set at Cranford, who pretended not to hear her, "but I have abandoned that."

"Perhaps I could bring the book by in the morning. Your appreciation of Bath will be heightened by it, I assure you. Would your mother object if I called?"

"No, why should she? We're staying with the Waplingtons in Henrietta Street."

"Are they relatives?"

"No, simply old friends of Mama's, whom she hadn't seen in ages 'til we came here."

"You don't live close by, I take it."

"In Westmorland, near Shap. My father couldn't come with us because of his health, so we won't be staying long. Perhaps only a few days."

Mr. Rowle studied her closely. "Surely you wouldn't come so far for only a short stay!"

"We had intended a month but . . . it's not decided yet."

Seeing that she did not wish to pursue the topic, he quickly changed its direction. "Strange that I've never been to Westmorland. It's wild country, I collect, more on the order of Scotland than most of England. Have you been to Scotland or Ireland? Lord, the adventures I've had in those two God-forsaken holes! And they talk of the West Indies as being uncivilized! There's a rogue behind every bush in Ireland, and a lunatic on every road in Scotland. Would you believe—But no, this is not the place to be telling blood-curdling tales! Forgive me! I shall say no more."

Nothing could better have whetted Trelenny's appetite, and she beseeched him to continue, in spite of the frequent disruptions to his discourse caused by the dance. He was, however, adamant on the impropriety of regaling her with such stuff at an assembly but hinted that were they alone he could tell her stories that would curl her lovely blonde hair. "I don't set the least store in niceties of that sort," she protested indignantly. "An assembly is designed for giving one pleasure, and I can see no reason why we should not be entertained in whatever manner pleases us."

But Mr. Rowle remained unmoved, switching to a teasing burlesque of the standard social chit-chat to which Trelenny had been subjected during the preceding portion of the evening. He did it so well that she was hard pressed not to laugh outright, but her eyes danced with such merriment that Mrs. Storwood felt a reflected glow in her daughter's obvious enjoyment. Cranford found little pleasure in the set, though for Mrs. Storwood's benefit he endeavored to erase the furrow between his brows, and answer her delighted remark on Trelenny's success with a certain evenness, which to the uninitiated might have been taken for grimness. The thought did occur to Mrs. Storwood that Cranford's attention had frequently wandered to the other couple, and she was just the tiniest bit inclined to think he might be a trifle jealous, a possibility which warmed her heart yet further. She was, in fact, in such high spirits by the end of the set that she allowed Mr. Wheldrake to claim her hand without the least hesitation after Trelenny was led onto the floor by a newly arrived friend of Cranford's.

Having found that the simplest way to engage his old flame in conversation was to discuss her daughter, Mr. Wheldrake proceeded to do so. "Your Trelenny appears to be enjoying herself, Maria. Have you met Lord Rissington before? No, I suppose not, but he would be a party to encourage if he took a fancy for your daughter—well heeled, an excellent understanding, charming manners, active in the House. The mothers of marriageable daughters in London despair of bringing him to the sticking point, but I'm persuaded he only needs to meet the right lady."

Mrs. Storwood took the opportunity of her daughter's going up the set with the young man to study him more closely. Of average height and average looks, there was nothing particularly striking about him except the openness of his countenance and the kindness of his eyes. No one would pick him out of a crowd, though one might choose to converse with him because of his apparent approachability. Trelenny obviously found him so, as she exhibited none of the stiffness her mother, knowing her so well, had detected earlier in the evening. This partner put her at ease, and Mrs. Storwood could only be grateful.

"I believe he's a friend of Cranford's, as Cranford has moved into his lordship's house in High Street. Do you know the other gentleman who arrived with him?"

"Anthony Bodford. A bit ramshackle, I fear, but harmless. Perfectly good *ton*, you understand, but he takes nothing seriously. I don't know him as well as Lord Rissington since he spends a great deal of time out of town. Comes from up your way, I believe. They're both members of Brooks."

This information, of course, was meant to convey their total social acceptability, but it would have had little more influence with Mrs. Storwood than with her daughter if the gentlemen themselves had not seemed so unexceptionable. Of more weight with her was that they were friends of Cranford's. She smiled benignly when Trelenny's hand was solicited for the next set by Mr. Bodford. Really, it was delightful the way her daughter had not had to sit out a single set during the evening.

Put at her ease by Mr. Rowle and Lord Rissington, Trelenny saw no reason to be intimidated by the stocky, smiling Mr. Bodford, who informed her that he had known Cranford forever, well, since they went to Eton together, came from Westmorland just as she did, and couldn't live but a matter of miles from Sutton Hall—as the crow flew. "Not that I'm one for allowing a lot of crows to fly about," he assured her modestly. "A great nuisance they are, and I consider it my duty to rid the estate of them. I have this old dog, Tagalong, who never misses a chance to come with me. Seems to have a personal vendetta against crows. Well, they're ugly, you know, and have such a grating cry!"

"Just so," Trelenny agreed, unable to stifle a giggle which bubbled in her throat.

"There now. I didn't mean to run on about crows, Miss Storwood. Wouldn't want to offend any of the old dowagers who happened to think I was referring to them. Did you ever see so many decrepit old ladies in one place before? I swear Bath has become a veritable nesting ground for every gouty old man and mawkish old lady. Do you know what I saw in the street today? You'd never credit it! This old fellow was hobbling along with a stick and couldn't for the life of him make it up onto the pavement. And who do you think came to his assistance? Well, *I* would have, you understand, but I was a distance down the street passing the time of day with Lady Jellybean—or something like that—I never can remember names. Anyhow, who decides to help the old gadger but this horridly bent old woman who can barely move herself! She was already on the pavement, don't you see, so she reaches out a shaky hand to grab hold of his arm, but latches onto his stick instead and boom! down the two of them go, sprawled all over the street. So they're puffing and panting and trying to regain their feet when along comes *another* human wreck. I excused myself to Lady Jellybean—or whatever—because I couldn't bear the sight of it all and was determined to get them all chairs and send them on their way, when the third fellow ... you know, come to think of it, I don't believe he could see so well, because the first thing he did was stumble over the old fellow's stick, which caused him to go reeling into the lamppost, and it started to sway back and forth like a drunken sailor. They really should use sturdier stuff for the lampposts here. Flimsy posts they are compared to London, promise you! And have you noticed they haven't any gas? Always proclaiming themselves so advanced and not a gas lamp to be seen. Now I ask you! Where was I?" he asked in confusion.

"You were about to tell me what happened to the poor fellow who fell into the lamppost," Trelenny prompted him as she bit her lip.

"Right-o. Well, he apologized to it, just as though he'd run into someone, you see, so I supposed he *didn't* see any too well. His hat had come off and he couldn't find it for the life of him, and a dog was wandering by and clamped it in his teeth and was about to make off with it—sometimes I think the little ragamuffins around here train their dogs to do such dastardly things. It's not the first time I've seen such a sight! Not to wrap it up in clean linen, Miss Storwood, some of these hounds are trained to steal! Yes, I know it's shocking, but there it is! The dog was running full tilt toward me by this time and the old folks were still struggling in the street. He jumped right over them—bless me if he didn't. I grabbed the hat from him and made to hand it to the fellow by the lamppost, but just then the old lady struggled to her feet and crowned herself with the beaver. Thought I'd assaulted her! I never! Started haranguing me, and a large crowd began to form, with someone lifting the old fellow to his feet and dusting him off, and another restoring the hat to its rightful owner. No matter what anyone said, the old lady wouldn't believe I hadn't tried to assault her, so I shagged off. Well, really, there was nothing else to do, was there?"

"N-nothing." Trelenny, her eyes sparkling with laughter, missed several steps of the dance and was kindly corrected by her partner, who never once faltered in the movements in spite of being so completely wrapped up in his anecdote. His store of amusing incidents was apparently inexhaustible and, in spite of the fact that he frequently interrupted himself to digress, Trelenny found him exceedingly entertaining and readily understandable. He had something to say about his two friends as well.

"Cranford is the best of good fellows. But you know that, I dare say. Tipped me the wink at Sally's to hush up about his camomile patch and all, of course, but you won't find him holding a grudge."

"Sally's?"

Tony had the grace to flush and mumbled unconvincingly, "Old friend of ours. Go to visit her in Kendal sometimes."

If he had not flushed or run a finger under his cravat, Trelenny would have thought nothing of it, but she had the most astonishing realization that they were discussing a representative of the demimonde, and she honored Cranford across the room with an incredulous stare, which he could by no means interpret, though he had every intention of finding out what Bodford had blabbed now.

On the subject of Lord Rissington, Tony was just as unconsciously forthcoming. "He'd found a spot for you and your mother, but he was perfectly happy to let me have it for my father. You don't mind, do you? Cranford says you're situated with Mrs. Waplington and won't need it. Rissington can get anything done—knows everyone. I was a good deal taken aback, I can tell you, when he introduced me to a bishop and a footpad all in the same afternoon. Not that he associates with footpads! Or bishops either, come to that! It was over a matter of his cousin's having a valuble old ring stolen, or some such thing. Rissington don't hold much with the Runners, so he went about trying to find the thing in his own way. Like I said, he gets things done. So don't be taken in by that cherub look of his! It's fooled more than one. He's up to every rig and row, promise you."

The magic hour of eleven arrived all too soon for Trelenny, though in truth she was not used to late hours and once or twice stifled a yawn behind her fan, while her eyes continued to sparkle with pleasure. But there was no prolonging the dancing beyond the appointed hour. The Lower Rooms might persist to midnight; the Upper Rooms would not fall into such laxity. Trelenny found herself bundled out to the arranged chair, where Cranford discovered as he walked beside that she was not of Lady Babthorpe's inclination. No sooner had the men begun to walk off with her than she lowered the window and exclaimed, "Wasn't it delightful? Everyone looked so elegant I was almost afraid to open my mouth at first. You should have danced more, Cranford. Doesn't Lady Jane attend the rooms?"

"She depends on her father's escort and he takes exception to crowded public places."

Trelenny looked crestfallen. "I didn't know. Could we invite her to join us next time? Or perhaps you could escort her. Mr. Wheldrake has offered to look after Mama and me."

"Has he? Very thoughtful of him. I shall remember to consult him in future."

"Oh, don't be so stuffy, Cranford. Mama thought you would not wish to be forever tied to us. You will have friends of your own to see and carouse with of an evening." She smiled impishly in the darkness. "I liked your friends. Mr. Bodford especially is so very entertaining."

"He talks too much," Cranford muttered, not meeting her eyes. If one wished to keep a secret, one certainly didn't share it with Tony. Imagine his telling Trelenny about Sally Reed's house in Kendal! Of course Bodford had protested that she hadn't understood, but Cranford knew better. Why else would she have bestowed that incredulous stare on him? "Shall I come by in the morning to take you and your mother to the Pump Room?"

"Dear me, no. I don't know if Mama will wish to go again, and I haven't the least idea when we would leave, even if we did."

"I'll call sometime during the day to see what plans you have for the evening."

"Don't hesitate to make plans of your own, Cranford. Mrs. Waplington has a stack of invitations which she says will include Mama and me. And Mr. Wheldrake—"

"Yes, I know. He will be happy to look after you. I doubt he understands the first thing about what that entails." The chair was set down in the hall and Cranford, grim faced, helped Trelenny out.

She allowed him to take her hand but quickly withdrew it when she stood before him. "I thought I behaved just as I ought this evening. Did I do something wrong?" When he made no reply, just held her eyes with his for a long moment, she swallowed nervously. "Goodnight, Cranford. Thank you for escorting us."

"Goodnight, Trelenny." Without another glance at her he turned and made his farewells to the rest of the party and strode from the house.

chapter sixteen

Although the maid Alice enthusiastically explained what she had in mind to do with Trelenny's hair the next morning —a wild concoction of ringlets and sweeping waves—her mistress shook a determined head. "I am going to have to have it cut."

Horrified eyes met hers unbelievingly. "Cut, Miss Trelenny? But you've *never* had your hair cut. I've not seen a lady in the whole of Bath who has such long, beautiful tresses as yours. Whatever would your Mama say?"

"I shall have it done properly. Last night there was a lady who looked so...so...oh, free and unencumbered with her hair all short and fluffy. When I complimented her on it she laughed and said, 'I had to have it all cut off for the scarlet fever last year and it has yet to grow in properly.' At first I thought she was teasing me, but it really was so! Imagine! She looked wonderful but was suffering agonies of mortification for her short hair. I shan't, Alice. I want to be different from everyone else. So I asked Mrs. Waplington who was the best hairdresser in Bath and she promptly said Monsieur Robert and I ordered that a note be sent him first thing this morning. I shall pay him from my own money. Now don't look so disapproving. It's *my* hair, after all. And don't go off to tell Mama; it's to be a surprise."

"She'll be surprised all right," the girl muttered darkly. "Why you should take such a notion I can't imagine, Miss Trelenny. I can make your hair look ever so elegant, and what would you want to do but look like someone's lost dog!"

"No one notices you if you look like everyone else."

"Mercy sakes, miss; you're hardly a familiar face in Bath! You'll be noticed enough just for being new here."

The truth of this statement did not escape Trelenny after the reasonable success she had enjoyed the previous evening. Nor could she claim that she was tired of the same old hairstyle, as each day in Bath had occasioned the testing of some new arrangement, with an infinite variety yet before her. But each seemed only an imitation, an artificial copy of the mode. She wished to be original, as original as one could be who had been inspired by another. Miss Tooker's black locks were kept ingloriously hidden under a fanciful creation of feathers and ribbons; Trelenny had every intention of displaying her blonde mop to advantage. Cranford might disapprove, of course; there was nothing new in that! He treated her altogether too casually. Just see how he had practically ignored her at the assembly the previous evening and told her afterwards that she was a burden to him. As though she were a childish nuisance and not a grown woman entering society! Well, he need not bother to escort them about! Mr. Wheldrake was more than willing to do so, and Mama was feeling guilty about imposing on Cranford, anyhow. For all Trelenny cared, Cranford could go off to flirt with Lady Babthorpe, discuss pottery with Lady Jane, drink with Mr. Bodford, or gamble with Lord Rissington. She would be a great deal better off without his condemnatory presence. And she would show him that other men didn't see her as an affliction.

An hour later Monsieur Robert minced into her bedroom in Alice's disdainful wake. He was, however, no less astonished and horrified than the maid when Trelenny advised him that she wished to have her hair cut short. The long fingers touched her silken tresses as he murmured, "No, no, madam. You have no idea what you ask! *Mon dieu*, what I could do with such hair. Cut it?" He uttered the words with loathing. "It is not the mode! And for you it would not do in any case. Such hair is an achievement! Such length, such texture. It should be worn as a crown!"

"If you cannot or will not cut it, Monsieur Robert, I shall have to call in another hairdresser," Trelenny told him sternly.

The little man experienced great distress as he snipped, none of which was unaccompanied by mournful declarations of disaster. Two inches at a time was the most he would allow himself, begging her to reconsider as each new length emerged, to be rhapsodized over for its greater desirability than any shorter length. Implacably Trelenny urged him to continue, though as the mounds of hair began to grow on the floor she did experience some qualms. Feeling that it was too late to turn back, she had begun to wonder whether her straight hair would behave in quite the way Miss Tooker's did. Perhaps it would lie limply about her head, untrainable by hot irons or combs, drab and disgraceful.

As Trelenny's apprehension grew, Monsieur Robert's appeared to diminish. "Ah, yes. Who would have guessed? That will do very nicely. You see, we have a bit of curl when it is short. With a little help from the rod..." His fingers flew about—touching, snipping, crimping, turning her this way and that until he was perfectly satisfied. For some time Trelenny had not been able to force herself to look in the glass, but now Monsieur Robert triumphantly insisted. "I am a genius! Look at it! It will be the *new* mode, I promised you. See what I have done!"

Trelenny saw, and she heaved a sigh of relief. Gone was the stylish long hair, replaced by a cap of fluffy curls that framed her freckled face so impishly that she very nearly hugged the small fellow, who was bouncing about in his ecstasy. "Yes, that is precisely what I wanted. I look quite different, don't I?"

Mrs. Storwood certainly thought so. She took one look at her daughter and reached for her vinaigrette with a shaking hand, unable to utter a word.

"Don't you like it, Mama?" Trelenny asked anxiously. "I know it is not the thing to have short hair, but I think it is just right for me, don't you, Mama?"

"I...I shall become used to it, I dare say. Your Papa was always so proud of your long hair...What he will say...I will write to him, of course, so that he can prepare himself."

"You don't like it," Trelenny said flatly, dropping into a large chair, her face despondent.

"Well, dear, it seems a little...brazen, somehow. But it will grow in time and can be pulled back into...do you realize that you won't be able to wear braids anymore? I think, yes, I am quite sure, that your hair is now shorter than Cranford's. What will he say?"

"Oh, I don't *care* what Cranford says, Mama! What

difference can that possibly make? He can have his hair cut shorter, if that will make him feel better. I'm sorry *you* don't like it, though. Monsieur Robert was rather pleased with it and thought it would start a new mode."

"I can't see how," Mrs. Storwood replied unhappily. "No one over the age of twenty would dare to wear such a style. I thought you were so intent on looking older, Trelenny."

"I was, but I don't want to look like everyone else, dearest Mama. Couldn't you—"

They were interrupted by the arrival of a footman, who announced that Mr. Morton Rowle had inquired if they were at home to callers. After one despairing look at Trelenny's hair, Mrs. Storwood drew a deep, shuddering sigh and said, "Yes, I suppose so. Please show him in."

All deference, Mr. Rowle first made his bow to Mrs. Storwood, who steeled herself for his inevitable astonishment at her daughter's rash morning's activity. But Mr. Rowle did not so much as blink when he turned to the girl. A quick smile broadened with an assumed complicity, almost as though he had expected such an independent action from her. "Enchanting. And much more appropriate, if I may say so, than the very proper style you wore last evening—" He checked at the frown gathering on Mrs. Storwood's brow and changed the subject. "I have brought you the book I mentioned. Perhaps your mother would enjoy it as well. It's a bit of a spoof on the manners of the day in Bath."

Trelenny accepted the book with due gravity, though her eyes expressed an eager anticipation, as she expected it to be a great deal more entertaining than *Evelina,* coming as it had from Mr. Rowle rather than Cranford. Despite her attempts during the correct half hour Mr. Rowle sat with them to encourage him to elaborate on the experiences mentioned the previous evening, he would not be budged from his mundane social discourse, directed mainly at Mrs. Storwood, who apparently found it wholly acceptable. Mr. Rowle did, however, press her hand on his departure, expressing the wish that she and her mother might walk with him the next day if it were fine.

Ever alert to her daughter's wishes, and comforted by Mr. Rowle's entirely unobjectionable performance, Mrs. Storwood went so far as to temporize. "That would be very pleasant—provided there is no chill or damp in the air."

"I could, perhaps, show you around the Abbey," he

suggested, "if that would be of interest. I confess to some little knowledge of its history."

Pleased by the serious nature of the projected expedition, Mrs. Storwood smiled her acceptance and Trelenny, conscious of the admiration in his eyes as he looked enquiringly down at her, grinned, "Thank you, Mr. Rowle. I'm sure we would enjoy a tour of the Abbey above almost anything."

"*Almost* anything?" he murmured quizzingly, as he slipped out the door with one last, laughing glance at her.

Trelenny turned to her mother, a bubble of mirth still welling in her, and commented, "He is the most exasperating gentleman."

"How can you say so?" Mrs. Storwood asked, a puzzled tilt to her brows. "I thought you liked him."

"Oh, I do." Trelenny reconsidered expressing her opinion on his choice of a destination for a morning's stroll, since it had occurred to her belatedly that the decision had rested solely on Mr. Rowle's assumption of her mother's preference. Instead she laughed. "You see, Mama, he thought my haircut quite suitable. I hope you won't worry about it, for I can always purchase a wig if people laugh at me."

"A wig?" Mrs. Storwood asked in a quavering voice, powerfully affected by the vision of some such item sitting askew on her daughter's head.

"Lots of ladies wear wigs, my dear. Did you see the short, plump lady in the puce gown last night? There can be no question but that she wore one. Nature could not possibly have contrived such a grotesque color. And it wasn't dyed, for at the nape of her neck a strand of white hair had escaped as though she were concealing some animal under her hat and its tail was hanging out."

"You do have the most vivid imagination." Mrs. Storwood sighed. "But I dare say there will be no cause for you to wear a wig. We shall see what Elsa has to say about your unique hairstyle. I wonder if she has left her room yet."

Before she had a chance to enquire, the footman came to announce the arrival of two more callers. Half-reconciled to her daughter's appearance, and delighted that Trelenny should have won so much recognition the previous evening, Mrs. Storwood promptly agreed to have them admitted. Lord Rissington and Tony Bodford had met on the stoop outside, the former bearing flowers, the latter a box of comfits; and a mock acrimonious scene had followed in which each had deplored the other's gift as unworthy, whether for its ephemeral or cloying nature, depending on the character of the giver. On entering the parlor, therefore, there was a certain amount of good-natured jockeying for position, each desiring that this gift should be presented first and with an appropriate comment on its virtues, but with nonetheless an attempt to win Mrs. Storwood's approbation and not her disgust. Owing to these overriding concerns, neither of the gentlemen at first noticed Trelenny's hair.

"I say, Miss Storwood! Won't you cut a dash!" Startled but enthusiastic, Tony Bodford uttered such phrases as *all the crack, slap up to the echo,* and *precise to a pin.* The box of comfits, all but forgotten, was carelessly consigned to a lyre-shaped music stand which inhibited his progress to have a closer view of Trelenny's short locks.

Lord Rissington was more restrained in his speech but no less so in his approbation. "You look astonishingly like a portrait of my great-aunt when she was a girl, Miss Storwood. Flying in the face of convention, she had her hair shorn just so on the eve of her presentation at court, and she was a great hit. Quite a life she had, too, come to think of it. Buried three or four husbands, all titled and well blunted, and had such a swarm of children that I can't keep track of half my relations today." Skirting the music stand with a great deal more dexterity than Bodford, he presented the flowers, his cherubic face beaming in triumph on his companion. "I make you my compliments, Miss Storwood. These poor blooms can but ill compare with your own radiance this morning but I beg you will, out of the goodness of your heart, accept them."

Desperately searching for his own gift, Bodford muttered, "Shabby bunch of greenery! Not even out-of-season stuff, if you will. I went all the way to Stall Street for the best comfits in town." His eye lit on the renegade box and he scooped it up, dislodging several sheets of music in his hurry. These fluttered to the carpet before he could retrieve them, and he was so intrigued by the carpet that he paused to exclaim, "Have you ever seen anything like this, Rissington? If you look very closely you can see—" He stopped abruptly and flushed at Mrs. Storwood's incredulous expression. "Sorry. Pay no heed to me. Just a fancy of mine, to be sure. The weave is a bit irregular, of course, but it could not possibly be of interest. Now where did I put those sugar plums? Ah, here they are. I thought Miss Storwood might like a box for her room. Not that she wouldn't share them with you, ma'am! There are more than enough for two people, or even more! Mrs. Waplington, I know, has a sweet tooth. Noticed her more than once eyeing the ... Well, there, that's no matter, either. What I mean is, hope you'll enjoy them, Miss Storwood."

Stifling a giggle, Trelenny allowed him to place them in the hand that did not contain the bouquet, saying, "Thank you, Mr. Bodford, It's a great deal too good of you both. Won't you sit down? I'll just ring and have these flowers put in water."

"You see, Rissington?" Bodford whispered aside. "You've just gone and caused her a lot of trouble bringing those weeds. Now a box of comfits is just the ticket. Sits right on any table and doesn't have to have water. All ready for the moment you find yourself sharp set and hours to go till the next meal. You should remember that for next time."

Ignoring this admonition with superb unconcern, Lord Rissington set himself to entertain Mrs. Storwood, and her daughter when she returned to sit with them. Being possessed of a remarkable memory (not to give the lie to his comment on keeping track of his relations, each and every one of whom he could name, give an age for and a place of residence, together with an astonishing amount of history), he found little difficulty in eliciting the names of those acquaintances Mrs. Storwood had lost track of and, more often than not, bringing her up to date on their whereabouts and recent activities. Knowing everyone was a hobby of my lord's, and perhaps that reason more than any other had induced him to dance attendance on the Storwoods, though Cranford's reluctance to speak of them may possibly have piqued his interest. Although Mrs. Storwood's delicacy of character and high tone of mind were not perhaps duplicated in her daughter, Rissington found Trelenny delightful, and hardly the sad romp Cranford had led him, in his cryptic remarks, to believe. Spirited, certainly, but with a reasonable regard for convention, as witnessed by her efforts to draw Bodford, who, if not precisely sulking, was certainly not in his element in the parlor that morning, into the conversation.

Mr. Bodford's unguarded and erratic manner did not recommend him to young ladies' parents, as well he knew, and he resented Rissington's ease on the present, as he had on past occasions. Unfortunately, they were often attracted to the same females, and Rissington forever won the advantage.

Because of his angelic face and wide blue eyes, no one suspected him of the least guile; and Bodford would be the first to affirm their judgment, though he could have told them a great deal that would have surprised them, nonetheless. And it was not necessarily that Bodford himself was suspected of guile, more often he was presumed foolish, which was just as far from the truth as the presumption that Rissington's temperament was as open as his countenance. A stocky figure, indeterminate features, nondescript brown eyes and hair all combined to make him an unprepossessing figure; and, when considered in addition to his penchant for saying precisely what came to mind, he was either dismissed as a loose screw, a slow top, or a frippery fellow. Often overlooked were his perpetual good nature (excluding the present circumstances), his expertise in every field of athletic endeavor, and his unfailing courtesy to the highest and lowest of his fellow creatures.

Remembering his delightful tales of the previous evening, Trelenny was endeavoring to show him to advantage before her skeptical mother, who had conceived the standard impression of Mr. Bodford during his first minutes in the room. "When does your father come to town, Mr. Bodford?"

"He leaves Westmorland in a week. Makes a stately progression, though, and I don't expect him for some time after that."

Trelenny felt she had not perhaps given him the most propitious opening, so she tried again. "I heard of a highwayman near Preston on our way here. Have you ever encountered any trouble on the road?"

A gleam appeared in his eyes. "Haven't I just! Last year I was going into Somerset to visit Thompkins. He lives near this little village called Luccombe and God help me the directions he gave would have lost a military scout. Well, it's nowhere, I promise you! Pretty country, you understand. Once I found the dratted place even I could appreciate how pleasant it was there, but I kept asking my way and no one had ever heard of it! Fancy that! I dare say there's not a soul in Westmorland who couldn't direct you to Kendal! Of course, Luccombe is a village, but I swear I asked this farm lad for the place when it turned out I wasn't half a mile from it—and he hadn't ever heard of it!"

Afraid that her mother was becoming restless by this digression, Trelenny asked, "And was it on your way there that you met a highwayman?"

"A highwayman? I've *never* met a highwayman," he declared emphatically. "Met a footpad once," with a significant look at Rissington, "but never a highwayman. Well, stands to reason, don't it? No highwayman's nag could outrun that pair of mine, could they, Rissington?"

"I shouldn't think so."

"But I thought you said you'd encountered trouble on the road." Trelenny persisted.

"I did," Tony agreed with the gleam returning to his eyes. "I was about to tell you. Wasn't but a short distance from the village and I could see the lights gleaming through the trees ahead, when I came around a bend to find a carriage slung right across the road. Whoa, I said to myself, this means trouble. Drew my pair up short, though it was a near thing. Stopped them just a squeak away from the carriage and sent my tiger to their heads before I had time to realize that there was only one horse attached to the landau. Well, I thought, one of the horses has gone lame and they've left him and taken the other to get help. But why would they have left the carriage straight across the road, I wondered? Sort of put me on my guard, don't you know? So I took up a pistol I keep under the seat and walked right up to the door and opened it. And what do you think I found?" He gazed on his audience with bright-eyed eagerness.

Rissington groaned; Trelenny smiled encouragingly; Mrs. Storwood waited rather longingly for the end of the tale.

"A naked woman! On my honor!" Oblivious to the fact that he had shocked Mrs. Storwood, Tony continued with relish. "And not a highwayman involved in the whole affair! First thing I did, of course, was take off my driving cape and give it to the poor woman. Seems her husband had driven her out of the house without a stitch on her back over some misunderstanding. Told his coachman to leave her like a newborn babe precisely ten miles from his estate, but one of the horses went lame and he'd ridden off to get another in the village. When the lame horse heard my carriage coming he tried to bolt, but just threw the carriage across the road. The poor woman didn't dare to get out and try to right the situation."

"Her husband did that to her?" Trelenny asked incredulously. "What happened to her?"

"I took her up with me in the curricle and brought her to Thompkins' place. His sister knew the woman, and eventually she was returned to her parents' home. They sued the husband; stripped him pretty near as well as he did his wife."

"I'm glad to hear it! What a despicable thing to do."

Mrs. Storwood looked as though she needed a whiff of her vinaigrette, but Trelenny was too indignant to notice. Lord Rissington considered it time he and Bodford took their leave, and mercilessly propelled the other man before him to the door. With an apologetic smile, he took his leave of Mrs. Storwood and Trelenny, managing to convey his hope that they would meet again soon over Bodford's mumbled, "Wasn't entirely in the right, you know, the wife, but I don't hold with such villainy as the husband's myself."

Before the door had closed after them, Mrs. Storwood dug her vinaigrette out of her bulging reticule and agitatedly waved it under her nose. "Whatever possessed him to tell us such a story?" she asked faintly.

"Don't be vexed with him, Mama. I think he's a dear, really. He didn't mean to upset you, I'm sure, just to entertain us with his escapade."

"Cranford would never have told us anything so improper! Imagine discussing unclothed women with us."

No, Cranford doesn't discuss it, he just does it, Trelenny apostrophized mentally with an embarrassed toss of her head. Gone was the long silken hair he had released from its pins that night, and she was *glad* it was gone!

chapter seventeen

Cranford had spent a disturbed night. Sleep proved elusive, so he rose from his bed, wrapped a dressing gown around himself, and struck a flint to light his bedside candle. Restlessly pacing about the room, an elegant chamber with an alcove containing two Hepplewhite cabriole chairs flanking a draw table, he noticed the copy of *Emma* and decided he would begin reading it to make himself drowsy. Before opening the first volume, however, he stared off into the shadowy room, unable to pinpoint what was discomposing him so. Trelenny, of course, he thought, running a hand distractedly through his hair, but this was not his usual state of mind concerning her. Ordinarily he would experience a moment's irritation or more sustained doubts of her behavior which lurked at the back of his mind. Was he too hard on her? This evening, for instance, he need not have ended their evening by impugning her. Surely it was cruel to depress her soaring spirits after so successful an evening for her. Three men at least had been more than pleased to share her company, had laughed and talked with her with evident enjoyment. Both Bodford and Rissington had questioned him about her after their sets, expressing delight in her freshness and enthusiasm.

And it was true that Trelenny was not just in the common way. Her own special charm was her eagerness and optimism about life and everything in it, her fascination and sympathy with other people, her ready adaptability to both good and bad fortune. They were not necessarily merely characteristics of youth, either, Cranford realized. A certain amount of caution would be acquired in time to blunt the edge of her frankness, but the joyous celebration of each day seemed unlikely to change, barring any disaster.

So why had he tried to spoil her evening? Perhaps because of her accusation earlier in the day that he wouldn't own to reading *Emma*. No, for all his irate behavior, he knew almost for a certainty that that was only a prank of hers, played in revenge for his perpetually pinching at her. He smiled ruefully at the memory of her haughty demand to be taken home, but another scene eclipsed that almost immediately—her laughing face raised to Mr. Rowle and again to Rissington and Bodford. Cranford had intended, if Trelenny lacked a partner for any dance, to solicit her himself, but there had been no need. She had managed perfectly well without his assistance, and somehow that rankled. Not that she had enjoyed the early part of the evening; Cranford knew her well enough to understand that she had been uneasy with her first partners. Even then she had not turned to him for support, though he realized, with chagrin, that he had given her no encouragement to do so, rather the opposite.

With an exasperated shrug, he decided that it was futile to delve further into the day's uncomfortable occurrences. Tomorrow he would treat her more kindly. Better yet, tomorrow he would avoid her, as she seemed to wish. Mr. Wheldrake could stand escort to the Storwoods, and Cranford would have an opportunity to do precisely what he wanted, though nothing occurred to him offhand. He unconsciously rumpled his hair and opened the book on his lap, forcing any further thoughts of Trelenny from his mind. Not once, until he encountered the note tucked in the third chapter, did he give a thought to Lady Babthorpe.

> Cranford dear, when you doze over this book, dream of me. My lord spends Tuesday night in Wells. I am forbidden to go out in the evenings save in his company, so I shall be at home alone . . . Clothilde will be at the rear entry at midnight. There is no risk. Don't fail me.

Cranford took the note to the grate and lit it from his candle, watching impassively at it flamed and turned to ash. The room was cold now and he shivered. Thoughtfully he retraced his steps to the alcove and placed a leather bookmark in *Emma* before discarding his dressing gown and climbing into bed. He did not dream of Lady Babthorpe.

Lord Barlow's house in Queen Square reflected his daughter's taste as well as his own. When Cranford arrived he was shown into a drawing room in such contrast to Mrs. Waplington's eclectic rooms that he almost smiled. Instead of the clutter of furniture, paintings, and mirrors, there was a refined simplicity ornamented by classical motifs and objects, which held no small interest for an antiquarian. Lady Jane and her father were entertaining a woman and her daughter unknown to Cranford but obviously on easy terms with the host and hostess. They soon took their leave, and after conversing with Cranford for a few minutes, Lord Barlow did likewise because of a pressing appointment.

"Did Miss Storwood go to the Assembly last night?"

"Yes, and was very well-received. Rissington and Bodford joined her entourage."

"Is Tony in town, then? I hadn't seen him."

"He arrived only two days ago and has been searching out lodgings for his father. Rissington found some for him."

"Naturally."

"A Mr. Rowle, too, seemed particularly interested in Trelenny."

Lady Jane frowned. "Is she an heiress, Cranford?"

"She'll have a handsome portion and a very fine property after her parents are gone. Do you know Rowle, Jane?"

"I've met him, and heard more." She turned earnest eyes on Cranford. "Don't let him get his clutches in that dear child."

Cranford sighed. "I was afraid so. He seems to have a vast appeal for her. She told me he had an air of adventure about him."

"Pooh! He's a thorough-going blackguard, but not everyone sees that. Changeable as a chameleon, wriggling his way into every potential advantage. Papa had a business dealing with him, and you know, Cranford, Papa is usually astute in judging character. Mr. Rowle has an astonishing facility for endearing himself to the most unlikely people. I wouldn't trust him out of my sight."

"He has a stepsister named Caroline Moreby?"

Lady Jane's eyes opened wide. "You have done some astonishingly rapid research, my dear fellow."

"No, I met a Mr. Laytham in Preston, on his way to the border with Miss Moreby."

"Did you?" Lady Jane laughed aloud. "You relieve me, Cranford. Gossip was rampant here as to what had become of her. It was general knowledge that the stepfather was attempting to force her into a marriage with his son, and that she was very reluctant. I didn't think she'd have the spirit to elope, though. Laytham? He would be the tall boy who took chivalry to heart. Miss Moreby was a substantial heiress from her grandfather. The elder Rowle has as much of an eye to the main chance as his son, I hear. Having married the mother, he intended to keep all the Moreby money in the family through his son. Poor Miss Moreby couldn't even keep her own mother on her side; the woman is a vacillating weed! When the girl didn't appear in society a week or so ago, it was rumored that she had been sent off to the country until she agreed to marry Rowle. I must admit I thought it likely. No murmur has escaped of the elopement."

"Is Rowle received?"

"Not everywhere. They're minor gentry, and the highsticklers won't have anything to do with them, especially since the father and son both act like merchants when they smell a deal brewing. Still, I've seen the young one in any number of good houses. If it weren't for Papa's experience, I suppose I wouldn't feel so strongly. You should warn Miss Storwood."

Cranford shook his head. "It wouldn't do any good, Jane. She'd just think I was interfering. Of course, she did try to assist Miss Moreby, but Trelenny would scarcely understand how a girl could let herself be pressured into marrying someone. She has a certain amount of experience in that line," he admitted with a mournful grin. When his hostess made no comment he continued, "And Miss Moreby didn't actually tell her about Mr. Rowle's attentions. It was Laytham who told me. Nothing coming from me would carry much weight with Trelenny. She'd think Miss Moreby poor spirited (as she did Evelina) for running off at so little cause. Trelenny has a great deal of confidence in her own estimation of people—and she's a babe in the wood."

"I could mention something casually. Really, Mr. Rowle is insidious, Cranford. Don't expect Mrs. Storwood to recognize him for what he is."

"Any help you can give would be appreciated, Jane. I

don't want to see Trelenny hurt. Possibly Rissington or Bodford will take an interest and keep her too busy to pay much attention to Rowle."

"Let's hope so." She would have asked if he had no hopes of winning Trelenny's interest himself, but the question seemed impertinent. "Would you like to see Papa's collection? It's been years, and he's added a number of pieces besides the wine cup."

"He's brought it with him? The whole collection?"

"All but the really large pieces, she said with a laugh. "He always does."

"A man after my own heart," Cranford said fervently, smiling. "Lead on, dear lady. And, Jane, I would be delighted to escort you to the Cheyney's this evening if you have a mind to go."

"Why, thank you, I'd be delighted. The Storwoods . . . ?"

"Trelenny tells me Mr. Wheldrake would welcome the honor, and I've a mind to pursue my own path for a while." He brushed a speck of dust from his coat and neglected to meet her eyes.

"I see."

Mr. Wheldrake was flattered to have his offer of escort accepted again, and without benefit of Mr. Ashwicke on this occasion. Amongst the half dozen invitations on her desk for the evening, Mrs. Waplington declared her intention to attend only three: a rout at the Hunsingores, a drum at the Cheynes, and lastly a ball at the Buttercrambes. Cards had come for Trelenny and her mother—for each of these occasions and the thought of attending *three* functions in one evening sent Trelenny into alt. She was so pleased with the white satin gown she wore and her new hairstyle with its solitary diamond butterfly clip that she almost regretted that Cranford would not see her.

At the Hunsingores she met Mr. Bodford, who, though addicted to the card table, found time to introduce her to several of his friends and kindly partnered her at one of the whist tables long enough to see her several pounds the richer, before excusing himself to the higher stakes in the back drawing room. Mrs. Waplington also rose a winner and announced that she was ready for her chair to the Cheynes, if the others could be persuaded to desert such good company.

Trelenny, flushed with her success, mounted the steps at the drum with every expectation of pleasure. If she was not mistaken, Mr. Rowle had mentioned the Cheynes that morning and she had hopes of finding him among the assembled guests. She was not prepared to find Cranford there with Lady Jane.

In spite of his avowed intent to treat Trelenny more kindly, Cranford felt as though she'd slapped him when he saw her. That beautiful golden hair that had reached to her waist—gone! Those silken tresses that had slipped through his fingers when he released the pins—vanished, to be replaced by a madcap fringe that floated on her head like a naughty angel's halo. He quickly transferred his stunned gaze to Mrs. Storwood, who shook her head unhappily.

"Good evening, Lady Jane," Trelenny said nervously, offering her hand and trying to avoid Cranford's fulminating glare. "I . . . I'm so pleased you had me to Queen Square to learn the waltz, for we're going to a ball next."

"I trust you will enjoy every moment, my dear. Your haircut is charming. How very clever of you to find something completely original. No matter what we do with mine, it's always an imitation of someone else's."

"Actually," Trelenny confessed, "I got the idea from Miss Tooker. Do you know her?"

"Yes." Lady Jane's eyes twinkled. "But I don't think she *chose* that particular style."

"Well, no, but I thought it looked like fun. And don't you think she'll feel more comfortable if someone else has short hair? She seemed rather miserable."

Lady Jane pressed her hand. "That was sweet of you. Isn't it wonderful when our own desires fall in with doing a good deed?"

An impish smile dimpled Trelenny's face. "Cranford once told me it's called rationalization."

"Cranford is marvelously *apt* sometimes." Lady Jane pointedly surveyed his scowling face. "Of course, at others he's a stuffy pedant. You know, I don't believe I've told you about the time he took Geoffrey to Newmarket. There was to be a match between him and Sir Lowell, but the night before—"

"Very well." Cranford spoke between tight lips. "Geoffrey shouldn't have told you that, Jane. Good evening, Trelenny. You are looking... well. May I get you a glass of punch?"

"Thank you, no," Trelenny replied stiffly. She touched a finger to the butterfly clip to assure herself that it hadn't come loose and began to back away from the couple. "It's all right, Lady Jane. I... I knew he wouldn't approve. Mama doesn't either." Flashing a hesitant smile at the older woman, she fled to her mother's side and managed to keep her eyes averted from Cranford for the entire length of their stay at the drum. Of course, the task was made easier by the arrival of Mr. Rowle, who teased and flattered her alternately, but she could not entirely lift her spirits to their former level and, except for leaving Mr. Rowle behind, she was happy enough to leave the Cheynes for the ball.

From across the room Lady Jane watched the departure of their party with worried eyes. "You are going to push her right into his arms with your disapproval, Cranford. Why should you care if she cut her hair? It looks adorable."

"She had beautiful hair, so long it came down to her waist, and it felt like silk."

Resisting the temptation to ask him how he knew, she responded astringently, "Then she probably had a great deal of trouble keeping pins in it, and that much hair piled about her head must have been most uncomfortable, and near impossible to keep tidy."

"She cut it to annoy me."

"You flatter yourself! She wanted to so something original—not look like everyone else. I have often had the same desire, but I lack the courage to carry it through. It's easier when you're young, of course, but still, I admire her."

"Admire her?" he asked incredulously.

"Yes, for not letting herself be hedged in by traditions and conventions. And don't tell me she isn't aware of the rules, for I have no doubt Mrs. Storwood is a perfect model of propriety."

"She is. Would that her daughter followed in her footsteps."

Lady Jane regarded him coolly. "If you feel that way, Cranford, I would advise you to abandon your pursuit of her. Trelenny doesn't need a heavy hand, merely a guiding one. There's Emily Harper beckoning to us. I should like a word with her."

Chairs were coming in and out of the Buttercrambes' brilliantly lit hall with regularity, and still there was a line of them before the door, as well as several carriages awaiting their turn to disgorge their occupants at the entrance. Bewigged footmen in truly manificent liveries showed no sign of haste as they opened carriage doors and lowered steps for their aristocratic employers. Let the common folk hurry; footmen were too conscious of their reflected dignity to fall to such vulgarity. Trelenny watched the scene with fascination and amusement but none of the trepidation her mother experienced. For Mrs. Storwood this was Trelenny's real testing, and she could not but feel that her daughter had put herself at a disadvantage with her unusual hairstyle. It was all very well for Elsa Waplington to laugh and call Trelenny a naughty puss; she had no daughter of her own to agonize over should the tide of opinion sway against her. Mrs. Storwood hardly noticed the satin-hung walls or the ice sculpture of a fabled sea monster; her eyes searched the room for some friendly, familiar face.

At her elbow Mr. Wheldrake murmured encouragement. "She'll do very well, Maria."

"But people are staring at her. That woman by the pillar is frowning and a gentleman across the room has lifted his quizzing glass with the most supercilious air. Oh, I shan't be able to bear it if they ostracize her. She had so longed for her first ball."

"Here's Lord Rissington coming to speak with her now. Never fear. Others will follow his lead."

Although Trelenny had not overheard the whispered conversation of her companions, she too had noticed raised eyebrows and knew a moment's alarm. How comforting it would have been to have Cranford at her side! But no, his brows had been raised higher than any here. She held her head proudly and forced a smile to her lips; *no one* could intimidate a Storwood. Impeccable birth, unassailable breeding, and a more-than-respectable fortune stood behind her. Her eyes flashed a challenge to any who dared malign or laugh at her.

As he approached, Rissington was struck by the figure she made. Incongruous, perhaps, the stature all dignity and the hair an elfin nonsense, but captivating, nonetheless. "If you are trying to frighten me off, I promise you I am made of sturdier stuff," he informed her valiantly. "He who has not been quelled by the eye of Her Royal Highness refuses to allow any mortal to so much as make him tremble. Though I confess to a certain weakness in the knees, I do implore you to honor me with this set, for the eyes of the room are upon me, and if I don't succeed I shall be shamed before them all."

"What a farago of nonsense! Have you met the Queen then? Is she so very forbidding?"

"I have and she is. Cranford didn't escort you this evening?"

"No. We saw him at the Cheynes with Lady Jane."

"He's always been very attached to the Reedness family. Shares a great many interests with Lady Jane. Old things, you know. Not my sort of style, but then, each to his own. *Will* you dance with me, Miss Storwood?"

"Certainly, my lord, if you feel your knees are strong enough to support such activity."

Mrs. Storwood breathed easier after that initial set. As on the previous evening, there was no shortage of men to solicit her daughter's hand, and, though she could not *quite* approve of the waltz, she was delighted to see that her daughter performed creditably. "I can see no reason," Mrs. Waplington declared, "that she should not dance it, though perhaps it would be well if Mr. Wheldrake led her out the first time. Rissington is itching to do so, of course, but let us err on the side of caution. There will be another later in the evening for his lordship should he still desire it."

And he did desire it. Constituting himself as Trelenny's escort in the absence of Cranford, Rissington propounded his extreme suitability as her partner above the claims of Mr. Bodford, who had just arrived and had yet to gain a solitary set with Miss Storwood.

"The two of you make game with me," she protested, laughing. "Mr. Bodford was so good as to see me through the shoals at the Hunsingores, and I believe I owe him this dance."

Surprised but pleased, Tony gallantly offered his arm. "Who'd have thought you'd choose me? It's the only waltz left this evening, Miss Storwood."

"I know. Aren't they glorious? I believe I could come to rank dancing the waltz second only to riding, given the opportunity."

"Frowned on it at first, the old tabbies. A lot of them still do. Won't have it danced in their homes, and sit about cackling like a bunch of geese while their eyes fall out trying to see who's holding whom too closely at someone else's."

If Mr. Bodford stumbled against music stands in crowded parlors, he did not have any difficulty on the dance floor. He was, in fact, a superb dancer, unconsciously graceful and offhandedly entertaining. Trelenny retreated to her mother's side flushed with pleasure, only to find Lord Rissington awaiting her there.

"I've arranged for the dance after this next, which you may recall you have promised to me, to be a waltz. I hope that meets with your approval," Rissington announced, his cherubic face beaming.

"Told you he could get anything done," Tony grumbled.

chapter eighteen

Trelenny calculated that it would be at least the following Thursday before they would hear from her father. It had not occurred to Mrs. Storwood that her daughter thought they would be summoned home, so she had not mentioned that her own portion of the letter, which Trelenny with scrupulous integrity had not read, had indicated her willingness to stay in Bath for her daughter's sake. Trelenny consequently expected to be summoned back to Westmorland in less than a week and threw herself energetically into the entertainments Bath had to offer. Saturday Mr. Rowle proved an excellent, personable tour guide of the Abbey, winning Mrs. Storwood's approbation and Trelenny's dissatisfaction. (She had not yet succeeded in getting him to tell her of his adventures.) The evening's occupation consisted of another ball at which she did not find him amongst the guests, though Lord Rissington and Mr. Bodford once again vied for her attention.

Sunday Cranford, formidably polite, escorted them to the chapel for services and took his dinner in Henrietta Street, but excused himself afterwards for an engagement with Lady Jane. By Monday Trelenny had convinced herself that he no longer intended to offer for her, and that she might rejoice in her new freedom, which consisted largely of flirting (so her mother with palpitating heart called it as she bid Mr. Wheldrake good night) with all three of her beaux at the dress ball in the Upper Rooms. Although Mrs. Storwood felt it incumbent upon her to have a small chat with her daughter about the decorum of dangling three men after her all evening, Trelenny just grinned and said, "Oh, pooh, Mama. It is but a game with them. Have you seen the least sign that any one of them is serious in his intentions? I promise you I have not! They are forever quizzing me and calling me Mistress Mary. They say I am quite contrary, but it is just what they expect. Oh, Mama, can it be wrong to have a laugh with them?"

"Well, no, dear, but they might receive the impression you are... a little... fast."

"How can you say so? Oh, I see what it is. It's Cranford's opinion you are *really* concerned for, is it not? You're afraid he'll not approve of all my beaux. Dear Mama, I hate to shatter your fondest dreams, but even you cannot doubt that he has desisted in his intentions. He only speaks when it is necessary, and then he is so coldly polite."

"But... but he asked your father for permission to pay his addresses to you, and he hasn't even *asked* you!" There was a suspicion of tears in her voice, and she busied her fingers sorting the threads in her box.

"Not formally, no. At Sutton Hall once..." Trelenny sighed. "He knew I wouldn't marry him then, Mama, and he was too proud to ask where he would receive a refusal. I think he is developing an interest elsewhere."

"You mean Lady Jane? Yes, I have noticed his attendance on her. But surely they are old friends, Trelenny. Cranford would not go back on his word."

"Pray don't talk so foolishly, Mama! I as good as told him I wouldn't have him, so he is free to court whomever he pleases." She caught her lower lip in her teeth to stop its trembling. How stupid to feel agitated about such a matter! Had she not for the past month and more declared her determination to reject him? Certainly he felt no remorse at her decision, and she was not so vain as to have wanted him to propose only so that she could give him her negative, so where was the problem? "I... I must go to my room and look out a shawl to wear with my dress tonight. The green one is snagged and won't do."

"Why not borrow mine? Or better yet, shall we go to the shops and find a new one for you? There were some beautiful cashmere ones in Milsom Street. Your Papa meant for you to have something special."

"Tomorrow perhaps, Mama. For the card party I shall borrow yours if you won't mind. I thought I would just read for a while in my room now."

"Are you feeling well, Trelenny?" her mother asked, all concern.

"Of course, silly. Must I feel ill to read a book?" She gave her mother a quick hug and abruptly left the room. Although Mr. Rowle had queried her as to how she liked the book he had lent her, she couldn't pick it up to read once she had gained her bedchamber. Instead she stared out the back window into the autumn garden, feeling as desolate as the day, which had become overcast and windy. As she watched, the rain began to fall, splashing against the sill and coursing down the panes, and it was a moment before she realized that her own tears had begun to fall as well. Dashing them away with an angry hand, she thought indignantly, well, really, it must be coming on to my time of month. How absurdly emotional I am! This really will not do.

Looking about the room for some occupation, she rapidly discarded the magazines and her needlework. Absently she opened the lid of her jewelry box, which played a cheerful tune hardly in keeping with her mood. She snapped it shut, but a most peculiar idea had formed in her mind. In the little room opposite, which she and her mother had been given as a sitting room, there was a pianoforte. Suddenly it seemed very important that she practice. No matter that it had been months, perhaps years, since she had done so with any serious intent. Today she did.

Two enormous rooms were filled with tables, some with green baize covers and a few with the two red and two black diamond-shaped marks denoting *rouge et noir* tables. Although a number of people stood about laughing and talking, the majority had settled down to the serious business of the evening—whist, piquet, quinze, macao, cassino, even faro. Mrs. Waplington allowed herself an evening at cards only once a week, for though she enjoyed the excitement, she very seldom found herself a winner. "You have to keep a clear head, my dear," she told Trelenny, "and I become so caught up in the game that I hardly notice my glass being refilled. And if it is full, I will drink it, heaven knows. Find a table where the stakes are low or moderate and don't hesitate to excuse yourself if the play gets over your head."

"Yes, ma'am. I shall try to follow your advice."

"Have you some money?" Mrs. Waplington dug in her

reticule and came up with five guineas. "Here, enjoy yourself."

"Oh, thank you, no. I have sufficient for my needs," Trelenny objected.

"I always think so, too." She laughed and pressed the coins into her guest's hand. "You would do me a favor, love, for I just know that tonight I shan't have the least luck."

Trelenny accepted the coins with every intention of returning them at the end of the evening. Her own money seemed more than enough for an evening's play, even should she be so unfortunate as to have bad cards. Never once did she doubt her skill. For an hour she partnered a young man with whom she had danced at the previous night's entertainment, and the following hour an elderly gentleman whose tendency to nap between plays caused her some confusion. With a certain amount of relief, she accepted Mr. Rowle's invitation to join a table playing at macao, though the stakes were so high as to make her feel slightly uncomfortable. At most of the tables there was a businesslike buzz of conversation, but at Mr. Rowle's things were different. Laughter and high spirits reigned supreme here, though drink held a notable place as well. No glass was ever below a quarter full that one of the participants did not wave a footman over to see it convivially replenished. Trelenny's five guineas were soon gone, and the stack in front of Mr. Rowle grew considerably.

Before another round could be dealt by Mr. Rowle, Trelenny rose a little unsteadily. "Thank you. I must look out my mother, so if you will excuse me..."

Mr. Rowle was instantly on his feet. "Pray don't deprive us of your company, Miss Storwood! Your mother and Mr. Wheldrake are just there on the sofa, and I dare say would be none the happier for being interrupted."

Trelenny turned startled eyes in the direction he indicated and found that indeed Mrs. Storwood and her companion seemed to be enjoying themselves to the exclusion of any other person in the room. Seldom did Mrs. Storwood look so animated as she did now, laughing and chatting happily to the apparent delight of Mr. Wheldrake. Uneasily Trelenny resumed her seat and allowed herself to be once again drawn into the camaraderie of the little group. Another half hour saw the disappearance of her own money and she rose again.

"There. I am cleaned out! Please excuse me."

Mr. Rowle's countenance registered shock, as though she had committed a social solecism. Again he rose and stood beside her but spoke in a kindly whisper. "I see what it is. You are not used to our Bath card parties. One never admits to being rolled up; it makes the other players uncomfortable, you know. We're a friendly group, Miss Storwood. Any one of us would be happy to accept your note of hand."

A hasty glance at her mother, still cheerfully engaged in conversation, assured her that that excuse would not hold. "Mrs. Waplington thought it would not be a good evening for her, and I dare say she is searching for me, longing to be on her way."

"Ah, your hostess misjudged the fortunes of the evening, it would seem, for I saw her not ten minutes ago when I slipped into the other room, a handy pile of coins by her side and twinkling on her companions in the most superior way."

Since Mr. Waplington had not attended them, and Trelenny knew no one else in the rooms well enough to make them an excuse for leaving her companions, she returned to her seat with a frown. Professing delight at her return, the others plunged straightaway into the game again and Trelenny knew the embarrassment of having a footman bring paper and pen for her to scribble a chit. She began to pray that her mother or Mrs. Waplington would come for her, but they did not. Despite her refusal to take another sip of her wine, or her concentration on the cards, she continued to lose. Each time she signed a new chit, the others smiled encouragingly and hurried on with the game.

At last she pushed her chair back rather violently and murmuring, "Excuse me!" she walked off before the others realized what had happened. Though Mr. Rowle was instantly on his feet he found himself addressing her retreating back. "Miss Storwood! You're not leaving!"

"Yes. If you will be so good as to possess yourself of all my notes, I shall redeem them tomorrow."

"But of course." He caught up with her, smiling. "There's no need to redeem them so soon. It is only a game, after all."

"I shall redeem them tomorrow."

"But you don't even know how much there is."

"Certainly I do," she replied indignantly, paushing before

they reached the sofa where her mother sat. "They amount to twenty guineas, and you will be paid tomorrow."

"Nonsense! It could never be so much! No more than ten, I should think."

"You will find the case to be otherwise, Mr. Rowle. Where shall I send the money?"

He cast a quick, nervous glance at her mother. "Really, there is no need, Miss Storwood. As I said, it was only a game. I'll tear up your notes."

"Don't be absurd! We weren't playing lottery tickets or speculation. Perhaps you will call tomorrow afternoon. I should be able to have the money by then."

Mr. Rowle bowed his acknowledgment, a sheepish grin on his face. "It's the very devil to hold the notes of one who means . . . no! At least I shall see you tomorrow. I shall count the hours."

"It will improve your arithmetic." Trelenny laughed, but she ignored his rueful expression and turned away with a heavy heart. Twenty guineas! Almost the entire amount she had left with Cranford, and only a handful of coins left in her room.

"Did you enjoy yourself, dear?"

Forcing a smile to her lips, Trelenny faced her mother and Mr. Wheldrake. "I like dancing better, but it was interesting. I think I learned a great deal tonight."

"You lost then?" Mr. Wheldrake asked, amused.

"Yes, but no more than I can afford, and there were compensations. May I sit with you? I haven't a shilling left."

Mrs. Storwood offered several guineas but Trelenny refused, and Mr. Wheldrake nodded approvingly. "You have learned something, my dear young lady. There's no use throwing good money after bad."

"No, nor anything else," Trelenny replied cryptically.

Both Rissington and Bodford had solicited Cranford's company, and Lord Barlow and his daughter would have welcomed his attendance at a musical gathering, but Cranford chose to spend the evening in his room, reading. He had sent no reply to Lady Babthorpe's message, having no wish to have it intercepted by her husband, and because the peremptoriness of it, after his efforts to refuse her kindly, had irritated him. A great number of things seemed to irritate him just now—not having his valet, staying with Rissington, the overcooked beef at dinner, even the fit of his well-worn boots. These last he had hurled into the grate when, having resorted to a boot jack, he had accidentally pulled his stocking off with it, and snagged the damned thing. Bath felt too small to hold him; he chafed against the inability to simply walk out to his stables, saddle a horse, and ride hell for leather across the countryside. Usually town life did not pall on him for several weeks, but he could not have borne to spend the evening being pleasant when all he really wanted to do was stomp around his room and curse.

If it weren't for that little vixen, right now he could be—where? Arguing with his father at Ashwicke Park? Alone in the partially furnished study at Coverly? In Kendal with a charming but idealized Cyprian? Cranford threw himself on the bed and glared at the ceiling. After a while he picked up the book and began to read, shutting his mind to any external thoughts and hardly aware that there were no Bavarian princes or daredevil captains in the story. There was plenty of food for thought.

As he was ordinarily an early riser, the footman did not hesitate to knock on his door at half past nine the next morning. Unfortunately, Cranford had read very late, falling asleep as the candle guttered, and had expected the luxury of sleeping until noon. Grumpily he called, "What is it?"

"A letter, sir. Marked urgent."

The first thing that occurred to him was that it was from Lady Babthorpe, castigating him for not appearing at her summons the previous evening, but the thought of Lady Babthorpe up and writing letters at this hour of the morning was ludicrous. His second thought alarmed him. "Bring it in!" Cranford had broken the seal and unfolded the sheet before the footman closed the door after himself.

> Dear Cranford: I am in immediate need of the money I left with you. Could you bring it to Henrietta Street this morning? If you have used the money as I asked, then I will approach Mama for a loan, so please bring at least twenty guineas of her money or mine with you. Should it be inconvenient for you to call, could you arrange to have it sent by

messenger? I regret causing you any inconvenience and am your most obedient servant

Trelenny

At least the little baggage wasn't in any irretrievable scrape, though God knew twenty guineas was hardly chicken feed. Cranford was aware that they had gone to a card party the previous evening and had no doubt she had lost the money gambling. Well, he'd done a lot worse his first evening at the card tables, he thought indulgently, and in all the years he had known her she had shown no unbridled gambling tendencies, so she was likely to be none the worse for her experience. A cautioning word might be in order, but he was certainly not the one to give it. He leaped out of bed and began to dress himself, though he couldn't remember for the life of him where he'd put his boots.

Trelenny had been standing at the breakfast parlor window for half an hour when she saw him come striding down the street. With a great deal of foresight she had sent her mother off shopping with Alice and had instructed the porter to show Cranford in to her, but now she almost shrank from meeting him. It would have been better if he'd sent the money by messenger. Maybe he wouldn't let her have it!

When he entered the room, his straight black hair impeccably groomed and the absurd black cravat tied in the most elaborate of styles, Trelenny hesitantly offered her hand and fearfully met his eyes.

"Trouble, Trelenny?"

"No, it's just . . . well, yes, I suppose you would think so. I wrote several chits last night when I was playing at cards, and I wish to redeem them as soon as may be. Have you brought the money?"

"Of course. I told you I would hold it for you."

"Thank you, Cranford. Would you like to sit down?"

He nodded and she led the way to the windowseat, where she perched on the edge and he leaned back and draped one long leg over the other. "Can I ring for tea for you?"

"No, thank you."

"I was afraid you'd be angry about the gambling."

"I've done a fair amount myself, Trelenny."

"Mrs. Waplington told me to play for modest stakes and excuse myself if the play got over my head, but I had a hard time doing that."

"Sometimes it's difficult."

"I shall be more cautious in future."

"I'm sure you will."

She lifted suspicious eyes from regarding her hands. "Cranford, why are you being so nice to me?"

A chuckle escaped him. "I suppose because I have grown used to your hair."

"Have you? I'm so glad. I think Mama has, too. Someday I will let it grow long again, when I'm old—thirty or so—but I like it this way. You're not angry anymore?"

"I never should have been. Forgive me." His dark eyes searched her face.

"Oh, Cranford, there's nothing to forgive." This was not what she had expected from him, but now the opportunity had come she clenched her hands tightly in her lap and said, "I shouldn't have teased you about that book. No one ever said there were princes and captains in it."

"There aren't. I should buy you a copy; I think you'd like it."

"You're reading it?"

"Yes, I borrowed it from someone. Trelenny, I've been itching to have a good ride. If I hired us some hacks, would you come riding with me this afternoon?"

A light flamed in her eyes and then died. "I can't. I'm . . . expecting a caller."

"I see. Well, it was just a thought." He stood up and dug her purse from his coat pocket. "You won't have much left. Can I lend you something?"

"I'll do well enough, but it's kind of you to offer."

"It's a standing offer, Trelenny." When he placed the purse in her hand he pressed her fingers firmly about it. "Are you enjoying yourself?"

"How could one not with so many exciting activities every day?" In her own ears her laugh rang hollow, but he did not seem to notice. "I've met dozens of people and everyone has been so thoughtful. They tell me Bath is nothing compared to London, but it's quite enough for me! And you?"

"I prefer London, but there's good company here this year."

"I like your friends: Lord Rissington, Mr. Bodford and ... Lady Jane."

Cranford could not fathom the peculiar look with which she accompanied this remark, but it moved him and he rumpled her golden halo affectionately. "And they like you, dear girl. Would you be willing to give up your gay social whirl to come to the theatre with Jane and me tonight?"

"No! That is, we are promised to the Wistows for dinner and a musical evening. Mama is especially looking forward to it."

"Another time perhaps. You haven't been to the theatre yet, have you?"

"No, and I should very much like to go but ..."

"As I said, another time. Goodbye, Trelenny. Give my best to your mother."

"I will." Clutching the purse to her breast, she watched him leave the room with a feeling of desolation, and ran to the window to follow his progress down the street. There was time to practice on the pianoforte before Mr. Rowle came.

chapter nineteen

Mrs. Storwood had returned from her shopping expedition in high spirits. "I have found the most enchanting reticule for you—shaped like a shell with a silver chàin. And tomorrow you must come with me to see the terry velvet boots. I feel sure they would be a perfect match for your brown levantine silk pelisse."

"Didn't you find anything for yourself?"

"Dear me, yes. Where is the package from White's? Ah, see for yourself. A white crape fan embroidered in silver, point lace lappets, and most beautiful black limeric gloves. There was a bonnet of black crape over black sarcenet, but I could not be sure it was suitable for me. The crown has twisted rouleaux of black crepe, crosswise, and the brim is lined with double white crape, with a black feather ornament in front."

"It sounds delightful."

"Yes, but a full bow of crape ties under the chin and I was not *sure* that my neck is quite long enough to support such a detail." She sighed. "Perhaps it is for a younger woman. I shall let you decide when you come with me. Madame Elise said it was enchanting but you know how these women are. They will flatter anyone into buying their most outrageously expensive hats. Not that I'm worried about the full brim, for it is so perfectly shaped as to provide almost a cameo effect. Well, there, you shall see it when we go shopping together. Have there been any callers this morning?"

"Cranford came by. He said to give you his regards."

Mrs. Storwood's countenance took on a slightly anxious cast. "You didn't quarrel with him, did you, love?"

"No, of course not. Actually, he was very pleasant, and invited me to accompany him and Lady Jane to the theatre this evening, but I told him we were engaged to the Wistows."

"Oh. With Lady Jane? Yes, I quite understand. Well, she's a fine young lady. Do you think we should call on her?"

"No, Mama. I have been to Queen Square, you will remember, but if you wish I will have Cranford mention to her that we would be pleased if she would call on us."

"Much the best, dear. You are quite right. Are we expecting anyone this afternoon?"

"Mr. Rowle said he would call."

In Mrs. Storwood's mind there was no comparison between Mr. Rowle and Cranford and she made no comment on this news. The young man was entertaining, presentable and polished, but she could not altogether like him, though try as she would she could not put her finger on the reason. Now with Mr. Bodford one could more easily explain a disinclination. Although he had recovered some ground in her eyes after the scene in the parlor, she could not feel easy on the score of an attachment developing between him and Trelenny. They were too alike in many ways, and he hadn't the authority to channel her spirits in a proper direction. No such objection could be made to Lord Rissington, it was true, but Mrs. Storwood had been warned about his penchant for flirting and never coming to the sticking point. And there was a certain levity about him which, endearing as it might be to her daughter, did not sit quite the same way with her.

It was gratifying, of course, to find Trelenny so well accepted, but Mrs. Storwood was almost relieved that her daughter did not appear in the least inclined to make a push for any of the young men. Not that Trelenny would ever be so vulgar as to toss her cap at anyone, but there were ways of letting a gentleman know that you would listen to an offer—the manner in which one dropped one's eyes or used one's fan. Of course, it was entirely possible that Trelenny contained no such artifice, but Mrs. Storwood believed implicitly that all females were endowed with the means to convey their wishes with never a word spoken. More likely Trelenny had no desire to encourage any one of the gentlemen, which was all for the best. Though with Cranford's defection and the time short until returning to Westmorland ... Mrs. Storwood was brought out of her reverie by the arrival of Mr. Rowle, who suggested that they might like to walk in the Sydney Gardens with him.

"We've not been there," Trelenny declared immediately, "and I have been longing to see them. They're only a step away, Mama. Should you like to go?"

Her daughter's eagerness always weighed with her, and though Mrs. Storwood would have been perfectly content with a nap after her morning's shopping, she consented. They had scarcely entered the gardens than she met an old friend and fell into conversation. This was the opportunity Mr. Rowle sought, and after a conspiratorial glance at Trelenny politely asked, "Would you object to my showing Miss Storwood about the gardens? We could meet you here at the arbor in half an hour."

"Yes, you two run along. I'd as soon sit here in the sun with Mrs. Lyegrove."

As they walked off together Trelenny said, "Mama has been shopping all morning. I really should not have pressed her to come with us."

"But then she wouldn't have allowed you to come, which would have sadly cast me down."

"Are the gardens such a treat then? I have heard there are concerts and illuminations and fireworks at night."

"For the daytime there are pleasant walks, the Merlin grottoes and the labyrinth, bowling greens, and swings."

"A labyrinth? Oh, I should like to see that. Do you know the key?"

"Yes, but I promise I won't tell you. You shall have the pleasure of finding your own way to the center."

"When I was young I tried to talk Papa into planting a labyrinth, but he said I would have outgrown it by the time the plants grew."

"I can't imagine he would want to give over the space a labyrinth would take."

"Pooh! Papa has thousands of acres and could well afford the space."

"I understand it's too mountainous to grow much."

"Ah, now there you suffer from a popular misconception, Mr. Rowle. There are dozens of fruitful valleys on Papa's lands and pasture for sheep and cattle in the mountains. Papa can let enclosed land at a guinea an acre, and good grass for more. His tenants grow wheat, barley, and oats and keep swine as well as milch cows and sheep."

"I hope he hasn't many tenants. What with his health so precarious that would be a great nuisance."

"I doubt he has more than four dozen tenant farms," Trelenny said casually, swinging her bonnet by its strings, "but he has an estate manager and two assistants to see to any matters that arise."

"You must have been lonely growing up here. I don't believe you have any brothers or sisters?"

"No, but Clare was not so far away—Cranford's sister, you know. I can't think what I would have done without her!"

"So Mr. Ashwicke lives very close to you?"

"His father, Viscount Chessels, owns the land to the north of Papa's but Cranford doesn't live there anymore. He has what Mr. Bodford calls a camomile patch in Sussex."

"I can see what appeal Lady Jane holds for him. There can be no argument that she will come with a large portion."

Trelenny regarded him coldly. "Cranford and Lady Jane have a great deal in common."

"So much the better!" He grinned engagingly. "I see his friends Rissington and Bodford are up to their old tricks."

"Tricks? How so?"

Mr. Rowle gave a rueful laugh. "Perhaps I shouldn't tell you. Some young ladies would be hurt by their game. I think you are made of sterner stuff, of course, and would see the amusing side of their prank. But still . . ."

"Come, Mr. Rowle, you cannot go so far and leave me suspended. What trick is it they play?"

"I should have said nothing," he offered, a sheepish expression on his face. "It's just . . . well, I should not like to see you harmed in any way, and I think perhaps they do not realize the gravity of the pain they could inflict."

"Really, whatever can you mean?" Alarm rose in Trelenny's eyes.

"You must not let on that I've told you! Honor among men and all that, Miss Storwood! I think I have a duty to tell you, though, and my own happiness may be at stake."

Trelenny blushed and looked down at the path.

"I've seen them do it before, you understand, or I would

merely think it coincidence. Last year a country girl came to town just as you did—for a short stay and under the chaperonage of only her mother. Both of them immediately fell into paying a great deal of attention to her, vying for her affections, as it were. They made a contest of the whole affair: who could win her heart first? Although I never actually heard them say so, I believe there was a wager riding on the outcome. Not that they had any intention of offering for her! On the other hand, you must not think that their intentions were *dis*honorable in the sense of ... well, you know what I mean. It was just a game. When it came time for the girl to leave town, they had an impartial judge determine who was the winner. There was—well, pardon my saying so—but a sort of scoring card: how many dances she gave one, how many languishing looks the other, that sort of thing. Rissington won hands down, of course. But I always felt sorry for the poor girl, thinking that one of them would offer for her." Mr. Rowle halted abruptly and surveyed Trelenny's shocked countenance. "I *knew* I shouldn't have told you! Nothing could be further from my intent than to upset you, Miss Storwood."

"No, no, I appreciate your consideration, Mr. Rowle. What a despicable thing to do! I would never have believed them possible of such villainy." Trelenny allowed her lower lip to tremble just the slightest bit. "Wretched girl! How I feel for her."

"I made sure you would enter into my sentiments in the matter, dear girl. Your sensibility does you honor. But don't repine. Forewarned is forearmed. I remember the snickers when Miss Ponsonby left town and I thought them dreadfully callous. For a week I stayed away from every assembly and concert because I could not bear such contemptuous ridicule. The poor girl was not to blame for her lack of sophistication. She had spent all her life in the country and had no idea how cruel and heartless society can be. *I* never heard anyone sympathize with her, I promise you."

"I am sure you felt just as you ought, and the others should be ashamed of themselves," Trelenny remarked fervently.

They had entered the maze and Mr. Rowle placed a hand on her arm, his eyes grave. "Please don't misunderstand me, Miss Storwood. The situation is not the same with you!

Anyone with eyes can see your beauty; anyone with a grain of perception can appreciate your charm; anyone with the least pretention to *ton* can recognize your innate poise, your refinement, your natural grace. Your innocence is not that of rusticity but of ingenuousness." He shook his head wonderingly. "To find such spirit and such sensibility in one woman! Such understanding and amiability. I had not thought it possible."

"You flatter me, Mr. Rowle." Trelenny nervously clasped her hands together and stared at the top button on his coat, which was gold and glittered in the afternoon sunlight.

"No," he said gruffly, "I fail to express even the hundredth part. Come, walk with me. I have never told you of my adventures in the West Indies. Should you like to hear of the day I encountered a ferocious beast or sailed into a smuggling ring?"

Trelenny was all rapt attention, her eyes aglow with admiration. "Oh, tell me them both," she breathed.

As he regaled her with anecdotes they wandered aimlessly (or so it seemed) through the maze. They passed several other strollers, but he was so wrapped up in the telling and she in the hearing of his exploits that they paid no attention to anyone else. At length Mr. Rowle looked about him with a bemused expression. "I'm afraid I've mistaken the way," he said ruefully.

"No matter." Trelenny opened the reticule which swung from her arm and extracted twenty guineas, while he watched, frowning. "I should like to repay my debt now, Mr. Rowle, before we return to Mama. It *was* twenty, was it not?"

"Well, yes," he said hesitantly, making no attempt to take the money.

"I was sure it was." She stood with both hands full, held out to him.

He muttered what might have been an oath and waved the coins aside. "I can't take your money."

"But you must! A gambling debt is a debt of honor and I would never renege on such a thing. Come, take them."

Reluctantly he emptied first one hand and then the other, dumping the coins in his coat pockets where they jangled against one another cheerfully. "Never again will I allow myself to be put in such a position," he said fiercely as he wiped his hands against his pantaloons as though to remove the taint of the money.

"You make too much of the matter, my dear sir. What is twenty guineas?"

So moved by her generous attitude that he could not express himself, he caught her lightly to him and kissed her. "Dearest of creatures! Most remarkable of women! How does it come about that one of your tender years has such nobility?" And because she made no protest, either of his kiss or his effusions, he kissed her again.

An ominous voice roared from a short distance away. "Trelenny! Where the devil is your mother?"

Showing no sign of embarrassment, Trelenny turned to where Cranford stood with Lady Babthorpe at the edge of the hedges. "She's with Mrs. Lyegrove in an arbor near the entrance, Cranford. Had you some particular need to see her?"

"I have a very particular desire to take you to her," he growled with a scathing glance at Mr. Rowle, who had uncomfortably backed away.

"But we have not reached the center of the maze yet!"

"It does not appear that you are likely to. This is about as far from it as you could get."

"Then what are you doing here?" she asked impudently, her eyes covertly surveying Lady Babthorpe.

The lady chose to be amused. "Our intent was much the same as yours, Miss Storwood—a little privacy."

"Well, Mr. Rowle and I will leave you to it," Trelenny replied with dignity. She inclined her head very slightly to Lady Babthorpe and threw Cranford a look of profound disapproval before adjusting the reticule on her arm and preparing to depart.

"*I* will take you to your mother, Trelenny," Cranford announced, "to see that you don't lose your way again."

Trelenny turned to Lady Babthorpe and Mr. Rowle, the former watching with amusement and the latter with displeasure. "If you would excuse us a moment, I would like a word alone with Cranford." Imperatively she beckoned him to follow her around the hedges, out of sight of the others. "You are making a scene, Cranford. Shame on you! If you take me back to Mama it will only upset her, for you are sure to be so

Friday-faced that she will assume something is amiss. *Nothing* could be further from the truth."

"Have you sunk so far as to consider allowing that jackanapes to kiss you a commonplace, my girl?" he demanded furiously.

"Don't be so stuffy, Cranford. There's no harm in it. In fact, I rather liked it." Her eyes danced mischievously at the thunderous lowering of his brows. "Didn't you bring Lady Babthorpe here to kiss her?"

"No, I did not!"

"Tsk, tsk. I cannot believe you are telling me the whole truth, sir. However, I will not impugn your word, as I know that makes you quite liverish. Cranford, have you any faith in my understanding?" When he seemed at a loss how to answer, she laughed. "Mr. Rowle says I have an excellent understanding, but there, he doesn't know me so well as you do, does he? Believe me, I know precisely what I'm doing, Cranford, and I'm having a marvelous time, so don't spoil everything, will you? I promise you we will go straight back to Mama."

Irritated, upset, even a little hurt, Cranford stared at her impassively for some time. "Very well, see that you do."

Impulsively, she stood on tiptoe and kissed his cheek. "Thank you!" And then she was gone, leaving him to sort out the conflicting emotions which raged within him.

"I tell you, Jane, she's the veriest child! *You* know what he is, and there she was allowing him to kiss her with nary a protest. By God, she told me she rather liked it! For heaven's sake, please talk to her. She wouldn't listen to me; I put her back up. But she's like a toddler on the edge of a cliff and you can't be *sure* she has enough sense not to try to fly. You said yourself that he's a very plausible rogue. I can't *bear* to think what the consequences will be if she marries him."

"No," Lady Jane said thoughtfully, "that would be disastrous. I'll call on her first thing tomorrow morning and see what I can do. Cranford, have you allowed yourself to become involved with Lady Babthorpe again?"

For a moment she thought he would not answer her. The reserved look shuttered his eyes and a certain stiffness about his shoulders proclaimed his withdrawal, but after a moment he shrugged and shook his head. "No. I have lost my taste for that sort of intrigue. Forgive me. Am I speaking too bluntly, Jane?"

She smiled gently. "We've always spoken as brother and sister. It is I who am being impertinent, I fear, but it occurs to me that Miss Storwood could put a great significance on your being in the maze with her ladyship."

"Oh, she will, the little baggage."

Lady Jane pursed her lips reprovingly. "The appearance of evil . . . you have set yourself up as a model of propriety to Miss Storwood. She can hardly see anything wrong in her kissing Mr. Rowle if you are playing fast and loose with a married woman."

"I can't very well explain to Trelenny what I was doing there. Actually, I had refused an assignation and Drucilla waylaid me in Broad Street, spitting fire, and I thought it only fair to give her an opportunity to vent her rage—albeit in a more private location. Mr. Rowle knows precisely the same, unfrequented spot in the labyrinth."

"I'm not surprised. It's time we left for the theatre if we don't wish to be late."

"I invited Trelenny to go with us but she was engaged."

Lady Jane cast her eyes heavenward and said nothing.

chapter twenty

The weather turned chill and dreary overnight, and a light rain had begun to fall by the time Lady Jane arrived in Henrietta Street. She was laughing and shaking the drops from her shawl as she was shown into the first-floor sitting room where Trelenny was practicing while her mother painstakingly removed two rows of stitches from a pillow cover she was embroidering. "I think we are about to have a Bath winter after all. Good morning, Mrs. Storwood, Miss Storwood. Was that you I heard as I came up the stairs? Your playing has improved tremendously."

"I've been working on it a little," Trelenny admitted. "Do sit by the fire, Lady Jane. Mrs. Waplington says we've been lucky in our weather so far, and that this is much more normal."

"I fear she's right. It's difficult to get a chair when the rains come, though, and some of them leak, so be prepared! My father is always threatening to order a chair of our own and have the footmen carry me about. What exquisite work you do, Mrs. Storwood!"

Trelenny was vaguely aware during the ensuing conversation that Lady Jane was observing her, and it occurred to her, dishearteningly, that perhaps Lady Jane wished them to be alone so she might discuss Cranford. Although Trelenny had no desire to be her confidante, and had to steel herself to suggest it, after a while she said, "Lady Jane, I wonder if you would like to see the new reticule Mama bought me yesterday. It's rather unique and I was debating whether to purchase one for Clare."

Her guest accepted the invitation with alacrity and

surveyed Trelenny's room with dancing eyes. "A most unusual decor."

"Yes," Trelenny laughed. "Mrs. Waplington meant to remove the prints and replace them with dogs or scenes of Somerset, but she forgot. Her husband uses the room for *his* guests, apparently. I don't mind them; they're rather charming."

"They may, perhaps, have led you to believe that a gentleman kissing a lady is a very natural thing, which it is, of course, but society has seen fit to place restrictions on who may do so with propriety."

"Cranford told you! What a mean, underhanded thing to do! Did he tell you he was there with Lady Babthorpe?" Trelenny could have bit her tongue but it was too late.

"Yes, he did. Don't make too much of that, my dear Miss Storwood. In the past . . . well, he has assured me there is no current . . . Lord, it is so difficult to know just how to put it."

"I understand what you are saying, Lady Jane. You need never hesitate to be frank with me. Mama didn't want me to be an ignoramus about relations between men and women and explained things to me some time ago." Trelenny busied herself searching in the drawer for the reticule as she said, "Cranford is very open with you. I would never have expected him to be so forthcoming."

"We've been friends a long time. I asked him."

"He wouldn't have told me if I'd asked him. He'd have told me it was none of my business."

"Would he?" Lady Jane grinned as Trelenny returned to her. "I feel sure he was about to say the same to me but changed his mind. Is that the reticule? I don't know Clare so well as you do, of course, but I think she'd be enchanted with it. Where did your mother find it?"

"At White's. She said they had several."

"Miss Storwood, I'm not one for beating about the bush. There is something I feel I should tell you, and with your permission I will do so. I think it's very important, or I wouldn't impose so on you."

"Please sit down." Trelenny made a nervous gesture toward the chairs, a sinking feeling in her heart. "I appreciate your thoughtfulness, Lady Jane." She was too agitated to notice the curious glance her companion levelled at her.

"My father and I come to Bath perhaps once or twice a

year, Miss Storwood, and I have an oppotunity to meet quite a few people when we are here. Some of the acquaintances are superficial, of course, and I would not presume to judge character on the basis of them. Others, for one reason or another, one gains more knowledge of, and feels confident in appraising. I do not think I am hasty in my determinations; years of social intercourse have confirmed me in the opinion that it takes time to gauge the virtues and failings of our fellow human beings. Now I *am* beating about the bush, aren't I? Miss Storwood, I have every reason to believe that Mr. Rowle is a contemptible villain."

"I know."

Lady Jane regarded her with astonishment. "You know?"

"Yes, I have suspected it for some time, but I knew for sure the other night. He's what my groom would call 'a nasty bit o' goods.' Really, how naive did he think I was? I am an excellent card player, Lady Jane; even Cranford could not dispute that. Mr. Rowle and his friends set me up! How could he think I wouldn't know? I had given him credit for some intelligence, at least."

Her indignation was so real that Lady Jane fell into gales of laughter. "You naughty child! Were you leading him up the garden path, then?"

"Well, I thought he deserved it. Twenty guineas! The better part of my quarter's allowance. And now I shall have to wait until next quarter to give Cranford some money for the trip. Do you know that Mr. Rowle's Christian name is Morton? Now I ask you, have you ever known anything good of a man named Morton? I beg your pardon! This is being prematurely judgmental, is it not? Still, it gave me some indication."

"What is it you are trying to do to him, Miss Storwood?"

"I have led him to believe that I am a magnificent heiress. God will forgive me for a few exaggerations in a good cause, won't He? I quadrupled the size of my father's estate and augmented his staff a trifle. You should have seen Mr. Rowle's eyes shine! I had the most difficult time refraining from laughing. Do you think I shouldn't have let him kiss me? I have wondered what it was like to be kissed," she said wistfully. "And I do believe it encouraged him to think I would welcome an offer from him."

"I . . . I dare say."

"Yes, and that is precisely what I have in mind. Oh, it's the most famous joke, Lady Jane. For the next week I expect him to pay me the most assiduous attention, and then he will work up the courage to approach my mother. I don't think I should let her in on it, you know, because I so want him to ask me. And then I shall laugh in his face. That's wrong, I know, but he owes me twenty guineas' worth of amusement, and I promise you I expect a great deal for my twenty guineas. The conceited coxcomb!"

"I shouldn't laugh in his face if I were you," Lady Jane said consideringly. "If I were doing it—and I think it splendidly appropriate—I would act as though I were vastly surprised and displeased with his presumption. Miss Storwood, the great heiress, to consider Mr. Rowle as a husband? Surely he was reaching above himself! Something on that order."

Trelenny's eyes sparkled. "You have hit on the very thing. I shall be extremely dignified and haughty as though he were a stable boy approaching me for my hand. Oh, I shall be so disappointed if he doesn't offer!"

"I don't think you have to worry about that," Lady Jane said dryly. "Once Mr. Rowle has the scent very little would prevent him from being in at the kill."

"Now you aren't to tell Cranford. He would not approve, you know."

"But—"

"Please, Lady Jane. I have told you in confidence. Even Mama doesn't know."

Lady Jane hadn't the heart to deny Trelenny's urgent appeal. "Very well, my dear, but he will be worried about you."

"I'll just stay out of his way. When I'm not around he doesn't think about me or what trouble I may be getting up to." She hastily picked up the shell reticule and returned it to her drawer. "I'm glad you think Clare would like one, for I have meant to get her something while I was here, and I shall have enough left for it. I wonder if the letters have been brought from the receiving office yet? It may be that Papa will have us come home, and then I wouldn't have an opportunity to refuse Mr. Rowle."

"You might be leaving so soon? Cranford had not mentioned that."

Trelenny was unable to tell if the news distressed Lady

Jane, who was too well-bred to show more than mild surprise. "We are supposed to be here for another two weeks, almost, but my mother was disturbed about Papa, so it will depend on what he writes."

"I see." Lady Jane rose and pressed Trelenny's hand. "I hope all is well with your father, and that you will be able to make your whole stay. It would be sad for you to leave so soon."

The eagerly awaited letter did not arrive that morning, but the next, and Trelenny breathlessly listened as her mother read its contents. They were to stay! There never seemed to have been any question about it in anyone else's mind but her own! Mrs. Storwood sighed a great deal, and Cranford, who had called to take Trelenny riding if she were free, accepted the verdict as a foregone conclusion. What he could not accept so readily was Lady Jane's report on her interview with Trelenny. When he had asked if she had been able to convince the girl of Mr. Rowle's undesirable character, she would say no more than "Miss Storwood is miles ahead of us, Cranford. Just let her be; she knows what she's doing." Although he had a great deal of confidence in Lady Jane, and they had been friends for years, he could not accept this casual dismissal of a potentially tragic situation. And the more he pressed, the more reserved she became until they had nearly quarreled over the matter.

His presence in Henrietta Street the next morning was the result of another restless night. He was plagued by dreams in which Trelenny figured as Rowle's wife, impoverished by his reckless expenditures and careworn by his neglect of her. Yet again and again he saw them kissing, her piquant face lifted to his with eagerness, a dream which never failed to bring him awake, distraught. And there was no solace in the reading of *Emma*. The kinship he had felt for Mr. Knightley from the start continued through the last page; and the recognition of Emma as an older Trelenny, with glaring faults and lovable virtues, wrenched him from the state of nervous suspension in which he had existed for days. What he had considered impossible had happened—he had fallen in love with the little imp.

The knowledge was not to prove an alleviation of his discomfort, however. He was no closer than he had ever been to winning her consent to a match between them, and, when he viewed the situation as rationally as he was able, he was not sure such a match would be a good thing—for her. Could he trust himself not to squelch her liveliness, or depress her ebullient spirits? Would he make allowance for her youth and inexperience or demand a behavior in keeping with his own recently acquired respectability? Surely both Bodford and Rissington were more likely to make her happy. Well, not Bodford, perhaps; that would be the blind leading the blind. But Rissington? Was he serious this time? Trelenny's offhanded acceptance of his pursuit had piqued his interest, certainly, but that did not answer the question. Rissington had a facility for sliding through that narrow alley of escape which barely precedes the point of no return: that stage at which one has paid such obvious addresses to a young lady that it amounts to a breach of honor not to offer for her.

Apparently some of these questions were on Trelenny's mind as well, he decided unhappily as they took the Claverton Down Road beyond the New Canal. Her eyes sparkled from the gallop he had agreed to once they turned right from the Sydney Garden and came to open country. "How I've longed for a ride! Somehow I had not expected that life in town could be so devoid of that simple pleasure. Mr. Rowle offered to take me riding once, but I didn't think Mama would allow me. Which reminds me, Cranford. Is it customary for your friends Lord Rissington and Mr. Bodford to pay so much attention to the same lady? I heard a tale which I do not credit, I promise you, but there was a grain of truth in it, I think."

"What did you hear?"

"That last year they made sport of a Miss Ponsonby, to settle a wager as to which could engage her affections."

"I should hope you wouldn't believe anything of that nature," he replied sternly. "Rissington and Bodford do have an unfortunate penchant for finding the same ladies of interest, it is true, but I would stake my honor that they never did anything so reprehensible. I wasn't in Bath last year but I remember hearing that Hugh Ponsonby's sister came here with her mother. She was engaged to a Major Brewster, I believe, and has since married him, so I think your bit of gossip was a mere fabrication."

"Probably. I had it from a most unreliable source."
"Who?"

"Just an acquaintance. Cranford, Lord Rissington is known for his flirting, isn't he?"

Cranford wished to be scrupulously honest in his answer and yet not undermine his friend's reputation. "It might perhaps be more fair to say that he has not yet lived up to the speculation he often provokes when he dances attendance on a lady. The gossips are all too ready to see in his slightest attentions the food they need for a blossoming and entirely imaginary match. Rissington is just the sort of fellow the matchmakers can't resist leg-shackling every time he does the pretty." He frowned at a row of entirely innocuous beech trees. "That is not to say that at any time he might not find a woman with whom he would choose to spend his life. I have never heard him denigrate the married state; on the contrary, he speaks of it with the proper respect and honor."

Trelenny giggled. "Do you know how pompous you sound, Cranford? Wherever do you learn such stilted language? All I wanted to know was if Rissington was a flirt, and obviously he is."

"I didn't say that!" he protested, but with a grin. "Perhaps he is, but you're leading him a merry dance, so I doubt it matters. He's a good sort, Trelenny, and Bodford, too, but Mr. Rowle ... God knows I don't want to set your back up, but do you know who he is?"

"Should I?" she asked, drawing in her horse.

"He's Miss Moreby's stepbrother, and the reason she and Mr. Laytham found it necessary to elope to Gretna Green."

An enormous grin spread over her face, making her eyes dance and dimpling her cheeks. "Is that so? How wonderful! Perhaps I shall get my money's worth after all."

A horrid suspicion was growing in Cranford. "You have some mischief up your sleeve, don't you, Trelenny? God, I could find it in my heart to pity the poor devil! Come, my girl, what wild scheme are you hatching?"

"Nothing of any moment, Cranford. Don't press me! My lips are sealed," she announced, making the childish gesture of locking them and tossing the key away.

"You could catch cold at this, Trelenny. Don't underestimate Mr. Rowle, I beg you. Does Jane know what you are about?"

Instantly the funning left her. "She won't tell you. She promised."

"Yes, and we are scarcely speaking to each other because of it."

Sadly penitent, Trelenny lowered her eyes. "You mustn't blame her, Cranford. Even to one's ... friends it is wrong to break a confidence. You didn't force me to tell you something I shouldn't once, and how much more so should you respect Lady Jane's silence?"

He ran a hand distractedly through his hair. "I wish you would tell me what you're up to."

"You make too much of it, Cranford. It's just a lark. Shall we turn back?"

"If you wish."

"Have you seen the Roman antiquities?" she asked brightly. "Lady Jane and the Earl must know where they are to be found."

chapter twenty-one

Mrs. Storwood, hands clasped nervously at her bosom, entered the sitting room one morning several days later to announce in a quavering voice, "Mr. Rowle desires to speak with you, love. That is, I have said he may address you. What else could I say? Your father isn't here. We have only a short stay left! Pray don't be hasty in your answer! I think you would be wise to insist on his meeting your father first if you... Trelenny, has he won your heart? I *cannot* be easy about him, try as I will. Don't see this as your only chance, I beg you. I have already determined to see that you get about more in Westmorland. And something could perhaps be arranged—"

Trelenny interupted her. "Hush, love. I have no intention of accepting Mr. Rowle, but you mustn't let on."

"You don't... Oh. I am so relieved. Shall I send him away?"

"Heavens, no! It is clearly my duty to see him; only then will he realize how determined is my refusal. You must give no sign to him of my answer, Mama."

"Yes, well, if that is your wish, dear."

Mr. Rowle's demeanor was nicely arranged to convey his respect, his hopes, and his nervousness on such a momentous occasion. Trelenny rose from her seat at the pianoforte to give him her hand, which he lifted to his lips for a fleeting moment. "How kind of you to call, Mr. Rowle."

"Did your mother not hint at my errand?" he asked, surprised.

"Should she have?"

"Why, no, not necessarily. I have the greatest admiration

for your mother and have no doubt she thought the matter best discussed between us without any comment forthcoming from her." This thought seemed to give him a great deal of satisfaction; in his eyes it spelled her accord with the match. "You could not have failed to note the development of my regard for you these past weeks, Miss Storwood. I fear I am not so artful as to have been able to hide it from you." He offered a deprecating grin.

Unmoved, Trelenny said, "Won't you sit down, Mr. Rowle?"

If this mundane comment gave him pause, he showed no sign. It was just the sort of inane remark a young girl would make to cover her confusion. Although he would have preferred her to sit with him on the sofa, the very fact that she chose to perch herself rigidly on a white and gold Greek chair of no notable comfort encouraged him to think that she did not trust herself in too close quarters with him. He smiled lovingly. "I have no need, I think, to tell you how I admire your understanding and amiability. Have I been remiss in mentioning your obvious beauty? I won't say that it doesn't weigh with me, but it pales into insignificance when compared with your noble spirit. Such goodness of heart is a rare quality, Miss Storwood, and to be prized above all else."

Trelenny wore a perplexed frown. "I am sure you are all graciousness to say so, Mr. Rowle, but is it not a trifle... presumptuous of you? My mother would not, I fear, wish me to listen to such encomiums from so recent an acquaintance."

He leaped to his feet and possessed himself of her hands. "You do not understand, my dear! I mean no disrespect. Quite the opposite, I assure you. My errand—nay, my mission in life!—is to make you my wife."

"Your wife!" Trelenny stared horror-stricken at his supplicating face. "Marry you? What can you be thinking of?" She tore her hands from his grip and, rising, walked agitatedly about the room. "My dear Mr. Rowle! I am an heiress, of a very old and distinguished family. It is my understanding that you have no more than a house in Bath. No estate, nothing. In fact, the house here is your father's and already inhabited by several people. You cannot seriously expect me to consider aligning myself with you. Why, I have every intention of forming a brilliant alliance, establishing a dynasty!" she informed him majestically. "I have enjoyed your company during my stay here and would not for the world cause you any distress, of course. Had I realized that you would presume to regard our acquaintance in such a light... Ah, I believe I understand. You are teasing me, aren't you, as you often do?"

A dull red suffused his face and he found it difficult to speak. "I do not consider the discussion of matrimony a matter for jesting, Miss Storwood. I thought you shared my... that is, you have led me to believe that you found me acceptable."

"As a companion during my holiday! You have paid tribute to me, as others have, and I sincerely thank you for entertaining me! I don't deny that you have made my stay an amusing one. For marriage, though, I must look a great deal higher than you!"

Angry sparks darted from his eyes. "Did it amuse you then to let me kiss you?"

"I thought it would." She sighed, meeting his eyes with a pitying gaze. "Perhaps your ardor is not what you imagine it, Mr. Rowle, for I can imagine a brother kissing a sister just so. I wouldn't be discouraged, though, for you may yet meet a woman who arouses some passion in you."

For a moment she thought she had gone too far. He clenched his fists at his sides and muttered through narrowed lips, "I doubt you know a great deal about the matter, Miss Storwood. If you have hopes that Lord Rissington or Mr. Bodford will offer for you, I fear you are sadly disillusioned."

"Offer for me? Why, of course not! Did you not yourself inform me how they treated poor Miss Ponsonby? I have standards, Mr. Rowle!" she informed him in a slightly raised voice. "Not only do I expect to ally myself with a man of birth, breeding, and fortune, but integrity as well."

"It is Mr. Ashwicke you have in mind, then?" he asked sweetly.

"God forbid! Did you not see him in the gardens with a married woman? Do you think it has not come to my attention that he has behaved in a most unbecoming manner with her? Let another carry such a burden about with her. The man I marry must come with a spotless reputation!"

"I hope you don't think my own reputation..." He

allowed the sentence to fade away, assuming in his turn a dignity born of experience and determination.

"I promise you I have not so much as considered your reputation, Mr. Rowle. Since you are not qualified on any other... on other accounts, it was wholly unnecessary. If I have in my inexperience led you to believe that I would welcome this offer from you, I must humbly beg your pardon. Not for the world would I foster such a hope in a man's breast where there is no possibility of his achieving his goal. You must admit that you have given no indication of serious intent. As with the others, there has been a great deal of high spirits and teasing, which we have all enjoyed, have we not? Not so do I see the man whom I shall marry. He will have dignity and reserve, a thorough understanding of politics and religion, very little taste for the senseless life of the *ton* and a desire to cater to my extravagant whims."

"And where do you expect to meet this man?" Mr. Rowle asked, his polite tone tinged with sarcasm. "In your Westmorland backwater?"

"Well, he might seek me out there; I imagine my fame will spread from Bath, don't you? However, I consider it more likely that I will meet him in London."

"I thought it was impossible for you to go to London because of your father's condition."

"Did you? I see. And you assumed that if I had not found a partner here in Bath, I would take any partner who suggested himself? A lowering thought."

Mr. Rowle was at the limit of his resources and his temper. With an exaggerated bow, he said coldly, "I am sorry if I have imposed upon you, Miss Storwood. I confess to having had no idea of the heights to which you aspire." She smiled benevolently on his sneer, further discomposing him. "If you will excuse me..."

"Certainly, Mr. Rowle. I do hope I shall see you at the Cosgroves' this evening."

As Mr. Rowle made his exit, blackly scowling, Cranford entered the house in Henrietta Street and allowed Mrs. Storwood to take him to the sitting room, where they found Trelenny convulsed with giggles. She covered her mouth and pressed her side, but could not control them well enough to offer Cranford a welcome. When she had recovered sufficiently, as she was forced to do under their reproving stares, she gasped, "It was worth the money, every penny of it. Did you see him?" Another burst of giggles overtook her. "And I never laughed in his face. Lady Jane was quite right; it was much more rewarding this way."

Mrs. Storwood, shocked out of her usual patience, said sharply, "I cannot see anything the least amusing in refusing an offer, Trelenny. You should be ashamed of yourself."

"Dear Mama, please don't be cross. He fleeced me out of twenty guineas, and he had every minute of his put-down coming to him. Imagine his thinking he could cozzen me into marrying him."

Although Cranford had understood a great deal more of Trelenny's remarks than her mother had, he could not feel easy about the situation. "Just what did you tell him, Trelenny?"

Under the piercing black eyes, all her amusement deserted her and she collapsed onto the sofa with a sigh. Instead of answering him directly, she sought her mother's eyes and said, "You will remember the card party at which I lost some money. Well, it amounted to more than twenty guineas and I knew that Mr. Rowle and his friends were not playing fairly with me. I couldn't say anything at the time and I found it difficult to leave their table. The long and short of it is, Mama, that I let him think me a great heiress so that he would offer for me, and I could refuse him. Lady Jane didn't think it wrong of me," she said with a defiant glare at Cranford. "It was much the same sort of thing you had her do that night Lord Babthorpe caused such a rumpus here at the card table."

Cranford was not impressed. "Lady Jane is a great deal more experienced than you in dealing with such people. What suggestion did she make?"

"I had intended to laugh at him, and she said it would be better to act surprised at his presumption, as though he were reaching too far above himself."

"Which he was," Cranford muttered.

Mrs. Storwood had resorted to her handkerchief, but not her vinaigrette. "I think, dear, that you would have been wisest to have had Cranford simply warn him off. Not that I condone what he did! Mr. Rowle has shown himself an unconscionable reprobate, but I'm afraid you are only too willing to indulge in such adventures, love. It would be a great deal more becoming in you to keep a distance from such a person and remain aloof from an escapade in which you do not show to advantage."

The censure, perhaps, was mild but having it delivered in front of Cranford made Trelenny feel like a naughty child, and an embarrassed flush stained her cheeks. "Yes, Mama. Would you excuse me?"

Her mother nodded, but Cranford stayed her with a hand on her arm. "Might I have a word with Trelenny before I go, Mrs. Storwood?"

Since another of Mrs. Storwood's firm beliefs was that men had a great deal more influence than women, she welcomed Cranford's intervention. A word from him would set Trelenny straight almost as well as one from the girl's father, she decided as she left the two of them together.

Trelenny stood with downcast head, biting her lip to still its trembling. Only when the door had closed did Cranford shake his head ruefully and laugh. "Dear God, I wish I could have overheard the whole scene!"

Startled, she lifted moist eyes to his face and said indignantly, "I thought you were angry with me."

"I am," he protested, still grinning. "What you did was brash, outrageous, and I would have expected nothing less of you. You are two of a kind, you and Jane, with too much liveliness for your own good." He withdrew a handkerchief from his pocket and patted her eyes. "Would that my words of censure had such an effect on you. Then I wouldn't have to be forever threatening you with dire consequences. Trelenny, I quite understand why you treated Mr. Rowle as you did; and I can't say that I, in the same position, would not have done the same, but I don't trust him not to cause trouble. You have given him a set-down that is bound to rankle, and he is just the type to spread some vicious rumor about you. It was he who told you that cock-and-bull story about Rissington and Bodford, wasn't it?"

"Yes, but I didn't believe it."

"And many people wouldn't believe a lie about you, but some would, and I can't view the possibility with any complacency. I'll keep an ear open."

"Thank you, Cranford. I didn't mean to cause you any trouble." She watched him return his handkerchief to his pocket. "You ... you won't be angry with Lady Jane, will you?"

"No, silly, I won't be angry with Jane." He rumpled her hair, smiling gently. "I have wanted to talk to you—"

The door flew open and Mrs. Waplington, beaming with pleasure and followed by a flustered Mrs. Storwood, hastened into the room. "The most wonderful thing has happened, Trelenny. Andrew must go to London for a month! How do you do, Mr. Ashwicke?"

Uncertain how to respond to such a greeting, Trelenny cast an enquiring look at her mother, who hesitantly took up the tale. "Mr. Waplington must leave for London next week on pressing business, and he plans to remain there a month. Elsa would like to take you with them and give you a taste of town life. I don't know what your Papa would say, but it seems too good an opportunity to be wasted. Cranford could escort me home, as we had planned, and Elsa would arrange for an escort for you when it was time for you to return to Sutton Hall. It's what you've dreamed of, I know, and possibly the only chance you will have."

Trelenny's eyes had glowed at the mention of going to London, but now they clouded. "Without you, Mama? Or Cranford?"

"I've promised your father I will return after our stay here, my love."

Mrs. Waplington gave a throaty chuckle. "You needn't worry, Trelenny. I shall take as good care of you as even your mother would. Ah, you'll love London. And after the success you've had here, who knows? I could ask for no greater treat than to introduce you to society, my dear. Well, aren't you thrilled?"

"I . . . yes! It's just that I can hardly believe my good fortune, ma'am. You have no idea how I have dreamed of such a chance." Trelenny clasped her mother's hands. "Is it truly all right with you? You won't fret or be miserable while I'm gone?"

"How can I when I know you are happy?" Mrs. Storwood declared stoutly. "There isn't time to write your father but I think he would agree, don't you, Cranford?"

Appealed to in such a way, Cranford resolutely put aside his own feelings and said, "Yes. He could have no objection to the scheme when Mrs. Waplington herself will be responsible for Trelenny." So easily it was settled, but of the four only Mrs. Waplington knew unalloyed joy at the prospect.

If Mr. Rowle spread any rumors about Trelenny, Cranford did not hear them. His decision to speak to her seemed premature in the face of her proposed journey to London. Let her have all the chances she could to find happiness before he approached her with his own proposal, he counseled himself in the darkness of his room at nights. If Rissington or Bodford followed her to London . . .

These were matters he did not discuss with Lady Jane. If he was preoccupied in her company, she never mentioned the fact. Her delight at Trelenny's coup with Rowle was untempered by his own sense of caution. "I hope you didn't scold her, Cranford. For myself, I would have given a great deal to be there when he offered."

"So would I," he admitted. "Her mother said anything that was necessary on the occasion, and I merely pointed out that he might take an ugly revenge for such callous handling."

"I hadn't thought of that. Well, Miss Storwood has enough champions to set the record straight, so I think we needn't worry."

But Cranford did worry—from a distance. He continued to escort Lady Jane, occasionally relieving Mr. Wheldrake, but that gentleman was more than willing to accompany the Storwoods; and when he was not available, Mr. Waplington unfailingly stood in. Cranford noted that Mr. Rowle managed to avoid most of the entertainments to which the Storwoods went, but that he made no effort to efface himself in any other way. As the time for Trelenny's departure for London drew closer, Cranford began to believe that his fears had had no basis.

The night of the Stanmores' ball, he was not engaged to either the Storwoods or Lady Jane as escort and he determined to stop in at the White Hart for any mail which might have arrived since last he was there. An invitation to join a friend for a glass expanded into an hour of reminiscing about their younger days, and he was just on the point of departing when an arrival caught his attention. There was something familiar about the fellow's face and unusual height, though in the dim hallway light he could not for a moment place him. When the landlord made a gesture toward Cranford, the gentleman turned and approached him with outstretched hand. "I am in luck, I see. I had hardly dared hope to still find you here."

"Mr. Laytham! I trust your journey was successful."

"Thanks to you and your friend," the young man said with a smile. He gave instructions for his luggage to be carried up to a room and asked for a private parlor. "Won't you join me for a moment? I can see you're dressed for a formal occasion, but I beg you will allow me to return what is yours."

The parlor to which they were shown was on the first floor overlooking the street, a snug room with the privacy Mr. Laytham deemed necessary for their conversation. When two glasses had been set before them and the waiter had withdrawn, he proposed a toast. "To Miss Storwood and Mr. Ashwicke, without whose assistance my wife and I could not have managed." He stared at the glass for a moment after he had taken a sip, then set it down and pulled from his pocket a purse, which he handed to Cranford. "I was asking the landlord your direction so that I might return this, with all the thanks that are due you. That night shall always live with me as a symbol of horror... and of the miraculous. May I be struck down if ever I ignore an opportunity to help a fellow being in trouble!"

Cranford accepted the purse and set it before him. "I trust Mrs. Laytham is well."

"Quite. I have left her with my family near Salisbury. She insisted that I come to search you out as soon as she was settled there. I have a letter from her to Miss Storwood, too, in my valise. Would you mind waiting while I get it?"

"Not at all."

He returned in a few minutes to place the sealed sheet beside the purse. "Caroline has a great deal of sensibility and credits Miss Storwood with preserving her sanity that night. As I told you at the time, nothing but the most dire necessity would ever have forced me into such a decision as to elope, not only because of society's view of such a̶ ̶t̶i̶o̶n̶, but because Caroline herself strongly felt the imp̶ ̶i̶e̶t̶y̶ of what she was doing. Alas, we had no choice. Her stepfather and stepbrother had gone to Cambridge to arrange the marriage settlement with her guardian, who had no inkling that Caroline was an unwilling partner to the treaty. Her own mother is unable to withstand the pressure her husband brings to bear on her and has, I fear, been treated to his temper for having allowed my wife to escape."

"Have you been to the Rowles'?"

"I've just come from there." Mr. Laytham drew a weary hand across his brow. "I had hoped to effect a reconciliation with her mother, at least, if not with her stepfather, but he would listen to nothing I had to say, and refused to let me talk alone with his wife."

"And the stepbrother?"

"He ignored me when I arrived, but I saw him later in the stables, ordering his traveling carriage."

"His traveling carriage?" Cranford's voice was sharp. "Do you know where he was going?"

"I have no idea," Mr. Laytham replied, surprised by the intensity of Cranford's regard.

"Tell me precisely what you saw and heard."

"I had left my horse there when I went in to see Mr. and Mrs. Rowle, and when I came to get it his horses were being put to the traveling carriage. Before he saw me I heard him insist on another rug and that the basket of food be put in the carriage rather than on the box with the coachman."

"Did he make any reference to a traveling companion?" Cranford was on his feet now, quickly thrusting the purse and letter into the pocket of his greatcoat.

Confused, Laytham tried to recall anything which might have given an indication. "No. Wait a moment! When the coachman mentioned a stain on the squabs, Rowle said something like, 'Don't bother with it. She won't notice in the dark.' Does that mean something?"

"Does he have a mistress?"

"None that I ever heard of."

"Oh, God. And there was no mention of where he was heading?" Cranford pulled on his gloves and headed for the door, pausing for the answer.

"Only a stop in the Crescent, not the destination."

"Damn him! Now listen carefully, Laytham. I need your help."

"I'm at your service." The young man was immediately on his feet.

"Mr. Rowle has offered for Miss Storwood and been turned down, and not in a manner which was likely to conciliate him. He believes her to be a great deal more of an heiress than she is, and your return is likely to presage his fall from grace in Bath. This hotbed of rumors won't spare him in any way. If the whole story isn't known, it can be invented, and not to his credit. He'll have no more foothold in society.

What you've told me leads me to believe that he intends to abduct Miss Storwood from the Stanmore ball in the Crescent. I may be wrong but I don't care to take a chance. I have to know where they're going if I don't get there before he makes off with her. Will you go to the Rowles' stables and find out what you can? Then come directly to the Crescent." He dug the purse out of his pocket again. "Here. Use what you have to to get the information you need." Before Laytham could agree, he was gone.

chapter twenty-two

The Stanmores' ball was in celebration of their daughter's eighteenth birthday, and for this momentous occasion they had spared no expense. Every room glowed with candlelight, footmen appeared at one's elbow the instant a glass needed refilling, the musicians were the finest Bath had to offer. Five rooms were entirely given over to the entertainment and several further ones as retiring rooms for the ladies and gentlemen. Trelenny had never seen so many jewels as flashed from ringed hands and encircled necks, sparkled amidst stylishly coiffeured hair and on matronly bosoms. The fairy-tale scene was not, however, the reason she kept glancing about the room. Lady Jane was already here with the Earl, but there was no sign of Cranford. This was to be the last dancing party she would attend before she left for London with Mrs. Waplington and she had counted on Cranford to partner her for at least one waltz. She had planned to tease him about teaching her, had looked forward to being held in his arms.

The fact that Mr. Rowle had just arrived did not disturb her. She derived no further amusement from her escapade and only wished to forget the entire incident. As she joined another set she was aware of his gaze briefly on her but she pretended not to notice. When she chanced to look in his direction again, he was no longer there. A few minutes later a footman approached as she and Mr. Inglestone were about to go up the dance.

"Miss Storwood?"

"Yes."

"There is a messenger from Westmorland at the back door asking for you. He says it's urgent."

"Asking for me?" Trelenny knew a moment's panic—what could it be but a man sent from her father and directed on from Henrietta Street—and she tried to still the wild beating of her heart before she spoke. "Take me to him." She excused herself to her partner and looked about the room for her mother, but could not see her. Was the news so desperate that her father (or someone else—awful thought) felt it must be broken more gently to her mother? Trelenny hastened down halls and stairways, past a multitude of busy servants all intent on their own occupations. The footman never paused, though he occasionally glanced behind him to make sure that she followed. She could hear the clatter below in the kitchens and the aromas of a dozen different dishes assailed her nostrils, though she barely noticed. The rear door on the ground floor was open and she could see a youth in riding garb, a bundle under his arm, his cap pulled down over his forehead, stomping to warm himself in the chill night air. No torch was lit without to throw its illuminating light on his face.

What happened next was so sudden that she could never afterwards recall in precisely what order events occurred. She was about to invite the lad into the warm hallway when the footman, who had stepped back to let her speak with the messenger, firmly thrust her out the door. A hand was clasped over her mouth, a voluminous, hooded cape thrown about her, and she was bundled into a waiting carriage while murmurs of doctors and ladies being ill seemed to pass illusorily through the darkness outside. The carriage door had scarcely closed when the vehicle lurched forward and gained momentum even as they rounded a corner, swaying dizzily. A hand remained over her mouth, muffling her cries, until it was replaced by a scarf tied behind her head.

With glowering eyes she recognized Mr. Rowle seated opposite to her but he paid little heed until he had concluded his instructions to the two other occupants of the carriage, who were set down several blocks further on to return to his house in Lower Borough Walls.

Now he turned to her and asked with exaggerated politeness, "Will you promise not to call for help if I remove the scarf?" When she did not nod, he shrugged. "Have your own way. It's a small matter and I would rather not trust to your word in any case. I wouldn't do that!" He clamped a hand tightly onto her wrist as she raised it to untie the scarf herself. "Let us understand each other from the start, Miss Storwood. From now on you will do exactly as I tell you if you wish to remain comfortable."

The measured, menacing tones had a certain effect. Trelenny did not doubt that he was capable of any villainy, but she could not resist a touch of bravado. Sitting up straight against the squabs, she folded her hands in her lap and twiddled her thumbs. Her initial impulse—to kick him—she restrained.

"I have always found," he mused, "that the lengthy process of laying plans and expanding them is fraught with danger. The chance of their being detected is magnified with each passing day. On the other hand, an idea brilliantly conceived and quickly executed seldom fails. See how smoothly my simple maneuver has gone. A ball night—dozens of unfamiliar servants about the house, hundreds of guests each intent on their own enjoyment—what could be better? I had only to see that your mother was not close by, introduce my footman, and the rest followed as night the day. I shall feel truly put out with your mother if she raises an outcry, but I think it unlikely. And even if she does, it will be only a matter of time before the whole of town realizes that you have run away with me. No one will be surprised, Miss Storwood. People have seen you welcome my attentions at a dozen assemblies and parties; Lady Babthorpe will recall your kissing me in the Sydney Gardens. And no one doubts that you're a romp, prime for a bit of mischief."

Trelenny's hands clenched tightly in her lap but she did no more than level a cold stare at him.

"You think you won't marry me?" He laughed. "You will. You have no choice, my dear. From all your mother has said, I gather that any shock is likely to aggravate your father's condition. And I think certainly the shock of knowing his daughter has spent a night in a man's ... company would sadly discompose him, were there not the mitigating effects of a marriage performed soon afterwards—in your mother's presence, of course. That will make it all right and tight with society."

He glanced out the window where the ghostly shapes of lone trees dotted the countryside. "I am going to remove the scarf now and you may make as much uproar as you wish, but it will do you no good. There is no one to hear you but my coachman and myself and I promise you we are not the least likely to be moved."

Her mouth felt dry and swollen when the scarf was removed. For some time she sat saying nothing, battling a desire to put her head down and cry. "Where are you taking me?"

"It is not necessary that you should know, but disillusion yourself of the idea that anyone will find you. We are not taking the road to Bristol or London, which would seem the logical routes of a runaway couple. This is my part of the country, Miss Storwood, and I know a half dozen villages off the main road where there are inns."

"I doubt an honest landlord would welcome an unwilling guest."

"For the right price, there are few who wouldn't accept one," he retorted cynically. "However, it won't be necessary for us to search one out. There is a fellow who would be more than willing to settle his obligation to me for so small a price."

Trelenny turned her head to the window and considered whether she had any avenues of escape.

When Cranford entered the Stanmore ballroom, his eyes quickly surveyed the company in hopes that Trelenny would still be there. He was reassured for a moment by the sight of Mrs. Storwood chatting comfortably with a matronly lady in one of the little chairs provided off to the side of the dancing. As he made to approach her, he caught sight of Lady Jane just leaving the dance floor and encountered her instead. "Have you seen Trelenny?"

"Yes, a short while ago." She turned her head to survey the shifting masses of people, but without success. "I don't see her now."

"When did you last see her?"

"The set before last, I believe, with young Inglestone."

Cranford placed an urgent hand on her arm. "Jane, there may be trouble afoot. I've learned that Rowle was having his traveling carriage stop here tonight. We must find out immediately if she's still here. I'll speak to Mrs. Storwood; bring Inglestone over if you would."

Lady Jane was not deficient in understanding. Her face

paled and she murmured, "Dear God! I'll be right with you."

It seemed imperative to Cranford that no commotion be caused by their search. He therefore approached Mrs. Storwood and her companion with a smiling countenance, bowed gallantly, and asked if Mrs. Storwood would honor him with the next set. Ever aware of her obligation to him, she consented, though she was not particularly in the mood for the rigors of the *Boulangère*. To her surprise he began to lead her around the dance floor toward the doors.

"Is something the matter, Cranford?" she asked hesitantly when they arrived in the hall.

"Have you seen Trelenny recently?"

"No, not for half an hour or so. She doesn't come to me after each set anymore since she is always promised several dances ahead."

"I must find her immediately. Would you check the ladies' retiring room?"

Surprised but willing, Mrs. Storwood departed and returned just as Lady Jane arrived with Mr. Inglestone. "She isn't in the retiring room. I wonder where she can have gone."

Lady Jane shook her head unhappily as she drew her companion forward. "Please tell Mr. Ashwicke what happened."

Embarrassed by the attention of three pairs of eyes, Mr. Inglestone nervously stroked his cravat. "Miss Storwood was approached by a footman while we were in the set and told that a messenger from Westmorland was waiting for her at the rear door. She asked to be taken to him."

"And you haven't seen her since?" Cranford demanded.

"No. Sorry, sir."

"Westmorland?" Mrs. Storwood looked faint, and Lady Jane encircled her waist with a comforting arm as she and Cranford shared a despairing glance.

"Thank you, Mr. Inglestone. Forgive me for interrupting your evening." Cranford's dismissal of the young man was hastily acknowledged and he beat a relieved retreat. "Mrs. Storwood, I have every reason to believe that no messenger from Westmorland but an agent of Mr. Rowle's was awaiting Trelenny outside. Have courage, ma'am. You must not let on that anything is amiss. Jane will see you home." He received a confirming nod and continued. "Should anyone ask, say

Trelenny has just been put in a chair—some indisposition—and you are following immediately. I'll find out what I can here and Mr. Laytham will hopefully bring me some word of their possible destination. Are you all right?"

Mrs. Storwood, ghostly pale and with trembling hands, drew a long breath. "Don't concern yourself with me, I beg you. Just find her, Cranford, and bring her back to me."

"I will do everything in my power." He turned away abruptly but stopped to say, "Thank you, Jane. I know I can depend on you."

At the rear of the house the torch had been replaced and the area was bathed in a flickering light where several chairmen and coachmen stood about blowing a cloud and discussing their betters with evident relish. Laytham had not appeared as yet and Cranford was able to gain only the information that a young lady, taken sick, had been hurried into a carriage and driven off. No one had taken much notice, and Cranford did not wish to make the incident seem any more significant than it did to them, so he stifled his desire to drain every detail and went round to find the lad who was holding his hired mount. From a distance he saw Mrs. Storwood and Lady Jane, Mr. Wheldrake and Mrs. Waplington descend the front stairs and depart. In a frenzy of impatience he mounted his horse but, having no direction to take, merely sat it uneasily, trying to rationally consider Mr. Rowle's nefarious design and not Trelenny's desperate situation.

Quarter of an hour passed before Laytham's horse came clattering up the street, but nothing could have been more welcome to Cranford than the wide, triumphant grin he wore. "You know where they're headed?"

"Haytesbury"

"I've never heard of it."

"It's on the way to Salisbury. Just follow me."

For some time they were silent, negotiating the chairs and carriages in the heart of Bath, but Cranford could no longer suppress his need to know that they were indeed headed in the right direction. "You're sure someone wasn't misleading you? I don't mean to question your knowledge, but it would be just like Rowle to have laid a false scent."

"You forget that I am familiar with his tactics, Mr. Ashwicke. For a guinea I bought the information that he was headed to Wells; for another and a promise to take the lad into my service I found his real destination. There can be no doubt of it. Rowle has had dealings of an underhanded kind with the landlord of the Bell there, and this lad has no desire to remain in his service. I had to take him to the White Hart before he felt confident enough to tell me the truth."

"I shan't ever be able to repay you, Laytham, but I'll see to the lad."

"No need. He's well enough, and I'm grateful for an opportunity to satisfy my debt to you."

"You've done that and more. How far is it?"

"Hour and a half in a carriage. Less on horseback, of course, if these nags can stand the pace."

When they had not overtaken the carriage by Warminster after an hour's hard riding Cranford began to have doubts. If they were going in the wrong direction there was no chance of reaching Trelenny before ... A soft curse escaped him and Laytham, understanding, said, "We'll be in time. Do you want to change here?"

"No! He's not much for speed but he's well bottomed." Cranford whispered encouragement to his hack as they left the town behind and once again lengthened stride. There was no use cramming him when Cranford had no idea how much further they had to go. Blessed with a sure-footed prad on a cold, black night, he had no wish to press his luck.

They had traveled no more than a mile further when they could hear a carriage ahead in the still night air, the jangling of harness and the thud of hooves announcing its presence before they could see it. Was Rowle fool enough to resist their rescue of Trelenny? Was he that desperate? Cranford raised his hand warningly "I would prefer to surprise them if possible. Do you know this country? Can we get ahead of them without being seen?"

"If we're quick about it. The road bends in a short while and there's a wood to the left. We'd have to cut across the fields most of the way, but a road skirts the wood."

"So that if we were on the road they wouldn't see us for the woods until they were upon us?"

"Right."

"Let's try it."

Their horses were tired and the route across the fields rough, with the necessity of opening and closing gates as they went, but once they reached the road they made up for the lost time. Standing back in the cover of the woods they could hear the approaching carriage and Cranford asked, "Would you rather wait here?"

"And miss the fun? Never! What do you want me to do?"

"Anything that will make the coachman draw in his horses. Ride toward him shouting—a flood, an accident, some danger in the road ahead. I shall deal with Mr. Rowle."

His black scowl made Laytham laugh. "Would it were me. I owe the fellow something."

"Now!"

Laytham spurred his horse forward yelling incoherently of all the possibilities at once, but his advent so startled the coachman that he instinctively drew back on the reins. As he did so, Cranford rode directly to the coach door and flung it open, leaped to the ground and confronted the two startled occupants. Rowle leaned forward to grab Trelenny but Cranford was faster. With lightning speed he had grasped Rowle's arm and pulled him ruthlessly out of the carriage onto the dusty road. Although no help was forthcoming from his coachman, who craned his neck to peer curiously at the unwonted activity, Rowle was in no frame of mind to let his prize slip so easily through his fingers. He leveled a kick at Cranford's shin that did not wholly meet its target but glanced along the leg, throwing him off balance.

As he put out an arm to catch himself against the carriage, Rowle leaped to his feet and struck a blow to the midsection. It was the last contact he made with his opponent. Infuriated by the fellow's gall, Cranford landed right and left in a style which would have pleased Gentleman Jackson and certainly flattened the likes of Mr. Rowle, who lay still in the road bleeding from his nose, with an eye rapidly blackening and swelling.

Cranford disgustedly turned from him and climbed into the carriage, where Trelenny had watched the whole with a sort of horrified fascination. "Are you all right? Did he hurt you?"

"I had no idea you could fight like that, Cranford! Where did you learn? Do you go to matches?"

"You're all right," he said dryly. "Have you no nerves, my girl? One would think you were abducted daily."

The animation left her face. "I was really very frightened," she admitted, allowing him to take her icy hands. "He intended to force me to marry him and for all he's a pipsqueak, he is a great deal stronger than I am, Cranford." A lone tear slipped down her cheek and she licked it off her lip. "I have tried for the last hour to think of some way to escape but only the most impossible things occurred to me. What good are fantasies when you are faced with . . . ? The only real thing I could think of was that somehow you would find us, even if I couldn't tear off bits of my petticoats to leave a trail. I don't know why I should have thought that was any more real than visions of lightning striking him dead, but I did. How did you find us?"

"I'll tell you in a moment. Let me get us headed back first."

She could hear his instructions to the coachman and the gentleman on horseback both of whom apparently acknowledged his authority, but the coldness of his terms to Rowle left her somewhat shaken.

"I will expect you to have left the country within forty-eight hours, Rowle. No whisper of this night's activities will pass your lips or those of any other. If one breath of scandal attaches to Miss Storwood's name, I shall know where to put the blame, and I don't think you would like the consequences. Lord Rissington and Mr. Bodford, as you well know, would not appreciate any damage done to Miss Storwood's reputation, and if I am not available to see to the matter, one or the other would gladly step into the breach. I hope you will not bother to deceive yourself that any one of us is more than capable of dealing with you. Your coach will be returned to your father's house, but you will be left here to make your own way tonight. Perhaps the walk will clear your head."

Trelenny caught only a glimpse of him sitting beside the road with his head in his hands before the carriage moved forward to turn in the road. Seated beside her, Cranford did not even glance out the window. "How will he manage?"

"I don't know and I don't care, but he will do it."

"Is Mama dreadfully worried?"

"Of course, but I had Jane go home with her to Henrietta Street. We'll have fresh horses put to in Warminster and make it to Bath as quickly as possible. You have Mr. Laytham to thank for your rescue." He proceeded to enlighten her as to the events of the evening, even remembering to hand her the letter from Mrs. Laytham, which she could not read in the darkness of the carriage.

When he had finished relating his story Trelenny said sadly, "Aren't you going to say 'I told you so'?"

"No, my darling girl, I am not. I feel as responsible as you do, and I am only relieved that you're safe and unharmed. Have you any idea of the agonies I suffered? No, and you have had quite enough of your own to occupy your mind. Forgive me."

The gentleness of his tone, his calling her his "darling girl," wrenched Trelenny as nothing else had that evening. Why had she been such a fool as to let him fall in love with Lady Jane? Why was it that the Rissingtons and Bodfords held no appeal to her when compared with Cranford? His was not just a familiar, reliable face anymore but the only one which mattered at all. How could she have been so stupid as to grow to love him only once he was out of her reach? Lady Jane and he were so very well-suited—their taste for antiquities, their love of music, their common friends. Trelenny could not even fault Lady Jane on her spirit; she was a lively woman whose natural refinement kept her within the limits of propriety Cranford so respected. They were the ideal match, and Trelenny had never felt so desolate in her life. She turned her head away to hide the tears which coursed down her cheeks.

"Are you hungry? There's food in this basket."

Trelenny gulped down a sob. "No, th-thank you."

Her shoulders shook and he reached for the carriage rug. "Here, let me put this about you! For God's sake, Trelenny, why didn't you tell me you were upset? I am a barbarian, aren't I? Of course you're upset!" He pressed her head to his chest and tightened his arms about her. "Poor little one. What a night you've had! Cry it all out, my dear. That feels better, doesn't it? It won't be so long before you're home with your mother again. She was very brave; don't worry about her. And Jane will know just how to best keep her spirits up." The more he tried to console her, the harder she cried, so he stopped speaking and stroked the short, fluffy hair until she at length raised her head to try to speak. When no words came she looked so distressed that he bent and kissed her.

If he had meant to console her, which is what he told himself, he was not prepared for her response. She clung to him as though for dear life and returned his kiss with a shy, moving earnestness which entirely disoriented him. Not that he desisted. Her very intensity swept him from the tender caress he had originally intended to a much more passionate embrace, which she, to his wonder and confusion, readily accepted. When they drew apart he stared at her unbelievingly. "Is it possible? No, it is only the shock you've had, isn't it?" Her eyes were luminously moist in the light from outside, and he realized that they had entered Bath. They would be in Henrietta Street in a short time. He shook his head to clear it. "Trelenny, you know I have spoken with your father, have meant to offer for you for some time. Is it possible you have changed your mind? Can you have decided to have me after all?"

Her throat ached at the necessity of her reply. "No, thank you very much, Cranford."

chapter twenty-three

In the uncertain light he tried to study her face but she turned from him, smoothing down her gown and saying sadly, "I know your father will be disappointed, Cranford, but he will adjust to a different match for you."

"My father has nothing to say to the matter."

She looked at him reproachfully. "How can you say so? He has pulled the purse strings shut on you and will only open them if you marry me."

"I don't need his money, Trelenny. Coverly is doing very well." A glimmer of hope appeared in his eyes. "Is that why you thought I offered for you?"

"Well, when you approached Papa, you didn't even like me!"

"But that's not true now! I admit that at the time I had another reason."

"What was it?" she asked bluntly, her chin coming up.

"It's unimportant."

"Not to me."

"Trelenny, when my mother died I was supposed to be there, and I had failed to come. I didn't know she was dying. She had written me a letter shortly before, telling me how you were growing into a young lady and she hoped one day we would marry. Lord, I caused her so much anguish! My father said that her dying words were to the same effect, that I should marry you."

"Then he lied to you. Mama was there, and all Lady Chessels wanted to tell you was that she loved you and hoped you would be happy. Surely Mama told you so."

"She would hardly tell me that my mother wanted me to marry her daughter."

"That's not the point, Cranford. Your mother wanted you to be happy. How could you think it would please her to do something you didn't want to do?" Trelenny glanced out the window to see the familiar houses in Henrietta Street. "We're here."

The carriage had barely come to a stop when she jumped down without the aid of the steps or Cranford's hand and rushed to the door, where the porter, bleary-eyed but relieved to hear the carriage stopping and see young miss, swung the door wide. "Where is my mother?"

"In the parlor, miss."

Trelenny raced to the door and flung it open but paused on the threshold at the sight which confronted her. The tableau struck brilliantly on her mind after the other trials of the day. While Mrs. Waplington, her husband, and Lady Jane had risen at the sound of approaching footsteps, Mrs. Storwood sat unaware in the circle of Mr. Wheldrake's arm. Her mother's eyes were red and she held a handkerchief to them, but her head rested against Mr. Wheldrake's shoulder until he cried, "She's here! Maria, Trelenny's safe."

Unable for an instant to believe her own eyes, Mrs. Storwood remained immobile on the sofa. Trelenny flew into her arms saying over and over, "I'm all right, Mama. I'm all right. He didn't hurt me. I'm all right."

"Oh, my love, thank God!"

The others turned to Cranford for details while Mrs. Storwood touched Trelenny's hair and eyes and chin to assure herself that it was truly not a figment of her imagination. "You must go directly to bed," she said irrationally. "Yes, that would be the best thing. You've had a great shock; I'll take you straight to your room."

Trelenny turned to smile at the others, only to see Lady Jane press Cranford's hand and hear her say, "Well done, my dear. You look fagged to death. Are you all right?"

"I'm fine," he replied shortly, then smiled apologetically at her. "Thank you for coming, Jane. Shall I see you home now?"

"If you would." She crossed the room to hug Trelenny. "I can't tell you how happy I am that you're safe, Miss Storwood. I hope you can forgive me for encouraging you in your plan to set-down Mr. Rowle."

"There is nothing to forgive, Lady Jane. I appreciate your coming here to be with Mama."

Although Mrs. Storwood took the opportunity to thank Cranford, who promised to come around in the morning, she was not deterred from her plan to see Trelenny immediately to her room. No assurance of her daughter's well-being was so strong as seeing her tucked fast in her bed and almost instantly asleep. She kissed the silky blonde head and sighed. "Life is fraught with pitfalls for you, my love. Thank heaven you have the courage to face them with dignity."

At the breakfast table Trelenny was especially cheerful in an effort to persuade her mother and friends that she had suffered no ill consequences from her misadventure. She gave a vivid account of Cranford's pugilistic skills and an impressive recitation of his coldly delivered demands to Rowle. Anyone observing her, even her very closest companions, could have had no idea of the problems she had wrestled with when she awoke early in the morning.

First, there was the problem of Cranford and Lady Jane. Trelenny flushed to recall her own forwardness in the carriage. Kissing him as though her life depended on it! What recourse had she given him but to finally make good on his word and offer for her? Her realization that she loved him had come too late, and much as she wanted to marry him, she could not in all honor accept him when she knew he had given his heart to Lady Jane. It was difficult to even resent Lady Jane, much as she wished she could. Not since Clare had she met someone she so liked and respected. Trelenny despaired of offering Cranford an acceptable excuse for her behavior should he press her; he would have to think the worst of her.

And her mother. Trelenny had had qualms before as to the intimacy growing between her and Mr. Wheldrake, but the scene upon which she had entered the previous evening had shaken her as nothing else could have. Reluctant to enter into the social whirl of Bath without her husband, Mrs. Storwood had leaned on Mr. Wheldrake for support and the relationship had grown into—what? In her own rush to savor every moment of her stay, Trelenny had not fully comprehended the dangers of placing her mother constantly in company with a charming, affectionate gentleman who clearly felt a great deal for her. Even in her thoughts Trelenny shied away from comparing Mr. Wheldrake and her own father. Not only did it seem disloyal but unfair. Who was she to say that her mother should deny the pleasures of society and be tied to the Westmorland wilds? Could this taste of high life have awakened Mrs. Storwood's longing for a different kind of life from the one she had? Refusing to consider the matter one inch further, Trelenny had come to a decision. She would not go with the Waplingtons to London but home with her mother to insure that her father suspected nothing of what had passed (if anything had), and to comfort her mother (if she needed it).

Since Mrs. Storwood was loath to let Trelenny out of her sight, Cranford found the two of them in the sitting room. Making up for her scanty thanks of the previous evening, Mrs. Storwood proclaimed her undying gratitude for the better part of half an hour during which time Cranford and Trelenny attempted to indicate to one another that they wished to speak privately. Neither of them was forced to ask her to leave, however, as eventually she was overcome by emotion and excused herself.

After an awkward silence Cranford said, "We reached no conclusion in our discussion last night."

"Did we not? I was sure we had."

"You had a misconception as to why I offered for you."

"I cannot see that makes any difference to the conclusion."

"Trelenny, come here."

They had not reseated themselves after her mother left and she had nervously walked to the window, as far as she could get and not appear positively rude. "Why?"

"Come here."

Though she did not hasten to his side, making a circuitous and lengthy progress about the various chairs, she did eventually reach him, her chin raised and her eyes fearful. When he took her in his arms and kissed her, she valiantly tried to remain passive but her own emotions were more than she could manage. She responded, as she had the night before, with every evidence of passion.

He released her, smiling ruefully. "Well?"

Flushed and angry with herself, she murmured, "That proves nothing but that I like to kiss."

"You did not respond that way when Rowle kissed you."

"No, well, I didn't like him."

"And you do like me?"

"Of course I like you."

"Trelenny, you act as though you like me well enough to marry me."

"I don't!" She sought desperately for some way to persuade him of her sincerity. "You're like your father, Cranford. Not always," she hastened to add at his stricken look. "But see what you did to Clare! That was autocratic and heartless, not the act of a kind, decent man. And you think of me as you do Clare, as someone to be treated as a misguided child. You aren't like that with Lady Jane! She's an adult and an equal in your eyes. But I'm not."

His hurt was evident and the pain in his eyes bothered her, but she refused to let him sacrifice himself. He said slowly, "I see. You're wrong, you know, Trelenny, but I can't prove it to you."

"Don't try! Please let's not discuss the matter further, Cranford. I have something very important to ask you. I want to go home. Will you take us? Tomorrow?"

"You don't want to go to London?" he asked incredulously. "I thought that was very important to you."

"Mama is more important."

"Trelenny, I shall take the greatest care of her."

"It's not that! Of course you will. I just want to go with her. I want to see Papa. I'm sorry to take you away from Bath right now, Cranford, but it's important."

"We were due to go in a few days anyhow." There was something here he didn't understand, but her dear face was politely masked and he knew it would avail him nothing to pursue the subject. "Very well. I'll have the traveling carriage here at ten."

"Nine?"

He tapped a restless finger against a chair back. "Nine."

The return journey was very different from its predecessor. Cranford purchased *Emma* for her, but had not the heart to read it aloud, and Mrs. Storwood could not erase from her mind the heartbroken Trelenny who had come to her when Cranford left.

"I did the right thing, didn't I, Mama?"

"Yes, my poor love, you did the right thing. Oh, how I ache for you."

"He'll be happy with Lady Jane. They're so perfectly suited. I told Cranford I want to go home tomorrow."

"But . . . but your trip to London."

"I couldn't enjoy it right now, Mama. Perhaps another time Mrs. Waplington will invite me."

Four days they spent in the carriage, each covertly observing the others: Trelenny thinking that her mother looked very sad, and Cranford, well, he had become impassive again; Mrs. Storwood admiring her daughter's perpetual good humor and wondering at the gaze Cranford bent on her when she didn't see him; Cranford hoping against hope that his letter to his sister would bring permission to tell her secret, and watching the mother and daughter for some answer to the perplexing aura of sadness which surrounded them.

As the countryside grew familiar Trelenny became more agitated by the minute. Cranford tried to distract her by enumerating the reasons Kirby Thore was believed to be the Bravoniacum of the Romans, though why he chose to bore her with such a subject he was at a loss to explain even to himself. When she responded, "Since Camden's time it was thought to be Galacum, but I suppose Horsley has proved that Appleby, agreeing more nearly to the distance in the Itinerary, holds that claim," he was dumb struck and uttered not another word until they drove through the gates of Sutton Hall. Forewarned by a note, Mr. Storwood was waiting at the front door, outwardly calm but filled with almost unbearable anticipation at being reunited with his family. Mrs. Storwood's eyes filled with tears the moment he came in view and she waved until the carriage stopped, impatiently waited for the steps to be let down, and raced to his waiting arms.

"Oh, James, how I've missed you!" And right in front of everyone she allowed him to hug her to him and kiss her for such a long time that Trelenny murmured, "Well, really! She would scold me for such behavior." But after a moment she smiled and sighed. "It's all right then. I should have known."

Cranford eyed her suspiciously. "Were you afraid an attachment had grown between her and Mr. Wheldrake? Goosecap! I could have told you it was no such thing."

"She saw so much of him, and danced with him, and they would talk for hours."

"About you and your father and his sons. Didn't you ever hear them?"

"Mama has a right to her privacy. I wouldn't have dreamed of eavesdropping on them."

"You have the most infernal sense of honor, Trelenny."

But Mr. and Mrs. Storwood had broken from their embrace and Trelenny, after one painful smile, dashed to her father to be almost as rapturously greeted as her mother. Mr. Storwood held her at arm's length then and surveyed the much maligned haircut. "I like it," he pronounced. "It suits you perfectly."

If Cranford's greeting from Mr. Storwood had been all cordiality and gratitude, that from his father was otherwise. Lord Chessels was immediately apprised of Trelenny's rejection and took it in very bad part. Cranford would have left Ashwicke Park but for the letter he awaited from his sister. And when an answer came it was in a surprisingly different form from what he had expected, and its delivery was not only to Ashwicke Park but Sutton Hall.

Although Cranford called twice in the week following their return, he took tea with the whole family and had no discussion alone with Trelenny, as neither of them made any opportunity. The sidesaddle was there, of course, and when she rode out she was unable to keep to her resolve not to think of him, but sometimes, when she practiced the pianoforte, she could dull the pain for a while. It was when she was playing one afternoon that a visitor arrived in the doorway of the parlor, unperceived until she spoke.

"Cranford didn't tell me you had advanced so far in your playing, Trelenny."

Her face lifted with an incredulous smile. "Clare! I didn't know you were coming! How long have you been here? Are you well? Are you happy? Are your daughter and Lord Hinton with you?"

"You haven't changed, I see," Clare laughed, "except your hair. Are you setting a new fashion with it?"

"I certainly hope so! Come and sit with me and tell me everything."

"That's why I'm here, love. Cranford, Thomas, and Catherine are with your parents, but I begged a word alone with you first." She bit her lip momentarily and then smiled. "No one but Thomas, Cranford, and I know what I am about to tell you, and I feel certain you will guard our secret as closely as we do ourselves."

Trelenny frowned. "If it is a secret, Clare, you have no need to share it with me."

"I don't mind. You have always been my friend and, in time, I might have told you because I had so indiscreetly written you that letter."

"Cranford told you I mentioned it! I never meant to! You see, I am not to be trusted with a secret." Trelenny hung her head remorsefully.

"You didn't really mention the letter, I gather; only that you knew I loved someone else."

"It was enough! I don't want to cause you pain by going over the past."

Clare shook her head serenely. "Listen a moment and you will understand that I no longer feel any unhappiness. When I wrote you that I had fallen in love with Alexander Bradley, I believed it to be true. Lord Hinton—Thomas—had been courting me and I was deeply attached to him when along came this dashing soldier. Papa was delighted with Thomas and immediately threw all sorts of nasty barriers in Alexander's way, and you know what Papa is, Trelenny."

"Yes."

"If he had done nothing, I probably wouldn't have taken any interest at all. His autocracy just cried out to be rebelled against. Cranford did, and that spring I did. Alexander and I met secretly as often as we could and thought ourselves head over ears in love. It was partly the excitement of a clandestine relationship, partly that he was a wildly lovable fellow." She sighed. "I felt the only way I could force Papa to let me marry him was to let Alexander compromise me."

Trelenny's eyes widened but she said nothing.

"Napoleon had escaped and rapidly built up an army. Alexander went off to fight in April, promising to return and marry me the moment the menace was over. It was not until after he left that I found I was increasing. I was terrified. I couldn't tell Papa, and so I did nothing for a month or so. Perhaps I hoped I might lose the baby, perhaps I thought Alexander would be back before I began to show." Clare twisted her hands in her lap. "Eventually I could stand the suspense no longer and I told Cranford. Lord, he was so understanding! Not once did he lecture me as I deserved to be for my folly. He set off for the continent immediately, but

Alexander was moved from place to place. By the time Cranford reached Belgium, Waterloo was underway but he went onto the battlefield to find Alexander. When he finally located him..."

Clare paused for a moment. She had never been in the position of telling the whole story before, and it was more difficult than she had expected. "Alexander died in Cranford's arms. Of course Cranford said nothing about my condition and told me Alexander's last words were of me."

"I'm so sorry, Clare."

"When Cranford returned we talked for hours and hours about what best to do. I was heartbroken and desperate, but he wouldn't let me make a decision until I grew calmer. In a few days he asked my permission to tell Thomas, who was a great friend of his, and who, Cranford believed, loved me enough to marry me, even when in possession of all the awful details. And do you know, Trelenny, he did." Her eyes sparkled with joyful tears. "Thomas is the most astonishing man. We were married early in July with the baby due in December, but he arranged for us to live away from everyone so that no one would know when she was born, and we could announce her birth several months later."

"But what if it had been a boy? His heir?"

"He would have done the same. I'm glad, for his sake, that it was a girl. She's the dearest thing, Trelenny, but we thought the longer we waited to show her to anyone the less obvious it would be that she is older than we say she is. I would hate for her to have to pay her whole life for my indiscretion."

"And Lord Hinton? How does he feel about her?"

"She's our baby, born out of the secret we share. Oh, Trelenny, I hope you will get to know Thomas. I can't imagine how I could have preferred Alexander to him for so long as a minute!" She wiped away the stray tear that had fallen and smiled. "So you see, my love, Cranford was not the least autocratic in the whole affair but the kindest, most helpful brother who ever lived."

"Oh, Clare! Is that why you have told me everything? Because I said I wouldn't marry Cranford for the way he had treated you?" Trelenny gazed horror-struck at her friend.

"Yes, my dear. He wanted my permission to explain to you and I thought it best if I came myself to tell you."

"But I only used that as an excuse!" Trelenny wailed.

"Don't you want to marry him?"

"Well, I can't!"

"Whyever not?"

"Because he's in love with Lady Jane!"

"Lady Jane Reedness?" Clare gave a gush of laughter. "Whatever gave you that idea?"

Indignantly Trelenny retorted, "It was *obvious*, Clare. He took her everywhere and was very attentive, and they are perfectly suited. Mama thought so, too, though it ruined all her hopes."

"Has Cranford never explained Lady Jane's situation to you, then?"

Trelenny had the sinking feeling that reality was escaping her. "No."

"Well, I suppose he wouldn't. Either it would not occur to him or he might not think she wanted it bruited about. *I* have known for years and I think she's the most courageous lady I ever met. Trelenny, she has loved her cousin forever, and he her, but he has spells or something and is quite dangerous during those periods. They always know when they're coming on because of the headaches he suffers, so there is time to confine him. Lady Jane couldn't marry him because of that, but he lives on her father's estate, and they are together a great deal of the time. The Earl takes her away to Bath or London when he's confined, and she never lets on. Cranford has known for years, of course."

"That wouldn't necessarily keep him from falling in love with her."

"He offered for you, didn't he?" Clare asked with asperity.

"Yes, but he had to because he had approached Papa before we went to Bath."

Clare rose and stomped to the door. "I wash my hands of the both of you. If he is too stupid to tell you, and you are too blind to see, that he loves you, you both deserve to be miserable!" On her exit she slammed the door.

Trelenny remained frozen in her seat and Clare joined the group in the drawing room, where every eye swung to her on her entrance. She lowered an exasperated look on Cranford and said shortly, "She thinks you love Lady Jane."

Now every eye swung to Cranford, but he did not gratify them by making any comment. Instead he rose and left them without even an apology, a certain sign of his inner turmoil. Trelenny was still sitting where Clare had left her, a glazed look in her eyes, when he came abruptly into the room and closed the door.

"What's this nonsense Clare talks about Lady Jane?"

"I... it seemed to Mama and me," Trelenny tried to point out in a reasonable voice, "that you had formed an attachment for her while we were in Bath."

"Well, I didn't. For God's sake, Trelenny, I told you that Jane and I had been friends for years."

"Even friends of long standing can fall in love, Cranford."

His gaze softened. "Yes, I know."

"She seemed the perfect wife for you. I tried very hard to be happy about it."

"Did you? But, Trelenny, when I offered for you..."

She lowered her eyes from his searching gaze. "I had made a fool of myself, letting you know how I felt. You never said you cared for me. I thought you were just honoring your word to my father."

"I didn't tell you? It's hard for me to express how I feel, Trelenny. Too many times I have had to swallow any emotions I might have had because of my father. Do you really think I am like him?"

"No. I'm proud of what you did for Clare."

"I'm relieved that everything has worked out so well." He crossed the short distance which separated them and took her in his arms. "I *do* love you, Trelenny. You will have to teach me how to express myself." And he bent to kiss her.

Sometime later she said, "You express yourself very well, Cranford."

Warner Regency Romances

□ **CHARLESTON TANGLE**
Joan E. Overfield
(D35-156, $3.50, U.S.A.) (D35-157, $4.50, Canada)
Set in Charleston, South Carolina, a charming story about a young widow who falls in love with a dashing English gentleman.

□ **THE DANDY'S DECEPTION**
Philippa Castle
(D35-008, $3.50, U.S.A.) (D35-009, $4.50, Canada)
A delightful romance in which a blue-eyed beauty and a handsome Earl find rapturous love, in spite of their families' interferences.

Warner Books P.O. Box 690
New York, NY 10019

Please send me the books I have checked. I enclose a check or money order (not cash), plus 95¢ per order and 95¢ per copy to cover postage and handling.* (Allow 4-6 weeks for delivery.)

___Please send me your free mail order catalog. (If ordering only the catalog, include a large self-addressed, stamped envelope.)

Name _____

Address _____

City _____ State _____ Zip _____

*New York and California residents add applicable sales tax.

They were the ideal match, and Trelenny had never felt so desolate in her life . . .

The gentleness of his tone, his calling her his "darling girl," wrenched Trelenny as nothing else had. Why had she been such a fool as to let Cranford fall in love with Lady Jane?

"Are you hungry? There's food in the basket."

Trelenny gulped down a sob. "No, th-thank you."

Her shoulders shook and Cranford reached for the carriage rug. "Here, let me put this about you."

He pressed her head to his chest and tightened his arms about her.

"Trelenny, why didn't you tell me you were upset?"

The more Cranford tried to console her, the harder she cried, so he stopped speaking and stroked her short, fluffy hair until she at length raised her head to try to speak. When no words came, she looked so distressed that he bent and kissed her.

If Cranford had meant to console her, which is what he told himself, he was not prepared for her response. She clung to him as though for dear life and returned his kiss . . .

Also by Laura Matthews

The Aim of a Lady
The Seventh Suitor
Lord Clayborne's Fancy
A Baronet's Wife

Published by
WARNER BOOKS

ATTENTION: SCHOOLS AND CORPORATIONS

WARNER books are available at quantity discounts with bulk purchase for educational, business, or sales promotional use. For information, please write to: SPECIAL SALES DEPARTMENT, WARNER BOOKS, 666 FIFTH AVENUE, NEW YORK, N.Y. 10103.

**ARE THERE WARNER BOOKS
YOU WANT BUT CANNOT FIND IN YOUR LOCAL STORES?**

You can get any WARNER BOOKS title in print. Simply send title and retail price, plus 50¢ per order and 50¢ per copy to cover mailing and handling costs for each book desired. New York State and California residents add applicable sales tax. Enclose check or money order only, no cash please, to: WARNER BOOKS, P.O. BOX 690, NEW YORK, N.Y. 10019.